Famous Writers School

Famous Writers School

a novel

Steven Carter

COUNTERPOINT
BERKELEY

Library of Congress Cataloging-in-Publication Data
   Carter, Steven, 1961–
   Famous writers school : a novel / Steven Carter.
      p. cm.
   ISBN-13: 978-1-58243-356-1 (hardcover. : alk. paper)
   ISBN-10: 1-58243-356-9 (hardcover. : alk. paper)
   ISBN-13: 978-1-58243-384-4 (paperback. : alk. paper)
   ISBN-13: 1-58243-384-4 (paperback. : alk. paper)
1. Authors—Fiction.
2. Authorship—Fiction. I. Title.
   PS3603.A779F36 2006
   813'.6—dc22

                                            2006023005

Counterpoint
2117 Fourth Street
Suite D
Berkeley, CA 94710

Distributed by Publishers Group West

10 9 8 7 6 5 4 3 2 1

Call for submissions from *TriHorn Review*. We're looking for short stories and essays under 3,500 words for a special issue on the effects of technology on hygiene in the modern era, and the resulting effects this has had on human relations. No erotica. Deadline: March 15, 200—. Send story with cover letter and SASE to *TriHorn Review*, Hygiene Issue, P.O. Box 1004, Trihorn PA 32543.

$500 first prize from *Wisconsin Poetry Review* second annual contest. This year's theme: The Wal-Marting of America. Poems must include at least one reference to Wal-Mart as an overarching and possibly destructive entity. $10 entry fee for each poem. No work will be returned. SASE for notification of winners. Deadline: May 1, 200—. Send to *Wisconsin Poetry Review*, Contest, P.O. Box 7, Waukegan WI 57899.

Get the time and space you need to do your best work. Writer's retreat in northwestern Georgia offers twenty wooded acres and spring-fed pond for private bathing. Rustic cabin with all the modern amenities. $495 p/week, $1,795 p/mo. Visit our website at www.writersgarret.net or call 888–555–9000.

Shakespeare was just another guy with a pen. What? you say. Well, at one time he was just like you, sitting there staring at a blank page with stories he wanted to tell but no idea how to do it. Don't let anyone fool you; *all* great writers have found themselves in that same spot and asked, How do I do this? Where do I start? No one is born knowing how to write—but that's where we come in. The *Famous Writers School* gives you the guidance *all* writers need in the beginning. Through a series of carefully structured lessons you'll receive instruction in all aspects of storytelling, and you'll receive thoughtful feedback on your work from a widely published fiction writer. You don't have to write in a vacuum any longer. You don't have to feel as if you're alone in a lifeboat, about to die in the middle of an empty ocean every time you sit down at your desk.

We're here and there's hope, if you're willing to take advice and work hard. Many courses like this one are simply con games designed to play on your deepest hopes and get your money, but we're not like that, and to prove it we offer a 100% money-back guarantee. To receive more information about our course, please send a SASE to Famous Writers School, P.O. Box 1181, Fayette WV 32111.

SWF, 34, novelist, former academic and product model (don't ask), seeks a more advanced SM writer for manuscript advice, talk and support, friendship, long meals, and possibly more. Smoker ok. Height and weight unimportant. Write to: Rio, P.O. Box 199, Pittsburgh PA 38891.

Publish your own book and fulfill your dreams with our complete editorial and publishing service. We have over fifteen years experience helping authors realize their goals and a staff of experts who critique your manuscript, proofread it, do the book and cover design, and obtain ISBN and LOC numbers. We give your book the tender loving

Famous Writers School
P.O. Box 1181
Fayette WV 32111

Dear Fellow Writer,
Congratulations!
By asking to receive this information, you've taken a step that requires a great deal of courage. How many times have you heard someone say, "I'm going to write someday" or "I have a story that would make a great novel?" Not many of us end up writing that novel, though. Why not? Well, that's a good question, and its answer is different for different people, so I can only tell you my own story.

It was a bright Saturday morning seventeen years ago when I first sat down to write fiction. In the next room, an unsigned divorce agreement lay on an unmade bed like a three-day-old mackerel whose odor I could not escape. I had a pack of Dunhills, a yellow legal pad, and an archaic fountain pen that my great-uncle, an RAF fighter pilot, used to write the love letters that convinced my aunt, an American Red Cross volunteer, to marry him, although now the pen stained my fingers if I so much as touched it. I also had a deep desire to be heard; to have my words be the hammer that knocked the camel through the eye of the needle.

Now, one of my favorite short stories is Chekhov's "Misery." It's about a horse cab driver who has to go out and work on the same evening he finds out his son has died in a faraway place. He keeps trying to tell those he meets about his son's death and his own grief but never finds a sympathetic listener, so, that night, unable to sleep, he gets up from his pallet in the barn and

3

goes into his horse's stall and tells her all he's been longing to say. It's a chilling and masterful story. Sitting at my desk that Saturday, I remembered it, thought about it, and realized the horse cab driver and I wanted the same thing. So I simply started putting words on paper. During a break to get a cup of coffee, I signed the divorce agreement, walked it down to the drop box on the corner, came back, sat down at my desk, unlocked and raised the rolltop, and kept writing.

I started writing every day. Sometimes I'd start as soon as I awoke and not stop until I fell exhausted into bed eighteen hours later. When money ran low I ate cheese and crackers and got my medical care from a doddering Taiwanese doctor at the VA; I didn't whimper and whine and go running back to the jobs where I'd already spent so many miserable years on my knees begging to be allowed to do ten dollars worth of work for eight dollars of pay so some mediocrity above me would have enough money to make his daughter neurotic.

So, at one time, I was a beginner, too. That probably goes without saying, but it's important you realize I wasn't sprung into this world knowing how to write. I also think it's important you know something about my credentials—after all, if you take this course, you're putting yourself in my hands:

Wendell Newton has published over seventy short stories, essays, and reviews in literary magazines. His collection of stories and occasional prose pieces, *Up From the Dust*, was published in 1997 by Three Mountains Press and was recognized as one of the year's top ten books by the Organization of Small Presses. Though Newton didn't try his hand at fiction until he was 27, he has been writing since he was a young man—in high school he won a statewide contest with an essay on the Battle of Agincourt. After majoring in English and minoring in French at Marshall University, he spent four years in the air force as a specialist in public relations, and in that capacity he wrote press releases and articles for base newsletters, and then he became speechwriter and personal secretary for a brigadier general, serving fourteen months in the Pentagon. After leaving the military he freelanced for a time, then took an editorial position with *America's Farmer*, the country's second oldest agricultural publication.

However, for the last eight years, Newton has made his living purely from his literary pursuits. When he's not working with his students in the *Famous Writers School* or writing himself, he publishes a literary magazine, *Upward Spiral*, and does freelance copyediting. His novel, *Out of Rain*, is forthcoming from Three Mountains Press. He lives in a home overlooking a beautiful river in the mountains of West Virginia with his two mixed-breed dogs, Duke and Daisy, and in his spare time he likes to play bridge.

All right, let's talk about the course. You complete six lessons that cover all the elements of fiction:

#1: Tell me the best story you've ever heard
#2: Put pressure on your characters
#3: Let your characters have their own lives
#4: Make it mean something
#5: What comes first, plot or character?
#6: Putting it all together

For each lesson you'll receive a teaching text and a writing assignment to complete and send back for evaluation. I usually read assignments within a week of receiving them and then mail my comments back. At the end of the course, you are invited to send me a story or even a novel manuscript, and if I think your work is publishable I will use my contacts to help the piece find a home.

The tuition for the course is $295, payable by money order, certified check, or personal check made out to *Famous Writers School*. That's less than half the cost of a university writing workshop, and if at any point you aren't happy with your instruction, just let me know and I'll refund the total amount of your tuition. Please send along with your payment the **application card** included in this mailing, and also please include a **personal statement** in which you tell me about yourself and your writing goals. If I can get to know you a little better, I think it makes me a better teacher for you.

Another thing. Everyone who signs up receives a free one-year subscription to *Upward Spiral*, which has published many former students of the *Famous Writers School*.

I'm signing off now, but as a P.S., I'm including some comments about the course from former students. Good-bye, and I hope to hear from you soon.

Sincerely yours,
Wendell Newton

The *Famous Writers School* is fantastic! I've completed the course and am now working on the novel I've always dreamed of writing about the well-heeled but spiritually bankrupt clients I served for years.
 —*Earl P., retired landscape architect*

My dream is coming true. I can't believe it. Thanks!
 —*Lois R., housewife*

Famous Writers School rocks! I've published two stories in horror magazines!
 —*Joe B., computer sales associate*

I was a student at one of the famous university writing workshops. My fellow classmates were for the most part literary effetes interested only in looking like writers as they sat in campus bars. I don't know why I signed up for the *Famous Writers School*, since most courses like this are a joke. However, I learned more in one story response

from Wendell than I did in listening to a whole year of blather from the more famous writers at the program I attended. If you really want to write, I suggest you pay the pittance Wendell asks and sign up for his course. You'll never have money more well spent.
—*Name and address withheld upon request*

This course isn't like the others. He actually helps you.
—*Macy P., respiratory therapist*

Famous Writers School opened me up to the possibilities of the written word.
—*Nancy Q., self-employed*

Newton is like Kafka, who was largely unknown during his lifetime, though he wrote groundbreaking fiction. At the end of the day Newton's work will be seen in the same light. He is so much better than the literary effetes who sneeze once and call it a story, sneeze twice and call it a novel, and then go on Charlie Rose to have their noses wiped.
—*Dr. Reston McN., university professor of English*

When I first signed up for the *Famous Writers School* course, I was afraid Mr. Newton wouldn't be open to helping me write a romance novel. However, I was wrong. He nurtured me every step of the way, and my book was just accepted at a publisher. I'm now in Europe doing research for my next book.
—*Sallie L., nurse*

———————

Dan Federman

Personal Statement

Hello, I'm 29 and work as a sales rep for John Deere. In college, though, I was an English major and I still read a book a week. I've also been writing everyday for two years and am currently finishing a novel that's sort of a detective story. I think detective writers are some of the best around. Writers like Jim Thompson and James Lee Burke, you actually stay interested in their stories, not like with Proust or somebody like that. My wife's a high school French teacher and she's crazy about Proust. Maybe that's why she stays in bed and complains so much. Ha-ha.

Being a writer first occurred to me in ninth grade. I got caught cheating on an English test and part of my punishment was to write a ten-page essay on why I shouldn't cheat. I wrote the essay, and on the last page when I was really straining to find things to say, I put down, "I shouldn't cheat in English because I might want to be a writer someday." Those words surprised me. I had no idea why I'd written them, but I never forgot them. For several years, though, I just fooled around with writing, only working on stories when the mood hit me and never finishing anything, until my wife got involved with Kaballah. I just got so tired of hearing about energy centers and the tree of life that I started going down to the basement in the evenings to write. In my opinion, Kaballah's about as legitimate as a daytime Emmy, but she defends it by talking about all the smart people who have believed in it, especially the philosopher Walter Benjamin because she knows I read him a lot in college.

Anyway, I feel I have the nuts and bolts of writing fiction down fairly well, and what I need now is some fine-tuning. I need an editor, and that's what I'd like from this course. For that reason, I'd like to send you chapters of my novel for the writing assignments, if that's okay.

I've just gotten a P.O. box to use for my writing business, so I need to give you an address change. Please send all further correspondence to P.O. Box 765, Newburg, OH 48771, and not to my home address. Thanks. I look forward to working with you.

Famous Writers School
P.O. Box 1181
Fayette WV 32111
March 12, 200—

Dear Dan,

Thank you for your enrollment in the *Famous Writers School*. I found your personal statement well written, a good indication that you have the ability to fulfill your writing goals. If you want to send me novel chapters, that's fine, as long as you revise them per the instructions in the lessons. However, this course will work better for you if you understand that I am your *teacher*, not your editor.

As for the genre writers you mentioned liking, they're okay storytellers, and they make good beach reads; however, please know up front that what we're trying to accomplish here aspires to more than that.

Sincerely,
Wendell Newton

Rio Jordan

Personal Statement

In the February issue of *Writing Life* my ad appeared right after yours. I'm Rio. I never would have noticed your ad and been led to begin this relationship unless our ads had been together, because I'm absolutely sick of school. I'm ABD in sociology, but eight months ago I realized I hated what I was doing and quit the dissertation. I was spending twelve hours a day reading articles that explored the pressing question of why teenagers get drunk and have sex, and I decided that wasn't how I wanted to spend the rest of my life. Actually, my dissertation was on how new technologies like cell phones and instant messaging affect patterns of rebellion in adolescents. Anyway, I'm lucky enough to have been blessed with a singing voice, so I do have a way to pay for my iconoclasm—I'm not an overeducated ward of the state—and most nights you can find me singing blues and torch at clubs around Pittsburgh.

What else to tell you about myself? Well, for one, I think Descartes messed everything up. The link between the intellectual and the physical has been lost. In my fiction I want to let my characters experience the world sensually, yet also have an intelligent conversation every now and then. In other words, I want to write about passion, passion between intellectuals, and not the kind you see in Bergman films, bogged down with all that Kierkegaard. That sounds silly, I know, but so does the idea of studying two languages to get a Ph.D.

Ever since I quit my degree I've been thinking of trying my hand at fiction. I've actually toyed with the idea since I was a teenager, and I almost majored in English instead of sociology. The past few months I've been jotting down ideas, keeping a journal. For instance, last week I saw a bee outside my apartment that had somehow gotten its body dyed purple, or a month ago an old man approached me outside a movie theater, carrying a paper grocery bag filled with nothing but saltines. He asked,

"Why are some of these women such liars?" I told him I didn't know. I bet you there's a story there.

Before I actually start writing, though, I want to make sure I have a reliable responder, and on nothing more than a gut feeling that wouldn't go away I sent off for the information on your course. I liked the tone of your ad and also the fact that you didn't kiss Shakespeare's ass. Just one question: Are those student blurbs real? If they aren't, it's okay. We all have to make a living. I just wondered.

As a lagniappe, I've enclosed a tape of a show I did this past winter. It was a cold, snowy Sunday night, the club was practically empty—I think the songs sound better if you know that. Just about the only people in the audience were my ex-husband and his girlfriend, but that's a whole different story and I've already gone over the one page you asked for. I do that all the time it seems, go on too long. Anyway, the recording's terribly rough, but I still thought I'd share it with you. It might help you get to know me better. I hope you enjoy it.

Famous Writers School
P.O. Box 1181
Fayette WV 32111
March 14, 200—

Dear Rio,

Thank you for your enrollment in the *Famous Writers School*, and I don't think what you said about Descartes is silly at all. His ideas on the mind-body split, while not totally deserving of dismissal, have had an undue and often destructive influence on the last five hundred years of Western culture. It's like we're a house divided. Why does the body have to be the *house* of the soul? Why can't we think of the soul as being a part of every cell of the body?

Also, don't worry about going over the one-page limit. When the prose is as interesting as yours, I can read all day.

I enjoyed the tape you sent, especially the slowed-down, dusky version of "Dust My Broom." It transported me to that mysterious place where you said you sang it. I could smell the wet countertops.

Now, as to your question about the blurbs: of course they're real, but I can understand why you might ask about them. The student testimonials for many correspondence courses are complete fabrications. But now that I've answered your question, I have one for you: What sort of products did you model? I've always found the lore of the advertising world in general, and the modeling world in particular, quite fascinating. You should consider using it in your fiction.

As soon as you're ready, send me the first batch of your work. I usually type up a response and mail it back, and I often speak with writers on the telephone after they receive my comments, in order to answer any further questions. We can work out the details later.

Good-bye, and I look forward to working with you.
All the best,
Wendell

Linda Trane

1. She is bigger than a breadbox.
2. But smaller than an ex-wife.
3. She has terrible hair.
4. But it's blond, and that's money in the bank.
5. She only gives gifts made with her own hands.
6. And the gifts she gives most often are red candles.
7. She has read and dismissed Freud, Horney, Adler, May, and Skinner.
8. Her favorite ice cream is vanilla.
9. She has been disappointed by life.

---

10. And also by her husband.
11. She no longer finds anything endearing or even remotely interesting about other people's children.
12. She has taken target practice with a compound bow twice this week.
13. She likes Daffy Duck cartoons.
14. She has not eaten pecans since a bad childhood experience.
15. She has not been to a movie theater for fourteen months.

Famous Writers School
P.O. Box 1181
Fayette WV 32111
March 19, 200—

Dear Linda,
Thank you for your enrollment in the *Famous Writers School*. I found your personal statement an interesting take on how to present a biography.
Enclosed you will find your first lesson and a writing assignment.
Sincerely yours,
Wendell Newton

Lesson 1

Tell Me The Best Story You've Ever Heard

One day I was waiting in the grocery checkout, scanning the magazines, when I looked up and saw a nurse from my doctor's office in the next aisle, unloading her cart. I knew her first name, Judy, and I'd always found her pretty but nervous, with jumpy eyes and a new hairstyle everytime I went into the office. She was still wearing her pink scrubs. I watched her hands move in and out of her cart. Her fingers were weighted down with rings, one on *every* finger, all cheap costume jewelry. I was struck by that. She'd never worn rings in the office. I realized she must keep them in her purse and put them on as soon as she got off work.

We ended up seeing each other out at the cart corral. It was full, and stray carts were scattered everywhere. However, Judy was trying to jam her cart into the back of the last one in the corral, backing hers away and ramming it into the other one's trapdoor, which didn't seem to want to open. As I approached she did that four or five times; I found it attractive that she wouldn't just leave her cart standing around. It was dusk, a misty rain was falling, the lights were on and everything looked smoky. When I reached the corral she looked up; I could tell she didn't recognize me.

"Looks like we've got a stubborn one here," I said and lifted the trapdoor on the cart in front of hers. She slid hers in.

"Thanks," she said.

"Certainly," I said.

Then without another word she walked away. I watched her get in her car, a green compact, which, I noted, had out-of-state plates.

Okay, you might say, but what's this have to do with me learning to write fiction? Well, the point is, stories are everywhere. This minor incident at the grocery has infinite fictional possibilities. New writers often ask, "How do you get story ideas?" but finding something to write about isn't the problem; the problem is *how* to write the stories all around you. Execution is everything. *Romeo and Juliet* has the same plot as a romance novel and in different hands *King Lear* is pornography. However, don't be misled: fiction isn't just thinly veiled autobiography or straight-out reporting. You often do start with something that really happened, like this meeting in a parking lot, but by the time you finish the story, it's usually quite different from your original idea, and this brings up another point: what *you* want the story to be isn't important. In fact, it's nothing. Nobody cares what you want. We're all dying. We have a finite amount of time left, and you want us to spend some of it with your story instead of eating ice cream? Good luck. So if you've got an opinion on gun control or globalization, bore your spouse with it, not us. Maybe you're an existentialist—great, put on a turtleneck and keep taking out student loans, but spare us your philosophy. I know all this advice doesn't jibe with our culture of self-esteem, but I don't care. What've I got to lose? The culture's failed, and your check's already cleared.

Ha-ha. Just kidding.

Before we get any deeper into this lesson, or the course in general, let me offer a quick mea culpa: I often teach by explaining my own experience as a writer. Why? Well, for one, a confession has more authority than a sermon and it's usually more interesting, too. But most importantly, I do it because you learn to write stories by studying stories, noticing how they work, what they do, and that's how I teach, by telling stories, not by giving a list of rules on how to plot your grandmother's trip to the bingo game. Cervantes, Melville, Faulkner, Woolf, Hemingway—they didn't learn from how-to-write books. They didn't do lessons on plotting and character development. They didn't sit with their legs crossed in a writing workshop. They learned from reading and studying stories, and in my course, that's how you'll learn, too.

The day I saw the nurse, I'd been writing for eight months. I went straight home and started a story about two people meeting at a grocery, but it went nowhere. I was determined it have a happy ending and couldn't figure out how to do that.

Then I called the nurse at work to ask her out, something I was planning to do anyway. She didn't remember our meeting at the grocery, so I brought up the last time I'd come into the office—I'd smashed a toenail and the doctor had to burn a hole in it to relieve the pressure of the blood building up under it.

"I don't remember that," she said.

"It was about two months ago," I said.

She was silent. Seconds ticked like hammers to the forehead. I was making a fist with my free hand. I couldn't think of anything to say. Finally I said, "I noticed your car has out-of-state plates. I thought maybe—"

"How do you know that?" she said.

"I just happened to see it at the grocery," I said.

"Oh. Well, all right. But how did you get my name?"

I hadn't considered the possibility of that coming up. I couldn't tell her the truth, though, which was that I followed her home from work one rainy day, watched her check her mail and go into her apartment, and then got soaked as I ran to the mailbox, got her name, and ran back to the car.

"Dr. Lean gave it to me," I said.

"I don't believe that."

"Well, I'm sure he meant no harm."

"Don't call me again," she said and hung up.

I don't mind telling this now, not at all. I know what I did was a little crazy, though I will say that in a different day and time, one less arid, it might've been seen as chivalrous. I never went to Dr. Lean again, either, but that doesn't matter: what matters is that the moment Judy hung up on me—the moment I heard that telephone crash in my ear—was the *exact* moment I understood fiction writing is not wish fulfillment. You just have to let a story be whatever it's going to be, and in the story I finally wrote about this incident, the woman in it is a mess. She's into astrology, tarot cards, numerology—cheap turquoise rings are just the tip of the iceberg—and things get messy.

The poet W. B. Yeats said all stories begin "in the foul rag-and-bone shop of the heart" and William Faulkner said stories are about "the human heart in conflict with itself." They're right, but how do you write fiction like that?

You start by telling me the best story you've ever heard.

A lot of courses like this open with an exercise where you write a two-page description of a tree in winter or a scene about an old man dropping a flowerpot on his cat. No one would read those things even if God came down in a cloud and held the paper. So I believe in jumping in with both feet and trying to write something you'd actually want to read.

Assignment: Think of the best story you know. It could be something that happened to you or to someone you know, or it could be a story you heard. Whatever it is, you want it to make us say, "That's great." However, stay away from current events or stories from history like D-Day—unless, of course, you actually happened to be there for the disaster that is your story's setting.

Next, just write down the story as if you were telling it to a friend. It's that simple. As you're writing, try not to worry about anything, especially whether or not what you're writing is good. This might prove difficult, but take heart. You're becoming a writer.

Dan Federman

Lesson 1

Mr. Newton,

I just wanted to remind you to please send all further correspondence to P.O. Box 765, Newburg, OH 48771, instead of to my home address, which is where lesson 1 arrived. That would be a tremendous help. Thank you.

1

My territory covers tractor dealerships in parts of three states and sometimes as I'm going down the interstate in the company Cavalier I drive past the exit where I'm supposed to make my call and stop at the first truck stop, flirt with the waitress, smoke, drink coffee, and think about places I could go instead of another tractor dealership.

The only good thing about my job is I meet a lot of secretaries.

One day I was in the southern Ohio farm country, in the office of a dealership manager who was making me wait since I'd arrived an hour late because of one my unscheduled stops, and across the room sat his secretary, a little blond stunner named Carrie who had just said hello and was still smiling.

—Where did you say you had your flat? she asked.

—On the interstate up near Phillipi.

—And it took you an hour to fix it? she said.

I shrugged and smiled.

—Guess I'm just a slow worker, I said.

She pushed her chair back and stood up. She was small and compact and her yellow dress was short, shapeless and loose. It looked like a good wind would blow it over her head. She stepped to a filing cabinet and put away a file folder, then banged the drawer shut.

—You from this part of the world originally? I asked.

—Born and raised, she said.

—So what do folks around here do for fun?

—Count soybeans mostly, she said.

She sat down again and busied herself uselessly with some papers, like an anchorwoman at the end of a broadcast.

—Is there anywhere around here to have a drink? I said.

She quit her paper shuffling and a couple of sheets fluttered to rest. She gave me a long look. Then she held up her left hand. Her wedding ring was silver with a dark groove around it.

—I guess you haven't noticed this, she said.

—Oh sure, I said. It was the first thing I noticed. Or maybe the third.

She smiled and lowered her eyes at the compliment. She smiled a lot and I liked that. The only time my wife smiled was when the waiter brought the next dish to the table.

—From the looks of it, you're in the same boat as me, she said.

—What, this? I held up my hand and twisted it back and forth, looking at my wedding ring. I just wear this to keep women from bothering me when I'm in bars, I said.

—Well, don't you just think a whole lot of yourself.

—Not really, but you'd have to get to know me better to find it out.

Then Joe Brockton, the dealership owner, opened his office door. He didn't say anything, he just stood in the doorway and stared. I grabbed my case and stood up and crossed the room smiling to beat the band.

—Mr. Brockton, I said offering my hand. So sorry I was late.

He looked at my hand like it was an IRS letter, then took it in his cool damp fat one and shook it weakly.

Joe Brockton owned not only the dealership but also eight hundred acres of land and three hundred head of cattle. He used to be partners in all of it with his brother, but then the brother died in a hunting accident and Brockton owned everything. I didn't know all the details, I'd just heard the story at another dealership on my route. Brockton was tall, fat, and very neat. His khaki work clothes had creases and his hair looked like it had its own bodyguard. He was probably fifty.

I sat down in front of his desk and got out a pad and pen.

—I'm here today just to check in, I said. To see how this year's line is doing and to see if there's anything we can do for you. Actually, though, we do have some new haying implements you might be interested in.

He didn't answer. He kept looking at me from up under his eyelids.

—I'll tell something you can do, he said.

—Yes?

—You can leave that little girl out there alone. I heard you talking to her. I heard what you said.

—Mr. Brockton, I'm not sure what you heard, but we were just having some fun. Some good-natured banter.

—She's my niece, he said.

—I see.

Neither of us said anything for a moment.

—You must be proud of her, I said.

—Her husband isn't worth a bucket of warm piss, he said. That's why I've got her on here, but I don't want her to get herself into even more trouble than she's in, so just lay off. Do you understand me? She doesn't have the sense God gave a goose. She's likely to do anything.

—I understand. You won't have any trouble out of me.

—Her husband can do about any kind of work, he said. Carpentry, brick and concrete, plumbing, but he's a layabout. Before I started her here, they were having to live on what she makes driving that school bus.

I nodded and tried to look concerned.

He ended up ordering a couple of the new hay rakes. On my way out, I said good-bye to Carrie, but that was all because Brockton was right on my ass all the way to the door.

I had one more stop to make that day, at a dealership over in Powatan. It's only thirty-five miles from Brockton's place but it takes an hour to get there because you have to take three different two-lane roads. The first one was curvy and bordered by hilly pastureland and about as interesting as a football interview. I turned on the radio and hit search twice, but a gospel station was all I could get. I left it there. The air conditioning on the piece-of-crap company car was blowing hot air so I lowered all the windows and loosened my tie.

2

My marriage was going to hell. I knew it and she knew it. We stayed together only because we had a daughter. Then six months ago my wife turned up pregnant again. She told me while we were eating supper and her voice had no more emotion than if she were telling me we had a new paperboy. Since neither one of us had been drunk for a while I had to try to figure out when it could've happened.

—That's great, I said, doing my best to look happy. I put a hand on her shoulder, but she didn't look at me. She kept staring at her plate, so I took my hand away. Then she stood up and left the table, leaving almost all of a T-bone steak.

—What's wrong with Mom? my daughter asked.

—Nothing, honey. She's just tired.

—Am I going to have a sister now?

—Maybe. Or a brother.

—Yay! she said.

I finished my steak and was still hungry, so I put my wife's in the microwave and cooked it a few more minutes, then ate most of it, too.

After driving ten minutes, I stopped at what I knew was the only store on my route to Powatan, a small white wood building that had two mechanical gas pumps, a gravel lot, and no name. I went inside and bought a soft pack of Camels, my first in two months, then sat outside the store on a couple of plastic milk crates and lit up. It tasted so good I wondered why I ever quit. Then I heard the two old men who had been inside the store start arguing. Their voices came through the screen door, an ancient thing that had a bread company ad on it, but I couldn't make out what they said. Finally one of them came out. The screen door banged shut behind him and he looked back through the dark wire mesh and shook his head. Then he looked over at me.

—Damn no-heller, he said.

—Excuse me?

—Not you, him, he said, nodding at the door. He don't believe in hell.

—Oh, I shrugged.

—You ain't one too are you?

—No, I believe in it, I guess. I just don't worry about it.

—Sure, there you go, he said.

He came over and sat down on a milk crate, his head a foot below mine. He took a twist of plug tobacco out of his overalls and used a Barlow pocketknife to cut off a piece. He wore a sweaty brown fedora with a little feather in the band, blue denim overalls and a cheap white dress shirt with a stiff collar. His shoes were brown and dusty and looked like they weighed three pounds apiece.

We sat there a minute, staring at the road. Nothing passed.

—Today's my birthday, he said.

—Well happy birthday, I said.

He spit. The juice landed in the dust neat and tight like a penny.

—Don't know how old I am, he said. Couldn't none of my people read or write so nobody got it down. But I got it figured somewhere between seventy-two and seventy-seven.

—How do you know today's the day? I asked.

He spit again.

—I don't, he said. When I joined the army I just picked a day
and wrote it in the front of a Bible to show them. Stuck by it ever
since.

I nodded, then flipped my butt away and stood up. He asked me
for a ride.

—Won't be any trouble, he said. It's just down the road here. I
got gas money.

He took his wallet-on-a-chain out of his back pocket.

I told him I didn't need any money, but he held out a dollar bill.
I shook my head, but he insisted and I took it. It was damp, and I
didn't like touching it.

3

—Daughter was supposed to pick me up, he said. Her and her
boyfriend, but I guess they're out getting doped up. She's been in
jail for stealing cigarettes, but she was supposed to get out this
morning. Did eleven months and twenty-nine days.

—That's a lot for stealing cigarettes, I said.

He leaned up and spit out the window.

—She could've done more, he said, falling back into the seat.
I've been afore that judge myself and she's a bitch. But my daughter's got three kids and that was a consideration.

—I see.

—She was going to stores real late and waiting until they wasn't
no one inside but the clerk, then sending those kids in to make a

scene, break something or whatever, and when the clerk left the register she'd run in and grab all the cartons she could and throw them in a trash bag and then run back to the car, which she would've parked a ways off from the store. Then the kids'd run out and that was that. Way she got caught was the car wouldn't start one night after she got the cigarettes and a deputy stopped and asked her if she needed any help. It's two in the morning and about ten degrees outside, and she's got three kids in the back of a Chevy Vega that's got a trash bag taped up over one of the windows, and she smiles and says no, we don't need no help, we're fine.

He spit out the window again.

—I never did get your name, he said.

—Doug Farnsworth.

—Fee Yates, he said. So what kind of work you do?

I told him.

—You been over to see Brockton today, he said.

I nodded.

—Hey, he said. Don't feel like having a drink, do you?

—Guess not.

—Mind if I have a quick one?

—Go ahead.

He reached under the bib of his overalls and pulled out a pint of whiskey. It was a brand I didn't recognize, Four Horses. He raised the bottle to his lips.

—Yessir, I guess we'll see if they's a hell, he said. Me, I ain't taking no chances. I'm making sure the Lord knows I'm humble.

He took a long drink. Then he screwed the cap back on and slid the bottle back behind the bib.

We rode a few minutes without speaking. Every so often he leaned up and spit out the window. Then suddenly the radio started cutting off and on and the dash lights were strobing. I knew what was happening. The alternator was getting ready to go out. I'd had it happen once before.

—Son of a bitch, I said.

—She's petering out, he said.

I made it to a pasture entrance where the roadside ditch was tiled and covered with gravel and pulled the nose of the car right up to the farm gate. Before I could turn the engine off it died. I reached to the backseat and dug my cell phone out of my sport jacket and turned it on: no service.

—They's a phone up here where I'm going, he said.

—All right, I said.

We got out, I locked my briefcase and jacket in the trunk, and we started up the road. Barbed wire fence lined the road on both sides and rocky pasture sloped up and away from the fence so steeply you couldn't see past the tops of the hills. It was like a tunnel with no roof. The air was hot and thick and we didn't go far before I took off my tie, folded it, and stuck it in my back pocket. The road was sticky underfoot and every so often you stepped in a pool of soft tar and left a footprint.

4

—Here we go, he said.

We were at the head of a logging road that started at the paved road, crossed a hayfield, then cut into some woods like a yellow gash and disappeared. The valley had widened. There was no fence anymore and only the first thirty or forty yards of land back from the road were cleared. The hay was knee-high, and behind the hayfields on both sides of the road wooded hills rose steeply.

We had walked for twenty minutes without seeing a house. I commented on that.

—That's cause it's all Joe Brockton's land, he said. And he don't need but one house.

—Is this house where we're going his?

—I guess you could say that, he said. It's on his land.

We started up the road. It was a washed out W, the ruts a foot or more deep. The shoulders were all hay or undergrowth, so we walked on the ridges of the W. My dress shoes weren't built for that and he stayed several paces ahead of me. He walked with his head thrust forward and with every step he planted his shoe hard like he was stomping on something. We passed through the hayfield and into the woods, where the grade steepened and the air was cooler. Just to make conversation, I asked him if he knew anything about what had happened to Joe Brockton's brother. Being in the woods, where you'd go hunting, made me think of it.

—Eton was having relations with Joe's wife was what I heard, he said.

That surprised me. I waited for him to go on, but he didn't.

—So you think Joe did him in? I said. I heard it was a hunting accident.

He still didn't say anything, so I let it go. It was none of my business anyway. I reached into my shirt pocket for a cigarette and discovered I'd left the pack in the car.

—Hey, I said. Mind if I try a chew of your tobacco?

He didn't answer.

—Hey, I said. I wondered if—

—Ain't got enough, he said without turning around.

5

The house was dirty whitewashed logs that formed a square the size of a three-car garage. It had a tin roof and a darkly cluttered front porch and sat in a sunless clearing on a knoll, and it didn't strike me until I saw it that no house here would have a telephone. There were no wires. As soon as we rounded a curve in the logging road and came in sight of the clearing four dogs of different sizes and indeterminate breeds except for one thin blue hound ran at us, not barking but quiet and low the way dogs do when they're going to attack. I stopped. Fee was ahead of me and when the first dog, the hound, reached him he slapped it across the face without breaking stride or looking at it as if he had expected to hit it as a matter of course the way you turn a doorknob to enter a room. The hound yelped and tumbled down the hill and the other dogs noisily surrounded it and it had to fight its way off the ground. I turned and started back down the hill.

—Hey, where you going?

I stopped. Fee was on the porch now, a man and woman standing next to him. They looked young and sullen. The woman had fair skin and long red hair and wore a man's blue button up shirt with the tail out and frayed shorts cut from a pair of khaki pants; her legs were chalk white and shapely. The man was a head shorter than her, wiry and monkeylike, wearing jeans and a black Jack Daniels T-shirt. His forearms were dark with tattoos.

Fee reached behind the bib of his overalls and pulled out a pistol and let it hang at his side.

—Don't rush off, he said.

I started backing down the road, smiling.

—I've got to find a phone, I said.

Fee raised the pistol level and at a forty-five degree angle and fired it to my right. At the explosion I tried to run but my foot slipped in one of the ruts and I fell. The dogs started toward me, but Fee made a sound that wasn't language and they stopped dead in their tracks.

—We was just about to have lunch, he said.

Famous Writers School
P.O. Box 1181
Fayette WV 32111
April 10, 200—

Dear Dan,
You have many obvious strengths as a writer, such as your ability to catch the speech rhythms of your characters and the fine sense of timing you show in some of your scenes; however, you need to reduce the drama here by at least half. In just twelve pages, we have an attempted adultery with Carrie, a horrific domestic scene with the wife, a description of felony theft that involves the use of minors, a vehicle breakdown, a pistol shot, and a kidnapping. It's enough to leave an Olympian breathless.

You should write your dialogue in the standard manner, and there are also several instances in which you use the present tense *spit* when you should use the past tense *spat*.

Sincerely yours,
Wendell Newton

Rio Jordan

Lesson 1

I'm having trouble with this assignment. Honestly, I expected the lesson to have more instructions about craft, but I still liked what you said about writing and I'm ready to jump in and get started. However, here's my problem: I know a lot of stories, but I'm not sure which ones I should try to write or even how to go about starting. I was wondering, could I run some of them by you and get your advice? I hope this is okay. If not, I understand. I was a teaching assistant for four years and I know you can get sick of hearing people's half-ass excuses. Once this kid in an intro to sociology class told me that he didn't have his homework because it had been his training weekend with his Guard unit. I told him he needed to learn to plan around things like that, and he said he thought serving his country was more important than reading about crime trends in Sweden. I asked him what he did in the Guard and he said he was in a water purification unit. But here's the kicker: after we finished talking about his homework he asked me to go for a Coke at the student union and I went! He was 24 or 25 and my divorce had just become final. See? I know there's a story there, I just don't know how to write it.

Anyway, here goes. . .

Idea 1:   One of the professors on my dissertation committee asked me to his house for dinner. He and his wife were in their early fifties and the professor had a reputation for being a sleaze, but he'd never given me any trouble, which surprised me, because I'd recently separated from my husband and everyone in the department knew about it because one day my husband came up to the TA offices waving around a sawed-off broomstick.

My professor had a cook, an older Hispanic woman, and she brought out the soup, something sweet and orange, then went back to the kitchen. We started eating.

"This is really good," I said.

"Yes, Mary does a wonderful job," the wife said. She cleared her throat. "Say dear," she said, "do you mind if I ask you something?"

"Certainly not. What is it?"

"Do you ever wear a wig?"

I hesitated. I wasn't sure I had heard right.

"Excuse me?" I said.

She and the professor exchanged a brief glance.

"I just wondered if you ever wore a wig," she said.

"Uh, no, I never have," I said.

"Well, I *love* to wear them," she said.

The story would be that, plus the rest of the evening. We watched *Rebel without a Cause* if that tells you anything.

Idea 2:   I once waitressed at a strip club and one night a guy came in who had won a silver medal in the 200 butterfly at the last Olympics. He had lost the gold in a photo finish and I remembered that on the medal stand he had been sulky about it. I was on the swim team in high school so I knew who he was, but I was probably the only person in the strip club who recognized him. To most people he was just another guy with his baseball cap on backward trying to stick a dollar bill between someone's legs. Anyway, when I brought him his third or fourth drink he got fresh with me. Stuff like that happened all the time, so I just laughed it off, but when I tried to walk away he blocked my path by swinging his legs out from under the table and lifting one of them up to block me. He was wearing shorts and had an Australian-looking tattoo on his thigh, a curlicue vine thing. It was the size of a cat. It hadn't been there during the Olympics. He had put on weight since then, too, and his face was puffy. He kept holding his leg up, smiling.

"Where do you think you're going?" he said.

I didn't answer. I gave him a tired look, then rolled my eyes and shook my head. His expression turned dark. I looked down at his leg. It was quivering now. He lowered it.

"I'm a customer," he said.

"You're in a strip club, for godssake," I said.

"Yeah, well, you are, too," he said.

I thought about asking him which kitchen cabinet he kept his silver medal in, but I didn't.

Idea 3:   When I was eleven, the pastor of my church got cancer. I can't remember for the life of me what kind it was, but it was incurable and the doctors said he had only a short time to live. His attitude, though, was great. Almost beyond belief. He insisted on doing his pastoral duties as long as he could, because, he told everyone, that's what he enjoyed about life. He delivered sermons, did weddings, counseling, visited the sick, and even preached a funeral. I had a terrible crush on him. He was just in his thirties and very handsome.

Then one evening I came home from a friend's house and my mother was sitting at the kitchen table weeping and my father was standing over her screaming. Uncooked chicken parts were thrown all over the kitchen and a bag of rice was spilled out on the floor. Our kitchen was so small it seemed like rice covered the whole floor like snow. Just as I reached the doorway my father grabbed my mother's neck and bent her over so her face was just above her knees. He was still wearing his dirty work clothes from the foundry where he was a shift boss, and he still had soot around his eyes.

"Go on, get down there!" he screamed.

Then he looked up and noticed me. She did, too. They both looked stunned, like they didn't know who I was. My mother started to say something, then stopped.

"Go to your room," my father said in a strained voice.

Long story short, my mother had just told my father she slept with Pastor Ron. Turns out after his diagnosis, he started sleeping with several women in the congregation. They'd go for counseling or whatever and it would happen on the leather couch in his office. The church secretary, an old woman at a desk in the next room, she heard it all, but she didn't say a word. What finally happened is a couple of wives confessed to their husbands, and then word got out and there was a whole slew of confessions. It was like a witch hysteria. Everyone was saying they had slept with Pastor Ron. His wife had a nervous breakdown. The very week she went into the psych ward, unable to remember her own name, he gave a sermon on the importance of tithing. The church was so full it looked like Easter. I was in the congregation with my mother. My father, of course, wasn't there—he never set foot in a church again the rest of his life. My mother had a bruise on her neck from where he had grabbed her, but she was dressed beautifully, wearing white gloves and a classy hat. Once during the sermon she leaned down to whisper something to me, but then hesitated. I could feel her breath on my ear. Then she just sat back again. I've always wanted to know what she was going to say. Maybe I could write a story where she did tell me something.

Idea 4:   Three months after our divorce my ex-husband brought a date to a club where I was singing. She was young but not pretty. Her hair was long, flat and greasy, the tops of her ears poking through it on both sides like baby mice, and her makeup looked like she'd put it on with a paint roller. She was also much too thin. They took a table in front of the stage and then sat there giggling and pawing each other like they were at the prom. I mean, they were holding hands for chrissakes. I was at the bar. They were facing me, and since the club wasn't crowded it was awkward. Finally I decided to go over and say hello just to prove they hadn't bothered me. I walked up to their table, smiling.

"Rob," I said.

"Rio," he said.

There was a pause, and then they both broke into giggles. When those had passed Rob started grinning, but the woman tried to stare me down.

"I just wanted to say hello," I said.

"Sure," Rob said. He nodded at the woman. "This is Alma, a friend of mine."

I smiled at her, wishing like the dickens I had just stayed on my barstool. She didn't respond, just kept staring a hole through me.

"Can't wait for the show," Rob said.

I said I hoped they enjoyed it, then went back to the bar.

During my set, the two of them did plenty of whispering and laughing. Then about halfway through, Alma started giving Rob down the road. I don't know what happened, but she threw her cigarette lighter on the table and jumped up, knocking over her chair, and started screaming and jabbing her finger at him. I was singing "Don't Get Around Much Anymore." The bouncer started toward them. Then suddenly Rob jumped up and threw a punch at Alma. I was shocked. Luckily the bouncer got there just in time to catch Rob's fist before it connected. He twisted Rob's arm behind him and started pushing him across the floor like a broom, and, believe it or not, I felt sorry for Rob. I wanted to mother and protect him. That was weird. But what was really strange was that Alma didn't leave. She sat back down and stayed for the rest of the set, never taking her eyes off me.

After I finished, I went back to the bar and sat down on a stool. The club was packed now. Suddenly Alma appeared out of the crowd milling around the bar. She was carrying this fifties-looking handbag, the kind your grandmother would have. I was scared. We looked at each other a moment. Her expression was empty.

"I'm sorry this happened," I said.

"I'm not," she said.

Then she turned around and left.

Idea 5:   I was in a Kmart the day before it closed its doors. The shelves and racks were mostly empty and the little merchandise that was left was scattered everywhere. Children were taking balls out of open bins and throwing them while their parents looked on with dull expressions. In one aisle, I saw a fat woman trying to climb some shelves to get a doll on the top shelf. In another, I saw two Pakistani teenagers with a shopping cart, one pushing, one sitting on the handle with his feet in the basket, but they didn't seem to be playing around. They looked serious, and they had three globes and about a dozen rolls of paper towels in the cart.

I needed to pee, so I found the bathroom. It was freezing in there and there were so many brown paper towels wadded up and thrown on the floor you could kick them like leaves. I did my business in a hurry, but as I was pushing the door open to leave someone on the other side pulled it open at the same time, and, lo and behold, I found myself facing Alma. I was in shock for a moment, then just really scared. She wouldn't move out of the doorway so I could leave. Her left eye was puffy and had a greenish yellow tint her makeup couldn't cover. Finally I stepped out of the way and she walked by me. The paper towels rustled under her steps. She went to the sink and looked in the mirror, then reached into the fifties-looking purse and pulled out a compact and started powdering her cheeks. I started out the door.

"Hey," she said. "Mind if I ask you something?"

I stopped and turned around. "What?"

"Is Rio your real name or just a stage name?"

"It's short for Riordan," I said.

"Well, huh. Isn't that something?"

"What'd you mean?"

"I don't know," she said. "You just must've had some really fucked-up parents."

I stared at her. I couldn't believe she'd said that. She snapped the compact shut and dropped it in her purse.

"So did Rob give you that black eye?" I said.

"Yeah, as a matter of fact, he did," she said. "The other night he was in such a hurry to get my nightgown off that while he was pulling it over my head he hit me with his elbow."

I gave her a look. "Yeah, right."

She shrugged. "Believe what you want."

"Did you follow me here?" I said.

"What'd you think?"

"I think you did."

"Then it won't matter what I say, will it? You've already made up your mind."

"Why are you doing this?" I asked. "Do you think I want Rob back?"

"You've been calling him."

"I've called him twice. Both times it was about divorce business."

"Yeah, right," she said.

Then the door opened and the fat woman I'd seen earlier came in carrying a doll in a box with a cellophane window. She was limping, dragging one leg behind her. The doll was supposed to be the tooth fairy. Lacy white skirt, bobbed hair, pretty like they all are.

"I wouldn't come back to this dump even if they did keep it open," she said and then went into a stall and closed the door.

Alma gave me this awful smile in the mirror. Then she started putting on the kind of glossy pink lipstick ninth graders wear. Behind the stall door, there was the sound of cellophane bending and crinkling, then the doll box hit the floor with a hollow sound. It was empty. One end of it stuck out from under the door.

I turned around and got out of there.

Okay. That's it. What'd you think?

You asked what kind of products I modeled. I did a lot of catalogue work, and finally I ended up doing mostly shoots for housewares and small appliances. I did can openers for Sears and several shoots for Tupperware. I did a lot of pots and pans. I don't know why they liked me for that kind of stuff. I guess I just have that happy wife look.

Famous Writers School
P.O. Box 1181
Fayette WV 32111
April 28, 200—

Dear Rio,
I think without quite realizing it you've written a story, and a very good one at that. That often happens—we do our best work when we're not trying to be *writers*. I'd like to publish this piece you just sent in the next issue of *Upward Spiral* and call it "Five Story Ideas," if that's amenable to you.

Cookware and small appliances—that's interesting. Believe it or not, I was actually in a commercial once myself. How it came about is quite a funny story. I won't bore you with it here, but it involved a local racetrack, that carnival game where you throw Ping-Pong balls at goldfish bowls, a nun carrying a bottle of Glenlivet, a little girl, and her father, whose hair looked like it had its own bodyguard.

And no, there wasn't a David Lynch film shooting nearby!
Again, very fine work.
All the best,
Wendell

Linda Trane's First Affair

The Poet swept me off my feet. First long telephone conversations, sharing intimacies, then meeting at cafés where we read our favorite poems to each other (his idea) and had long talks over bitter, oily coffee. The fattest croissants I've ever seen.

It finally happened one spring day in an unsteady rowboat in a cove on a lake. Tall pines on three sides. A picnic basket in the boat.

Afterward, promises made.

The Poet asked me to go to the drive-in with him. I told him we'd have to wait until my husband was out of town and my children could be left with their grandparents. He said the drive-in was open from April through October. Finally we went. Holding hands, eating out of the same popcorn bucket and flimsy bowl of nachos. Splitting a mammoth candy bar. Later, a remembered innocence in our fumblings. Clothes everywhere. In the background, the voice of Schwarzenegger.

The Poet likes to eat. I start going to his house to cook for him in the early afternoon, two or three times a week, before I pick up my children at school. Pork roast or beef roast with the vegetables in the pot or one of the casseroles he likes. I never see him, though. He's always behind the closed door of his study, working. Occasionally I hear a cough. Our deal is I'm not to bother him, but one afternoon I try to coax him out. Wear the black vinyl miniskirt he likes, spend extra time on the hair. Get the casserole started, then go to the study door. Say sweet things. Behind the door, silence. I touch the doorknob, pause, then open the door. He looks up pen in hand, stomach pushing against the desk. Mouth tight. Eyes fierce. John Brown minus the hair.

"Need something?" he asks with irritation.

I hesitate. "Nothing," I say.

I step back and quietly close the door and go back to the kitchen. I take the casserole out of the oven, hamburger, onion, potatoes, tomato sauce. I spit in it. Then again. Then I return it to the oven. I sit down at the table and start a crossword.

One day, the Poet takes me to lunch in a distant town. We eat at a fish place, then check into a mom-and-pop motel for an hour.

As we're leaving, the Poet unlocks and opens the car door for me, and, at exactly the same time, an attractive Hispanic maid walks by on the sidewalk and distracts him; his eyes on the maid, he closes the door too soon and the edge of it slams me in the jaw as I lower myself into the car. I make a noise that's not quite a scream and fall into the seat. After a moment, I taste blood. I spit it out on the asphalt. With my tongue I find the cut inside my cheek. The Poet is superficially solicitous but obviously irritated. The maid comes over. I spit more blood.

As I look at the blood on the asphalt, I realize what a terrible idea this affair is.

From the maid, I accept a plastic bag of ice and a white washcloth.

That evening my mouth starts bleeding again during supper. I tell my husband I slipped and fell and hit the banister as I was carrying a load of laundry upstairs.

I write a short story based on this incident. I give it to the Poet and he sits in an armchair reading it. I'm on the couch with a cup of tea. When he finishes he looks up. Not bad, he says. But Chekhov had a story like this. Woman spits blood and feels sorry for herself. Might want to look at it. Called A Gentleman Friend. He does a better job of earning his ending.

I smile and nod, then take a pistol from between the sofa cushions and shoot the Poet three times in the chest.

Famous Writers School
P.O. Box 1181
Fayette WV 32111
May 1, 200—

Dear Linda,

Nice writing, though I had hoped in this assignment you would try to construct more scenes with dialogue. You just had one very short one. I would suggest doing more in future work.

I'm not sure I like calling a character "the Poet." It seems too allegorical, and that makes readers feel manipulated. Also, it's not a good idea to kill off the Poet. This is a move new writers often make, thinking a surprise death makes the story dramatic; however, if you think about it, what it does is cut off any possibility of drama. Nothing new and interesting can happen to a character who is dead.

Sincerely yours,
Wendell Newton

Lesson 2

Put Pressure On Your Characters

One fall evening at the end of a long day of writing, I couldn't find the cap to my heirloom fountain pen. I always put it in one particular pigeonhole in my rolltop desk, the third one from the left on the top row, but it wasn't there. I started searching my desktop. I had planned to take a stroll before dark, but the sun was quickly sinking and in my hurry to find the cap and get outside I knocked over the mug with the likeness of Gogol on the side that held pencils and paper clips, and this in turn toppled my little metal statue of Balzac, which knocked askew a stack of index cards, which was what I had recently begun composing on after learning that's what Nabokov did.

I decided to leave the mess until I had more time to deal with it. I braced a hand on the desktop and started lowering myself to the floor to search for the cap, which put me nose to nose with my mess just long enough for it to get under my skin. I stood up and straightened the desktop. Then I got down on my hands and knees and looked under the desk. The cap wasn't there. I stood up again. There was now a patina of dust on the knees of my trousers, two uneven white discs that I brushed away, and the cloud produced was thick enough to hide Tinkerbell or any other muted Victorian sexual fantasy.

I went to the kitchen for a broom, then swept under and around the desk. Then I started searching through the pigeonholes. I took two unopened bills out of the first one and stuck a finger in it to feel around for the pen cap. When I pulled my finger back out, an uneven line of gray filth was clinging to it.

I went through all forty-two pigeonholes with a rag on the end of a ruler, but the cap wasn't there.

I slammed down the rolltop, locked it, put on a fleece jacket, and left the house for my walk. It was dark by now, and on the sidewalk I angrily strode from one green pool of arc light to another, watching my loafers appear and then disappear as I stepped into the next patch of darkness. I didn't know why I felt so uneasy about the lost cap. I knew it had to be somewhere in the house because I had started writing at six that morning and hadn't come outside until this walk. I was certain I would find it sooner or later, yet its disappearance still irked me terribly.

I then lived in a quiet old neighborhood in town, not the country idyll I inhabit now. As I passed the old homes with their huge trees, nothing more now than outlines in the dark, I began to smell the woodsy burning odor I associate with fall and which still seems to enter the evening air along with the first chill, though hardly anyone has a fire anymore. Where does that odor come from today? At once I was filled with nostalgia for sights and faces that had once been and were now gone, and also for those hopes I had once held but no longer did, such as the possibility of transcendence through the smile of a woman, or the first stumbling steps of a child, or putting the final period on the novel that would make the Japanese come visit my grave.

All right, let's stop here. What can we learn from this story? Well, I hope this: that the character in this story, ostensibly me, has had pressure put on him by something very simple, the loss of a fountain pen cap, and that has led him to feel a deep sense of loss about other things. How such an inconsequential loss started this chain of events, I don't know, but it did, and for our purposes that's all that matters. Take, for instance, bed-bound Proust and his little madeline. That cookie started a novel longer than three Bibles, so just remember that the circumstances that put pressure on your characters don't have to be big bludgeoning things. Divorce, bankruptcy, unwanted pregnancy—they're all fine in fiction, but sometimes it says more about characters if they're disturbed by something that seems insignificant.

All right, but do we have a story yet? Is it enough for a character to realize that he's lost hope? Not really. What's interesting about humans is that we keep brushing our teeth despite the horrific existential facts facing us, so I believe we need more action here. Let's see what happens:

I walked several more minutes, until I reached the house where I usually stopped and turned around, a grimy old Cape Cod where there was always a dog tied in the backyard and an ancient woman sitting at an upstairs window. The dog was a sad, defeated little fellow who was never off his tether, a heartbreakingly small circle around his dog house worn down to smooth dirt. I had often paused on the sidewalk and considered going into the yard to make friends with the dog, though he was so dulled by his hopeless situation he never paid me any attention. The old woman, however, was a different story. She *always* glared down at me from the window, her figure like a small child's at the dinner table, only her head and shoulders rising above the bottom of the window. She always wore a high collar, even in summer. Her face was brown and withered, almost mummified, which made her fierce gaze even more unnerving.

Under that gaze, I never entered the yard to befriend the dog.

Then one spring evening the dog was gone, and in his place was another dog that looked almost exactly like him, except for black markings on his chest. Just the day before I had seen the first dog in his house. The new dog wasn't yet accustomed to his lot and was barking like a banshee and had his tether wrapped around a hind leg. When he saw me, his barking intensified. I looked up at the window; the old woman was there, her gaze fixed on me.

So, on the evening when the fountain pen cap was lost, I stopped at the house and saw this second dog, by now accustomed to his lot and lying on his side in his circle of dust. I looked up at the window and saw the old woman, feebly backlit, staring down at me. But this time, a Raskolinov-like courage came over me, and I fixed my gaze back on her; after a moment, her mouth grew tight as if she were refusing a spoon of porridge. We stared at each other a minute, and then I looked away and strode into her yard.

"Hey, there. Hey, buddy," I said. The dog raised its head and I squatted down and began stroking its back. It immediately turned its belly to me. I looked up at the window again: the woman's mouth was moving behind the glass as if speaking, but then, as if a trapdoor had given way under her, she dropped straight out of sight.

I was baffled. I waited for her to appear again, but she didn't. I thought her chair might've toppled; I thought she might be coming outside. By now the dog was standing up under my hand, occasionally reaching out a paw and resting it on my knee. A gnawing fear grew in me: had she suffered a heart attack?

I stood up. The dog jumped up and put his paws on me. I considered letting him off his tether, but decided I was no Russian madman, and after a final look at the empty window, I left.

At home I ate a poor supper. I tried to read but couldn't concentrate, and finally went to bed. But I couldn't sleep and tossed and turned for an hour. Finally I got up and started scouring the house for the pen cap, and at two in the morning, after searching for almost three hours, I found it inside an empty coffee mug in a kitchen cabinet. I had no idea how it got there. I took the cap out and then threw the mug against the wall above the stove, shattering it.

For two weeks I didn't go by the old woman's house. I was afraid of seeing a funeral wreath. However, when I finally did go by there, the dog I had petted was gone and it hadn't been replaced. An empty tether lay stretched out in the yard, and, strangely enough, a dead goldfish was lying near it. As for the old woman, she was back in the window again, looking down at me with the same fierce gaze.

Assignment: Look back at the material you wrote for lesson 1 and find places where you can make something happen that will put pressure on your characters. For instance, in the example above, I have the character do something he had been afraid of doing, enter the yard to pet the dog. This put pressure on him, as did the old woman's strange disappearance. Keeping these examples in mind, revise the material you wrote for lesson 1, incorporating two new ideas into the story. However, don't be surprised or disheartened if you try an idea and it doesn't work and you have to try a different one. That kind of failure is common.

Dan Federman

Lesson 2

Dear Mr. Newton,

I have some questions about the comments in your last letter. I'm sure you know that detective fiction is written with an eye to keeping the reader interested. Fairly exciting stuff happens every few pages, and I think my opening chapters are within the bounds of what most detective fiction does. I also think the chapters accomplish what you said in lesson 2 about putting pressure on your characters, so if I toned down the action the way you suggested, I would actually be going against your advice. I guess I'm just confused about how to proceed. For instance, in this last lesson you mentioned Proust and his madeline and used that as an example of what we should do, make a story out of something insignificant. Well, no offense, but I've never found Proust interesting. I've tried to read him several times and have never been able to get farther than a few pages. It's like he thought every idea that popped into his head and every word that dropped out of his mouth were pure gold. I think he would've been a better writer if every day for about a month someone had walked into his room, stood smiling over his bed for a minute, and then punched him in the stomach.

You also suggested I write my dialogue the standard way. I'm sure you know this, but I do my dialogue the way Joyce did. I've seen others do it that way, too. Also, I think it would be better to leave all the *spits* as they are, and not change them to *spat*, which sounds too formal for my narrator.

Finally, I'd like to remind you once again to please use my new business address, P.O. Box 765, Newburg, OH 48771, instead of my home address. I really need you to make this change in your records. No need to go into details, but let's just say a certain Kabbalist in my house doesn't think this is the best way I could've spent $295.

6

The cabin was one big room. In the middle was a long table with five KFC bags on it. The table was the kind they have in schools, with foldout legs. At the two long sides were backless benches made of split logs, the wood gray and worn smooth. The log walls were gray and smooth too and light shone through them at odd spots where the chinking was gone. On the back wall a stone fireplace big enough to hold a tricycle was full of beer cans and fast food trash; a paisley couch with the cushions missing and its matching chair sat in front of it. Everything in the place looked like it had been pulled out of a Dumpster except for two corners where electronics still in the box, televisions, DVD players and car stereos, were stacked to the ceiling.

—Grab you a seat, Fee said. He laid the pistol on the table and sat down.

I sat down across from him.

—Get the fuck up, the wiry guy said. Me and her sits together.

I stood up and went around the table and sat down next to Fee. His pistol was a .38 and it was now eighteen inches from my left hand. He didn't seem worried about that, though. The young woman sat down across from Fee. You had to look twice to see she was pretty. She didn't have on any makeup, her hair was half combed, and the sourness of the room had seemed to attach itself to her, but her eyes were big, an odd shade of pale blue, and arresting despite their dull expression, or maybe because of it. Her cheeks were high and delicate with two doll-like, almost identical constellations of freckles; the rest of her skin was pale and smooth and looked like you could drink it.

—This is my daughter I told you about, Fee said. Melinda. And this is her boyfriend, Fluke.

Melinda nodded at me without expression, and Fluke fixed me with a dull stare that looked like he was watching a snake digest a rat.

—Let's say the grace, Fee said.

I thought he was kidding, but he put his elbows on the table and steepled his hands, closed his eyes and started. I was so surprised I didn't even think before I reached for the pistol; my fingers were almost on the butt when Fluke locked his hand around my wrist and jerked my hand away and slammed it down, making a hollow thump and setting the table wobbling. Fee didn't open his eyes. He just kept praying, saying things so ornate they sounded like they should've been in needlepoint on the wall of the Queen's bathroom. Fluke was leaning over the table, grinning in my face. His teeth were the color of dishwater.

Fee finished, opened his eyes, and reached for one of the bags. Fluke released me and fell back into his seat.

—What do you want with me? I said and my voice came out shaky.

—Don't know yet, Fee said.

—But you were. . . you told me there was a phone here.

—Yessir, I did. I got no idea why I said that. It just came out of me.

He got a meal box out of a bag. Melinda and Fluke were already eating. Fee pushed a bag toward me.

—Help yourself, he said.

I shook my head.

—It's got a breast in it, he said.

Fluke put down his drumstick and fixed me with an exaggerated grin.

—He's *skeeered*, he said drawing out the word. I don't know where I got the courage, but I just stared at him. His grin quickly disappeared and his face stiffened. He put his fingertips on the edge of the table, like a gunfighter in a movie, and this displayed his tattoos, which were a mishmash of bad van art—an eagle, a skull with a snake threading through it, a fist holding a thunderbolt. I looked at them a moment. Then I slid off the bench and stood up. Fluke jumped up and stood in front of me, his chest stuck out and his hands clenched into fists at his sides. He looked like an eighth grader doing *West Side Story*.

—I'm leaving, I said. You want to try to stop me, go ahead, but I don't think you will. I think you're the kind of people who just like to catch a frog and put it in a jar and look at it but you're not sure why.

No one said anything.

—People saw you get in the car with me, Fee, I said. If I don't come back home tonight, you're going to be the first place the police look.

Fee cleared his throat.

—Could be, he said. But if they's no body, they's no crime.

7

I started backing toward the door. Fee watched me over his shoulder. Fluke started toward me, but Fee held up a hand and stopped him. I backed out the doorway onto the porch, glanced around for the dogs, then stepped off the porch and, still watching the cabin over my shoulder, went down the hill to the logging road. Fee appeared in the doorway. He cupped a hand at his mouth and made an odd sound and immediately the four dogs appeared from the woods and formed a semicircle ten yards in front of me, blocking my way down the road. I stood there a moment. Then I bent over and gathered up three chunks of gravel the size of golf balls. I took a step forward to see what the dogs would do. They didn't move. They kept their heads lowered and watched me.

—Don't do that, Fee called.

—Fuck, let him, Fluke said from inside.

I threw one of the rocks and it passed six inches over the head of the blue hound and skittered down the road. He didn't move. He just started panting, his tongue hanging out.

—That ain't a good idea, Fee said.

I looked at the dogs, then back up the hill at him. He didn't say anything else. He just went back inside.

8

I stood there for maybe two minutes, looking at the dogs and thinking. Then I moved up the hill, away from the dogs. A moment later, they slid off into the woods again, two on one side of the road and two on the other.

I was in a kind of shock, I think. I was starting to understand I might not get out of this. An hour ago I had been tooling down the road having another crappy day at work, and now I was some idiot's whim away from death.

I had my back to the cabin, so I turned around and faced it. Where I was standing was shady and the ground was covered by brown needles and rotted leaves and silver mottles of sunlight coming through the trees. I couldn't stop thinking that sunlight might be the last I'd ever see. The last time death had said hello to me was a car accident my junior year in college. A drunk in a pickup truck hit me on an access road, and I had to have a couple of surgeries, my spleen had to be removed and one lung was collapsed. I wasn't in a coma, though, I knew what was going on, and every face that appeared at my bedside was either grim or heartbroken. I thought if I managed to live, things I hated like going to class or listening to my girlfriend Joan talk about her stomachaches would seem wonderful.

And for a while they did. For a while after I recovered everything seemed precious and it was during this euphoria that I asked Joan to marry me, and the very next weekend we drove to a wedding chapel in the Smokey Mountains. However, it wasn't long afterward that I found myself getting perturbed again because I didn't have a postage stamp when I needed it, or I made it to a movie ten minutes late, or I got a soggy piece of fish in a restaurant. Things got back to normal, only now I was married.

Standing in those woods, though, every glimmer of light and dried out needle seemed precious and I didn't want to lose them, and I swore to myself that if I did make it out of this alive, I was getting divorced. Life was just too short.

9

I went back inside. They were all at the table, drinking. Fee had his pint in front of him and Fluke and Melinda were sharing a Mason jar that held a clear liquid, moonshine I was sure. When I came in they stopped talking. I sat down next to Fee, then pulled over the last KFC bag. I had decided my only chance was to ingratiate myself and do whatever they wanted, then hope for someone to find my car and start looking for me.

—Who said you could have it? Fluke said.

—We got more company comin' it seems, Fee said. They's a chance he might want to eat.

—That fat S.O.B.'ll be all over it, Fluke said, and then he drank from the Mason jar. His eyes already had a bright wild look from the alcohol.

—Now that's an unkindness, Fee said.

Fluke laughed and took another drink.

—Hell, he said.

—Yessir, they is one, Fee said.

—Yeah, well dammit, who cares? Fluke said. I'm sick of hearing you flap about that.

Fee smiled sedately. Then Melinda undid two buttons in the middle of her shirt and fanned her hand back and forth in the opening.

—Here, have you a drink, Fee said. He pushed the pint over to me. I picked it up, took a sip, then pushed it back to him. He pushed it to me again.

—Get you a good one, he said.

I took another drink, a long one. The liquor took my breath going down and my eyes watered up.

—Here you go, Jim Dandy, try some of this, Fluke said. He pushed the Mason jar across the table.

—In a minute, I said.

—Puss, Fluke said.

Suddenly the burning in my belly turned to warmth and then it hit my head and I felt all right. I smiled at Fluke. He didn't like that. I tilted the Mason jar on the table and swished around the moonshine. There were tiny black specks in it.

—Your liquor's got bugs, I said.

—That's charcoal, dumb ass, Fluke said.

I lifted the jar and smelled. It had no smell.

—Fluke's just learning how to make it, Fee said. So far he's about the only one who'll drink it.

—She's drinking it, Fluke said and jerked his thumb at Melinda.

—That don't mean nothing, Fee said. She could drink Prestone and think it was grape pop.

—Yeah, well, this shine is good, Fluke said.

—Then why's it got charcoal in it? Fee said.

I took a drink of it. It didn't taste like anything.

—See? He's drinking it, Fluke said.

Then it felt like boiling water was in my gut. No warmth came, though, only a lost, sick feeling like I had gone from the first twenty minutes of a drunk to the last twenty, when it feels like one more drink will poison you but you still have to take it. I tried to stand up. They didn't know that, though, because I didn't make it past thinking about it. I thought to look for the pistol. It was still there on the table, inches from my hand. Then for some reason I thought about a girl I knew in high school, saw her sitting on the end of a diving board in a gold bikini, swinging her legs.

—There's the pistol, I said.

They were talking and didn't pay me any attention. I grinned at Melinda. She looked back at me with a dull stare. I picked up the jar and took another drink.

—There's the pistol, I said again and started laughing.

Then the pistol disappeared and I looked at Melinda again. Her eyes met mine this time and I smiled.

—I like your shirt, I said.

Fluke came up from his seat and slapped me. It felt like an angry woman had hit me. I told him that. That made Melinda laugh, so he slapped her too. Gave her a rosy glow. Fee was laughing.

—Why am I here? I said and started laughing too.

Fee said something, but I didn't hear because Melinda touched her face.

10

Her fingernails were dirty. When I stopped looking at them, Fee and Fluke were gone. I looked at her again.

—You don't know how happy you could be, I said.

Then suddenly Brockton was next to me.

—He's drunk, Fee said.

—I'll get his ass sober, Fluke said. He hit me like a woman again.

—We want him drunk, Fee said.

—What're you gonna do with him until it's time? Brockton said.

—Keep him here, Fee said.

—Why? I said.

—Cause we got some cows that need to be mounted, Fluke said.

I stood up. Swaying, I looked at all of them. The bench fell and spun in circles that went through my feet. I leaned on the table.

—I just see the one, I said.

Fluke gave me another one of his woman hits.

11

They disappeared. Only she was left, sitting across the table from me with the pistol in front of her. That was okay.

12

I woke up, my head on the table. The pistol was in front of her, eye level with me. I could smell its oil and the burn from where it had been fired earlier. I sat up, and my head sloshed and throbbed. I shut my eyes against that, then opened them again. She was watching me. Her face was blank. We kept looking at each other. Then finally she spoke.

—I ain't got nothing on under this shirt, she said.

—Huh?

She started unbuttoning it.

—What time is it? I said and looked at my wrist but my watch was gone.

—They're gone, she said. Won't be back till supper.

—Where are they?

—Checking plants. They got to go all over.

—Plants?

—Pot, she said.

She finished unbuttoning her shirt and looked at me with the faintest of smiles.

I grabbed for the pistol but missed and knocked it off the table. It hit the plank floor and spun away.

—Don't worry about that, she said. I'm gonna let you go.

—Huh? I said.

—I'm gonna catch it tonight whether you're here or not, so I don't give a shit.

We kept looking at each other. Finally she looked away and gathered the flaps of her shirt together.

—Just go on then, she said. Don't take that pistol, though. It's Daddy's.

I stood up and went across the room and picked up the pistol, then went to the door and stood there squinting against the light. I turned around.

—Do you want to go? I said.

She laughed a mean hard laugh, but then she seemed to think about it a second. She shook her head.

—Fluke's gonna get me a lawyer, she said. Get my kids back.

—There's other ways to do that.

—Oh yeah? What? You gonna pay?

—There's programs, I said. Things like that.

She shook her head.

—I been in programs, she said.

—Well, it'd be better than. . . this, I said.

—Look, you want to help me out? Fuck me real quick and then get the hell out of here.

—What do they want with me? I said.

She didn't answer, so I turned and started out again. Behind me she said:

—They're doing business with some new people, but they don't trust them.

I turned around in the doorway.

—Bunch of Mexicans, she said. Fluke and Daddy are supposed to deliver the first load of pot tomorrow night, so they was gonna make you drive the truck in case this bunch was planning something. They was gonna pay somebody to do it, but then they cooked up making you do it.

—How do they think they can make me? I said. What would keep me from. . . I don't know, driving that truck straight to the sheriff's station?

—Well, because if you did that, the sheriff'd point his gun at you and tell you turn right around and deliver that shit where you're supposed to.

—What?

—You don't move as much pot as they do in a little place like this without the sheriff getting his share, she said. And anyway, they took your wallet and keys. Your car's probably gone by now, too, and they might even make a copy of your house key. So if telling you they was gonna shoot you wasn't enough, they was gonna use your family against you.

Then she stood up and came around the table, holding the flaps of her shirt together in one hand. She approached me, her free hand held out. She had that faint smile again.

—Why don't you give me that pistol? she said.

13

We did it on that couch that didn't have any cushions. The uphol-stery was rough and scratchy and smelled like a wet towel in a hot car. After it was over I didn't want to kill myself, but I didn't want to go outside and plant flowers either.

She told me if I'd leave the pistol she'd keep the dogs off me. I agreed because I didn't think I could shoot four moving dogs in five or six seconds. She called the dogs with one of those odd sounds and got them around the back of the cabin and gave them the left-over chicken bones. There was no good-bye from either of us.

As I was walking down the logging road, stumbling sometimes because of my shoes, my head cleared a little. I decided since there were no houses nearby I'd go back to my car and retrieve my cell phone—I could still get into the trunk through the fold-down rear seats—and then keep going down the road until I hit a spot where I had service or came to a house where I could make a call.

I turned the last bend in the road and came in sight of the open-ing where it entered the woods—it looked like a tall bright door-way—and then I had to stop and vomit. It had some blood in it. When I was done I tried to spit the bad taste out of my mouth, but I had cottonmouth and couldn't get much saliva worked up.

Suddenly I had the strange feeling I was being watched. I glanced up from my stooped position and didn't see anyone, then stood up and looked all around.

The blue hound was sitting fifteen or twenty yards back up the road.

I started walking again, watching him over my shoulder. He fol-lowed me, keeping some distance between us. I stepped into the woods and searched until I found a stick about the length of a base-ball bat, then got back on the logging road with it and walked out of the woods and onto the paved road. The hound kept following me.

Famous Writers School
P.O. Box 1181
Fayette WV 32111
April 23, 200—

Dan,

You can copy the forms of Joyce until the "moocows" come home—a dash instead of a couple of little squiggles, it makes no difference—but it's useless to copy the forms of the masters without having a handle on the artistic orthodoxy that gives their work substance. Picasso was a realist, my friend, for years and years, and a damn good one at that, and only after he had learned to paint an apple that looked like an apple did he produce the groundbreaking work he would be acclaimed for. Of course, you might counter and defend your imitation of Joyce by saying that Picasso's great talent was stealing, as many art critics have pointed out. Certainly, every artist steals. However, when one steals, he must steal brilliantly.

As for your resistance to my advice to modulate the action in your novel, well, each man chooses his own meat. But I can say this with all certainty: fiction is about *moving* the reader one way or another, nothing else, and though sensational sex and violence might titillate for a while, soon the reading experience is like taking a stroll down a nude beach with a beloved aunt—one isn't quite sure where to put his eyes. The sex here also happens too conveniently, even for a genre piece. Even a detective story has to make claims toward verisimilitude. I think the problem is that you're ignoring my advice from lesson 1, which is that writing fiction is *not* wish fulfillment. Women, on the whole, aren't like the ones in your novel or the ones most detective fiction writers create—in detective fiction, women are usually just ghostly constructs of a pliable feminity that exists only in the male imagination. Hitchcock did a quasi-parody of this in *Vertigo*, and if you persist in your current course, I'm afraid that all that will be left for your protagonist to do is fall into an empty grave, as Jimmy Stewart does in that movie.

You mentioned you're married. So, when writing women, think about that experience, its likely complexity, and go from there. Ditto for sex. However, if you don't rethink your approach, the subtle misogyny in your novel will ultimately undermine any interest it might hold.

As for Proust, ignore or even pummel him, as you suggest, it makes no difference. He's still there and must be dealt with, and you would be wise to learn the lessons he teaches us.

Your address has been changed in my records.

Sincerely yours,
Wendell Newton

Linda Trane's First Affair, Cont.

The Poet doesn't really die. It's just a starter pistol. After our argument he takes me on the hardwood floor.

For Christmas I go to Disneyworld with my family. While my husband takes the children to the tropical paradise swimming pool, I call the Poet from the bathtub. I tell him one slip and the cell phone could drop in the water and electrocute me, so he should be careful what he says. I tell him I feel like maybe I want to die anyway, maybe today is the day, I can no longer distract myself with a constant stream of holidays, errands, books, music, shopping, conversation, food, exercise, sex, news, movies and cars. I haven't said a prayer since my wedding night, I tell him, when I asked God that my husband and I not be the kind of people whose parties make good short stories. But look at us now, I say. The other day Bob was talking about a couple we know and he said, They're a good team.

I stop and wait for the Poet to answer. He doesn't for a moment. With my free hand I push the water and watch the waves slap my feet.

Tired of holidays, are you? he says. You ought to try one of mine on for size. Try not lying around a two-hundred-dollar-a-day hotel room feeling sorry for yourself, with three people who love you at least *some*—and probably the best they can—one short elevator ride away. Tonight you'll eat shrimp and drink champagne. If that's all just too much for you to take, run the minivan your husband's paid for into a telephone pole.

You know, I think I want to end this, I say.

Go ahead, he says.

You're a jerk, I say. Like most men I've known.

That says more about you than it does men, he says.

Suddenly there's a knock on the room door.

Someone's at the door, I say.

Probably your husband.

No, he's got a key.

Oh, so you let him have one, he says.

Another knock. Then, weakly:

Estelle? Estelle, wake up.

Someone at the wrong door, I say.

So it is your husband, he says.

You just don't stop, do you? I say.

Another knock, more insistent.

Estelle? I've forgotten my nitroglycerin.

Oh my God, I say. It's some guy who needs his nitroglycerin.

Well, tell him he's at the wrong room, he says.

Hold on, I say. I set the phone on the commode lid and stand up; the water sucks and whooshes. I step out of the tub and go to the bathroom doorway, four feet from the room door.

I'm sorry, I say in a loud voice, but you've got the wrong room.

No answer. Then I hear a noise that could either be the thump of someone falling or a door closing down the hall.

Hello? I say loudly.

Still no answer.

I'm dripping all over the floor, so I grab a towel off the rack and spread it on the floor, then pick up the phone and start pushing the towel around with my foot. I tell the Poet what's happened.

Did you think of opening the door? he says.

It could be a trick, I say. And I'm naked.

Then just stay on the phone with me, he says. If something happens, I'll call the Disney corporation and alert them.

Funny, I say.

Has the door got a chain? he says.

No, but one of those slot and bar things that's just like one.

Then this is easy. You won't even have to get dressed. Just put the slot and bar thing together, then stand behind the door and crack it. You'll be able to see whether he's there or not.

That's a good idea, I say. Hold on. I lower the phone, slide the bar into the slotted arm, then crack open the door and peek around it. An old man is across the hallway, leaning against the wall and watching the door. He looks confused. He's wearing a thin blue vest with several medals and military insignia pinned on it, a bolo tie with military insignia on the medallion, and a baseball cap with the name of a navy ship stitched on it in gold letters.

Hi, I say.

Hello, he says. I'm looking for three-oh-one.

This is three-oh-one, I say, but my family has been in this room for several days.

He nods. He looks up the hallway, embarrassed.

Is this an emergency? I ask. Could I call the desk for you?

No thank you, ma'am. Sorry to have bothered you.

It's really no problem, I say. I heard you mention nitroglycerin.

He shakes his head and starts away.

Really, I say, but he keeps walking off. I'm about to raise the phone, when suddenly I hear Bob's voice.

Hey, he says.

He has come down the hall from the other direction. I smile at him, then shut the door so I can undo the slot and bar. I raise the phone.

. . . going on there? the Poet is saying. Are you—

Gotta go, I whisper, then set the phone on the high luggage rack next to the door, above a row of empty hangers. I open the door, staying behind it to hide my nakedness, and Bob comes in the room. He shuts the door and then we stand facing each other. His face, shoulders and arms are burned pink. He looks me up and down.

I put the kids in day care, he says.

I raise my eyebrows and nod.

Why were you looking out the door? he says.

Did you see that old man in the hall?

Yes.

He knocked on the door, I say. He thought this was his room.

We have sex. It seems to take forever. Somewhere in the middle I start thinking I forgot to turn off the phone. When we're done, I get up to go to the bathroom. After I step around the corner that hides the bathroom from the rest of the room, I grab the phone, go into the bathroom, shut the door and raise the phone.

Wendell? I say. Are you still there? Wendell?

Famous Writers School
P.O. Box 1181
Fayette WV 32111
May 1, 200—

Dear Linda,
You created more scenes in this lesson, so good work on that. However, I think your prose is probably a bit too punchy. Try throwing in a sentence every now and then that is so ornate it sounds like it should be in needlepoint on the wall of the Queen's bathroom.

Also, I would still advise against calling a character the Poet, and I would not call him Wendell, either. If that's meant as a joke, then fine, the joke's been made, but now you need to pick another name for the character. If you have trouble doing that, I find it often helps to search the obituaries.

Sincerely yours,
Wendell Newton

Rio Jordan

Lesson 2

Dear Mr. Newton,
Thank you for offering to publish my work. I'm truly honored. However, I'm afraid I'm going to have to decline. I'd just rather not have "Five Story Ideas" in print. For one, I don't feel it's good enough, but also, all five story ideas are true. They're also very personal, except for the one about the Olympic swimmer, although I'm not crazy about advertising the fact I waitressed in a strip club either. I just did it for a couple of months, but it was while I was married. I managed to keep it from my husband by telling him I was participating in a sleep research project at the university and that was why I was gone half the

night. If he'd found out, I wouldn't have blamed him for being upset. You had to wear this cheap little dress and to make tips you had to flirt. I know there's a school of thought that says this situation is empowering to women because it turns the male power structure on its head, and they trot out Marx and Foucault and Lord knows who else to make their case, but I doubt they have any idea what it's like to let a sweaty guy put his hand on your ass at 1:00 A.M. because you're hoping he'll leave you the change out of a ten. Anyway, I'd just rather not have those stories published.

What I would like, though, is to develop one of them into a short story. In my last letter I asked if you could give me feedback on which idea would be best to develop into a story, and I guess because you liked the piece as a whole you didn't offer any suggestions. I've been considering writing about the pastor who got sick and slept with all the women. However, when I sit down to write I don't know where to begin. So what I'm going to do is free-write about that whole incident, and I'd really appreciate it if you could read what I come up with and give me some advice on how to proceed. I know this might seem a funny way to go, but I've reached my wit's end and don't know what else to do. I sit down at the computer every day, and then just sit there and sit there, looking at the screen. I write a sentence, read it until it disgusts me, then delete it. That goes on for hours.

Thanks for your help.

I've never had a good relationship with a man. Is it Pastor Ron's fault? Is he the shifty and untrustworthy Ur-man and now I must constantly seek him out and try to change him? No! Even if that is true, it's kind of stupid, not to mention whiny. I did once tell Susie Blakely I was going to marry Pastor Ron. It was in Vacation Bible School and I made a wedding cake out of Playdoh, then got the teacher's matches out of her cigarette case and stuck them in the cake for candles and lit them. I didn't know wedding cakes didn't have candles. All I'd seen were birthday cakes. I couldn't get the matches blown out. It made a nice little fire and the teacher screamed and got everyone out of the room. She put out the fire by stomping on it. She said she burned her heel. She bent me over and made me look at the skin. Then she dragged me downstairs to Pastor Ron's office. This was the only time I ever talked to him alone. He was wearing a white shortsleeve shirt and a thin dark tie and a Bible and some other big books were on his desk. He was writing on a yellow pad and smoking a cigarette. An air conditioner rattled in the window behind his chair. His office was the only place in the church that had air. He looked up and smiled when we came in and the teacher was all fluttery. She told him what I had done. He said okay, she better get back to the children, he'd take care of it. She left and he asked me to sit down. The chair was black leather. He looked at me, squinting as he took a puff on his cigarette. I was so embarrassed. I thought I was going to cry. I looked at the floor.

"You know who Smokey the Bear is, don't you?" he said.

I kept staring at the floor and nodded. The carpet was red.

"Okay then," he said. "So what does Smokey say?"

I looked up and said quickly, "He came to our room but he didn't really say anything, the teacher read some stuff and he gave us rulers," and then I looked at the floor again.

"Okay, but what was the general message?" he said.

I shrugged.

"Riordan, look at me," he said.

I did. He was smiling.

"Let's just forget about Smokey," he said. "I know you understand what you did was wrong. I also know that you're a young lady now, much too old to be doing these kinds of things."

I nodded.

He said we probably ought to pray and ask for forgiveness. We bowed our heads. I peeked to see if his eyes were closed. They weren't. He was looking at something on the yellow pad and holding his cigarette out to the side. I shut my eyes again.

"Amen," he finally said aloud.

I opened my eyes.

"Okay. I think we're all squared away here," he said. He smiled. "You know, Riordan, I have trouble believing your mom doesn't supply you with enough cake at home, so that you have to start making them here. Her pineapple cream cake is the best thing at our potlucks."

I nodded.

"What were you making? A birthday cake?"

I nodded.

"Whose birthday is it?" he said. "Not yours, is it?"

I shook my head.

"Well, all right. You better get back up there. Try to stay out of trouble."

I slid out of the chair.

"And don't let Mrs. Berkee make you feel too bad," he said. "I think her heels are always red."

I nodded and ran out of the office.

The only other older guy I ever had a crush on was Dr. Stoddard, my American history teacher in college. He was forty and fairly nice looking and his lectures were fun to listen to. I always liked him as a teacher, but I didn't have a crush on him until one day in the middle of a sentence he stopped talking and got a funny look in his eyes and then dismissed the class. I went to the student union for a Coke, but later I went by his office. I felt a little forward doing it. The door was closed and I knocked. He opened the door, looked at me a moment, then turned his back and said, "Come in, Riordan." His office was usually neat as a pin but now most of the books were off the shelves and the file cabinet drawers were open and papers were stacked everywhere. The office was just a complete and total mess. A radio was playing.

"Is something wrong, Dr. Stoddard?" I said.

He was standing behind his desk—wait a minute, someone's at the door.

My pizza's here. Pepperoni and mushrooms. See, I'm putting everything on the page. No filtering. When I heard the bell I was afraid it might be Alma. Yesterday I called Rob to tell him I found some of his old family photos and Alma was there. I could hear her bitching in the background. Rob and I spoke for all of a minute and a half, but later that night Alma called me. I didn't know it was her at first, but whoever it was sounded like they were on a pay phone. I could hear traffic in the background. I said hello and a voice said,

"This is your last warning, bitch."

I asked who the hell this was, and the fact that she had to tell me seemed to make her even more angry.

"You're *gonna* know me before this is all over," she said.

"Look," I said, "I wouldn't get back with Rob if he gave me a salary. He's yours, lock, stock, and barrel. But if you call me one more time, I'm calling the police."

"Go ahead and do that. I am the police," she said.

"What?"

"Badge number three-four-eight-eight. Eleven-year veteran."

I almost laughed. "If you're the police, then I'm Barbra Streisand," I said.

Then I heard a dog barking. It sounded like it was right next to the phone. It kept going, and she didn't say anything.

"What's that?" I said.

"That's Red Sammy," she said. "You're gonna get to meet him soon." Then she hung up.

I called Rob on his cell phone. I told him what had happened and asked him if she was really a cop.

"Yeah, that's how we met," he said.

"What?"

"I was doing stress workshops for the department," he said.

Someone called three more times last night. I let the machine pick up every time, and all three times there was nothing but a dog barking on the message. It sounded like that same dog. Then about four this morning, a weird light came in my bedroom window. My apartment is street level so you get the glare from streetlights and headlights, but this was brighter than that, almost blue. I'd been home from my gig for an hour and had just turned off the lights and gotten in bed. When the light just kept shining on the wall across from the foot of my bed, I kind of freaked. I thought maybe it was the spotlight on Alma's cruiser. But as soon as I got out of bed and went to the window the light disappeared. I didn't see a car or hear one drive off.

Okay, back to Dr. Stoddard. That day in his office when I asked him what was wrong, he just shook his head and said, "I'm resigning my position."

"Oh," I said.

He didn't offer an explanation. We just stood there looking at each other across the desk.

"Do you mind me asking why?" I said.

"I'm sorry, but I'd rather not discuss it."

"Well, okay, but I'm really sorry to hear it. I think you're a great teacher."

"Thank you," he said. "That means a lot."

"Did something happen?" I said.

He shrugged.

"But it's the middle of the semester," I said.

"Semesters," he sighed, "are the teaspoons academics use to measure out their lives." He shook his head. "I'm absolutely sick of hearing them take their tedious positions on tedious questions that end up in journals that sit in libraries and never get their spines broken until some other tedious argument needs to be made so someone can keep his job repeating the same information year after year off a yellow legal pad." He paused. "You know, Riordan, I guess if you really want to know why I'm quitting, there's no reason I shouldn't tell you. Not now."

"I do. I want to know," I said.

"Well," he took a deep breath, "it's because I don't think I can take seeing one more twenty-year-old girl raise her arms above her head to stretch, pull her shirt up, and expose that tanned slice of smooth belly around her navel."

I kind of fell for him right there. I couldn't believe anyone would actually tell the truth like that. Two weeks later we slept together. The whole time we were together he never could relax, though. He kept saying, "You know I'm still going to give you the grade you make," and whenever we got together he always insisted we go in separate cars to this town an hour away, and even there he refused to go into a restaurant. He'd check into a motel, pay cash, and then make me go out and get something and bring it to the room. What bothered me most, though, was he ended up finishing the semester instead of quitting. I think he's an academic dean somewhere down in Florida now.

Pastor Ron. It was just after we got word that he was dead (murdered in El Paso outside a bar. Apparently he went in there flashing his money. Not long after his wife went into the psych ward, and he disappeared along with eight thousand dollars from the church account) my mother cornered me one afternoon after I got in from school. She was sloppy drunk. She sat at the kitchen table with her rum and Coke, leaning over and kissing me whenever the whim hit her and talking about Pastor Ron.

"Now there was a *man*," she'd say. Or, "If I'd been married to him, I wouldn't be sitting here like this." Or, "Ron made a woman feel like a woman."

I wanted to go to my room. But I knew she'd start crying if I did and when Father got home he'd find her upset and want to know why. I wouldn't really get in trouble, but it'd just be a bigger mess, so I sat there. I was used to it. Finally, though, during one of her lulls while she poured a drink, I said:

"I've got homework. I guess I better get started."

She didn't answer right away. She just kept looking at me.

"You know, I didn't really do anything with the preacher," she said. "It's not like your father thinks."

I stared at the table and nodded.

"We just made out," she said. "You know what that means, don't you?"

I nodded again.

"And how do you know that?" She giggled, then paused. "You've already let them, haven't you?" She gave me an appraising look. "Well, that's all right," she said. "You're a pretty girl."

Then she put a hand on my shoulder and leaned in close.

"Go on, do your math," she whispered. "See how much good it does you. I made straight A's, too."

I left home at eighteen. I sang my way through community college, five or six nights a week in cover bands, and I made good enough grades to get a scholarship for the last two years. Then I went to work for the city and married Rob, who was my supervisor (Rob, Dr. Stoddard, Pastor Ron—I think I'm starting to see a pattern here). He was engaged to someone else when we got together, a third grade teacher. I'd met her several times at the office, a lovely woman. I felt like absolute trash for breaking them up, but I was in love and it seemed like I couldn't help myself. The teacher was devastated when Rob broke it off with her. She quit her job and moved out west somewhere, and Rob and I got married after being together for two months. Then I went back to school and got my master's at night and started doing the modeling because we needed the money and because Rob wanted me to—he liked the idea of being married to someone he could call a model, even if I was just standing next to vacuum cleaners. Then I went back to school full-time and got all the way to the dissertation before I realized I couldn't go it another step. I got divorced, and now here I am, singing again. What does Pastor Ron have to do with any of it? I don't know. All I know is I never saw myself being where I am now. I wanted a family, a decent career, an ordinary sort of life, not this mess I've got now. I thought maybe I could at least write about it and make some sense of it that way, but it seems like even that isn't going to work out.

Okay, there it is. God, what a whiny mess. I'd say you've got your work cut out for you. And again, thanks so much for your patience with me.

I was intrigued by your mention of the commercial you did and how it came about—a goldfish game and a nun with a bottle of gin? Sounds wacky! If you've got time to tell me, I'd love to hear about it.

Famous Writers School
P.O. Box 1181
Fayette WV 32111
April 25, 200—

Dear Rio,
I'm sorry you're not going to allow me to publish "Five Story Ideas." I will certainly honor your wishes, but I *must* disagree

with you about the merit of the piece. It's a wonderful story, and I'll try one final campaign against your objections.

Although, as you said, all five stories are true and personal, it's highly unlikely your readers will have any notion of that. In fact, I can say with certainty they'll never know. Think of memoirs. These books are supposed to be "real" and "personal" but is it likely everything they say is true? I doubt it. It seems certain these writers fabricate events because pure tedium is at the heart of most of existence: *Open the car door, close the car door. Realize the keys are still in your pants pocket. Lean over and awkwardly reach into your pants pocket. Discover the keys are in the other pocket. Curse, lean other direction and retrieve the keys.* See? And who can call these writers' hands on their overdramatized addictions and comebacks, all the preening that makes them look like eighth graders doing *West Side Story*? No one, because no one but them knows what happened.

However, I still admire your integrity and humility in refusing publication. Despite your many and obvious talents, you still have the prescience to know the task ahead of you is daunting and that there is much to learn. I wish all my students had this attitude. I'm currently working with a fellow who has had the temerity to suggest he has nothing to learn from Proust. I've kept the gloves on with him so far, but I don't know how much longer my patience will last.

As for your difficulties with writer's block, please know that's not uncommon. You might find this hard to believe, but there are days when I find it difficult to jot down a coherent grocery list.

Now, as for the story you're working on, I apologize for not making the sort of comments you requested. I believe the Pastor Ron episode is excellent story material. I think it'd be best to start with your childhood meeting with Pastor Ron, move to your mother's confession to your father, then finish with the scene where you and your mother are in the kitchen. Simply flesh out these episodes and you should have a humdinger of a story.

All right, I think that finishes all our business, and now, as you requested, I'll describe for you my brief, unexpected, and odd foray into the world of advertising.

One day, in a fit of rage, I went to a carnival. A small traveling show had set up in a parking lot at the edge of the commercial district two blocks from my house. The Kiwanis or Optimists or some such group was sponsoring it, for a good cause certainly, but all afternoon as I tried to write, tinny bells, whistles, horns, and muted screams came faintly into my room, and groups of neighborhood children formed a constant parade of carnival traffic up and down the sidewalk, making an uproar like a pack of chimps. I closed all my windows, but still the noise seeped in. Finally I slammed down my rolltop, locked it, and changed out of slippers into a pair of shoes I wouldn't mind burning when I got back. I don't know what I had in mind when I left the house, except to go and glare at every person and machine ruining my afternoon.

I entered the carnival and started down the small midway. I won't describe what I saw because you know what a carnival looks like. However, I couldn't understand how parents could put their children on these creaky, greasy, slapped-together machines that would sling them with wild speed and that were all tended by sullen, yellow-eyed men.

Finally I came to the tent where the goldfish game was set up. A large square of goldfish bowls sat at waist level in the middle of the tent, and I stood looking at it from behind a plywood counter set up on sawhorses. The bowls were hardly big enough to hold a good swallow of water. Stuffed animals hung from the ceiling of the tent and around its four sides, and a laconic teenager barked out an indifferent sales pitch. He wore a white T-shirt tucked into jeans held up by a tooled leather belt too big for him, the excess tucked down the front of his pants like an obscene arrow. He had just one customer, a little girl of five or six, and she shrieked as each Ping-Pong ball she tossed bounced off the fish bowls. She wore a pale pink dress with lace at the neck, and behind her at the edge of the tent stood a precisely coiffured man in a navy blue suit, who I imagined was her father. After each throw the little girl would turn around to see his reaction: sometimes he pasted on a smile and nodded, but usually he was looking off at something—if that were the case, the girl would quickly turn around and throw again.

I sidled up next to the little girl and handed the barker a dollar; he wordlessly put down five Ping-Pong balls in a thin trench notched into the plywood counter. The little girl looked at me. I smiled at her.

"Hi," I said.

"Hi," she said.

"Looks like you're doing great," I said.

A look of pride flashed in her eyes.

"I've almost caught a fish," she said.

She picked up a ball and threw it. It hit the rim of a bowl, bounced, fell, bounced again, and landed on the ground. She looked at me.

"Almost," I said.

She nodded. "Your turn."

We took turns throwing. When she ran out of balls the barker always put down five more in front of her; I figured her father must've paid him in advance. I didn't look at her father again. I preferred to pretend he wasn't there and that she and I would go on throwing Ping-Pong balls on this bright spring day forever.

Finally another customer stepped up to the counter next to me, a prettily plain woman of around forty carrying an electric blue stuffed snake and a small canvas shopping bag. She set these things down on the asphalt between us. I saw that her bag held a Glenlivet box.

"So, where did you win that?" I asked, smiling and then nodding at the gin.

She smiled back. Her teeth were straight and white, she had clear pale skin and short black hair with the odd strand of gray. She wore loose blue jeans, a plain white blouse, and Ben Franklin sunglasses. When she spoke her accent was Irish.

"There's not a game where one may win that," she said. "That one must be bought, I'm afraid."

"And dearly at that," I said.

"Aye," she said, laughing.

She introduced herself to the little girl and me as Mary; the little girl told us her name was Tess, and I told them mine, and then we took turns throwing.

After several tries, one of Mary's throws landed in a goldfish bowl with a plop.

"You caught a fish!" Tess yelled.

The barker picked the bowl out of the square and handed it to Mary. The small fish in it swam wildly; there was so little room it looked as if it were spinning in place.

"If you hit two you can trade up for anything on this row," the barker said, pointing, and then went back to his stool.

Mary looked around me at Tess. "I've already got too many goldfish at home," she said. "Would you be able to take this one for me, Tess?"

"Yeah!" she said.

I smelled her father before I saw him, a strong whiff of cologne. He was standing right behind us, smiling.

"That's a very nice offer," he said, "but I'm sorry, she just can't take a fish home."

"Please, Dad," Tess said.

"I'm sorry, Tess, no," he said.

Mary's lips were tight and she asked the question I wanted to: "Then why did ya' allow her to play th' game?" she said.

The father shrugged.

Mary said, "But didn't you think it possible—"

"Like I said, you made a nice offer." He looked down at Tess and held out his hand. "Come on, honey, we've got to go," he said. But she didn't take his hand. She had tears in her eyes.

"Sir," I broke in, "I understand this really isn't any of my business, but is there *any* way I could possibly convince you to change your mind?"

He looked at me and sighed. Then his eyes moved from me to Mary. They stayed there too long, like he was sizing her up. They moved back to me. He kept staring. I tried to make light of it and brushed at my hair.

"I'm not attracting flies again, am I?" I said.

He said, "You know the soft drink Dr. Ale?"

"Yes," I nodded. It was bottled locally, tasted like sugared dishwater, and was quite popular.

"Dad, can I have the fish?" Tess said.

He told her maybe, then gave her two dollars and sent her to buy some cotton candy.

"I work for Dr. Ale," he said when she was gone. "We're shooting a commercial today out at Topping Downs, but I found out a couple of hours ago our two actors aren't going to make it. A man and a woman. Apparently they met at the audition and started going out and last night they both got food poisoning. We're working on finding replacements right now, but I don't know if we have. I've got to get to a pay phone and find out. If they haven't found anyone, you two look about right. We've rented the lounge at Topping for the afternoon. There aren't any lines. You've just got to look happy as hell to be drinking Dr. Ale."

"I'll do it," I said, "if you let your daughter keep the fish."

I looked at Mary; she sighed, rolled her eyes and nodded.

"Okay, it's a deal," he said.

"What guarantee do we have that you'll actually let her keep it?" I said.

"Hey," he said, "I'd let her keep forty fish if she wanted them. It's just her mother."

Tess was coming back toward us, carrying a pink beehive of cotton candy that completely hid her head.

While Tess and her father went to make the phone call, Mary and I sat down at a picnic table between a couple of food trailers. Right away, as if to defuse any romantic tension, she told me she was a member of an order of nuns that had a house in town. I told her I was a writer. Our conversation was pleasant.

In ten minutes, Tess and her father were back. Tess was smiling, a crust of pink cotton candy on her lips. That afternoon, Mary and I were commercial actors.

All best,
Wendell

Lesson 3

Let Your Characters Have Their Own Lives

Several years ago I befriended a nun. To protect her privacy I'll call her Mariel. We met by chance one afternoon at a carnival and she ended up inviting me for dinner that night at the small brick ranch she shared with four other nuns. All five of them looked somewhere in their thirties or forties and their vocation was taking care of shut-ins and the elderly. It was one of the nun's birthday, and we had chicken cooked on the grill, corn on the cob, potato salad, chocolate cake and homemade vanilla ice cream. The party was lively. These women were bright, earthy, and always laughing.

Not long after dark, as we sat around the dining room table drinking Tom Collinses, thunder sounded, and as if on cue Mariel and the others got up and started placing buckets and pans throughout the house. I offered to help, but they said I wouldn't know where to place the receptacles, so I sat there while they bustled around. Finally Mariel approached the table with a red plastic bucket with a chewed-up rim. She was wearing Ben Franklin sunglasses even though we were inside—she'd recently had a procedure done on her eyes that required she wear them all the time for a few weeks.

"Better scoot, or you're likely to be soaked," she said.

"I could use a good washing," I smiled.

"Aye, I don't doubt that," she said.

Then she gave me a smile and a nod that said *move*; I stood up and scooted my chair down the table and she placed the bucket where my chair had been. Then we found ourselves standing close together, and the moment was something like a surprise encounter in a Jane Austen novel between a Mr. Somebody and a Miss Someone. I looked at her hand hanging at her side and a strange impulse seized me: I reached out for it, and, when she realized what I wanted, she blushed. I only had thoughts of lifting her hand and giving it a queenly kiss of thanks, but I realized I was making her uncomfortable, so I lowered my hand and said:

"So what happened to that bucket?"

"A little stray that we took in here chewed it up. We called him Paco. He disappeared a couple of weeks ago, though. We've looked and looked for him. We don't know what happened."

"I see," I said. "I'm sorry."

She nodded, gave me a faint smile and then hurried off.

When they finished, there must've been twenty-five or thirty buckets and pans laid out in the house, and when the rain finally started, it looked like it was sprinkling inside. All the drips hitting metal or plastic produced an almost musical tattoo.

During the height of the storm I felt the need to visit the men's room. Sister Farah, the birthday girl, red-headed, freckled, and a little drunk, directed me to the backyard.

Everyone laughed, and then Mariel told me the bathroom was at the end of the hallway.

"But pay no attention to the colors in there," said Sister Joan, a pert Sandy Duncan look-alike.

"And remember, *we* didn't do it," said Sister Toby, who looked like an attractive plus-size model.

"Yes, but *Mariel* was here when it was done," Farah said and they all laughed.

"But you know I had no hand in it," Mariel said. "I was the new one in the house then."

"I don't know if I want to see this," I said.

I got up and went down the hallway, sidestepping a couple of dishpans, and then stood in the bathroom doorway, groping for the light switch. I turned it on, stepped inside and shut the door. The bathroom was insane. A kaleidoscope of colors. The commode was dark purple, its tank gold. The white porcelain bathtub had rows of tiny dots in all colors on its side. The walls and ceiling were painted in vertical stripes of seven or eight colors. The toilet paper holder was peach. I pulled back the shower curtain: each four-inch tile in the enclosure was a different color. There was no discernible pattern to the mosaic and it hurt my eyes to look at it. I shut the curtain.

When I went back out, the women were laughing about something to the point of tears. Smiling in the awkward way you do when you come upon a scene like that, I sat down again.

"Well, what'd you think?" Farah said.

"What happened in there?" I said.

"Oh, when I came into this house, things were a bit, I don't know, shall we say *different*," Mariel said. "A wee bit blowsy."

"A couple of those sisters ended up getting long rests," Trudy said.

"Why don't you paint over it or clean it off?" I said.

A couple of them shrugged and shook their heads.

"Too much work, I guess," Mariel said. "We've got enough to do as it is."

We kept talking and drinking. Like everyone else, I got a bit drunk, and around ten the party started breaking up. I thanked them for having me and said I'd have them to my house soon. Mariel walked me out to the front porch. The rain had slowed to a gentle shower. She asked if I wanted a ride home, but my house was only a few streets over, a ten-minute walk, so I told her no, I enjoyed walking in the rain.

"And thanks again for having me over," I said.

"Aye, we enjoyed having you."

Then there was an awkward moment, a pause akin to the one earlier in the dining room.

"What would you think about me putting a roof on this house?" I said.

"What?"

"A roof on your house," I said. "If you can get the shingles, I'll take off the old roof and put on the new one."

"You do that kind of work?" she said. "I wouldn't have thought that."

"I used to make my living doing it," I said. "I had my own handyman service. Carpentry, plumbing, electrical, whatever was needed. I learned it from my father, who was the caretaker on an estate in central New York. It belonged to a man who owned race-horses."

I stepped off the porch into the rain and walked into the yard. I looked up at the roof. It was a dull silver against the dark sky.

"Why hasn't it been fixed already?" I said.

"The order has no money for it," she said.

All right, we've seen two things so far that will help us write fiction: (1) the characters haven't been what we would expect them to be, and (2) the other details haven't been typical, either. Take, for instance, the nuns. Imagine how Hollywood would botch them up. Movie nuns are either good-natured figures of fun or drawn and bitter frumps, although occasionally there's one who's a tortured mix of religion and sexuality who looks like a swimsuit model and plays a flute. Or take the drippy house and its grotesque bathroom.

They'd likely become cheap slapstick, not a touching backdrop for a group of kind and loving women.

So let's see how these characters actually develop when they're allowed to have *real* lives—the kind you'd want for them if you were writing good fiction—and not the cardboard cutout jokes the movies would choose for them.

I was walking home in the rain, happily drunk, when the enormity of my lie hit me: I'd never done any sort of handyman work. I couldn't drive a nail without sending myself to the emergency room, and to this day I don't know why I lied. It's just not in my nature. I'm wracked with guilt if I accidentally grab two newspapers out of the coinbox instead of one. But that evening, I spent ten more minutes on the front porch talking Mariel into letting me put on the roof, and then we went back inside to see what the others thought, and we decided I would put on the roof as soon they could raise the money for the shingles. Before I left, Sister Farah even called someone at the church to see if they could do a fund-raiser.

At home, I made a pot of coffee, then sat in my dim kitchen for a long time with my head in my hands. Finally I got up and went to the living room and unlocked my rolltop desk, retrieved my checkbook and savings passbook from their pigeonholes, and took them back to the kitchen. Between the two accounts I had almost twenty-six hundred dollars. I needed new tires on my car, so there was a hundred and fifty I couldn't spare. Two hundred dollars would take care of my expenses through the end of the month. So I had roughly twenty-two hundred dollars that could go toward a roof. I figured the job would cost three thousand, and, after some soul-searching, I knew what I had to do: I had a French first edition of *Swann's Way* given to me by my former wife. She bought it through the mail from a dealer in Marseilles and presented it to me on my twenty-fifth birthday. Given my heavy use of the book, it was now in poor condition and not worth the fortune it might have been, but it was still worth enough to keep a houseful of nuns warm and dry.

The next day, I got up early and drove to Pittsburgh, offered the Proust to six book dealers, and ended up selling it for seven hundred and thirty dollars.

Back in town by early afternoon, I went to the nuns' house. Farah answered the door. She seemed rushed and said she wouldn't be home long because she had a client to visit. Mariel came into the living room and said she was making lasagna for supper and I was welcome to stay. I thanked her, but said what I had come for wouldn't take long. I asked them both to give me five minutes, and we sat down.

"I know what this is about," Mariel said. "Now that there's no gin pouring, you've changed your mind about the roof."

"No, I haven't," I said.

Then I admitted my lie. I pulled out a bank envelope and laid it on the coffee table.

"There's enough money there for the roof," I said, "and again, I'm sorry. I know you've already involved others, too, so I can go to them if you want and—"

"Yes, you *can* tell them," Farah said heatedly. Then she stood up and went down the hallway and into a bedroom, slamming the door.

"Pay her no attention," Mariel said. "Today she got to the house of one of her clients and paramedics were there. The woman had just died. It was the old lady who lived down the street in that big old Cape Cod, Miss Blair. Farah had been taking care of her almost two years."

That was the same woman who'd had the dogs tied up in her yard. Though my incident with her had been some time ago, the news still sent a chill up my spine.

"I'll accept your apology, but not your money," Mariel said. "Hardly fair, I think. Get you in here and get you drunk, and any fool knows men promise the moon when they're drunk."

"I insist," I said.

"I'm sorry, but no," she said.

"If you won't take it," I said, "I'm going to give it to your order as a dedicated contribution, to be used only for putting a roof on this house."

She thought about it.

"All right," she said, "but you keep eight hundred. The fund-raiser at the church can buy the shingles."

"All right," I said.

"Will you stay to supper?" she asked.

"Thanks, but another time," I said.

I figured I had just enough time to make it back to Pittsburgh before the book shop closed. I drove my poor Dodge Dart as if it were an ambulance and what was usually an hour and a half's trip was accomplished in just under an hour. I twisted my way through streets in an older section of the city, then made the final turn I thought would put me on the block where the shop was, but nothing looked familiar. I drove around for several minutes but couldn't find the shop.

I won't bore you with the details of being lost in a large city during rush hour in late July in a car without air conditioning; finally I drove home in the humid dusk, drenched in sweat and defeat. At home, I consulted a map and discovered I'd had the wrong street name in mind and had been looking for a street that didn't exist.

By eight-thirty the next morning, I was sitting outside the book shop in my parked car, and right before nine, the old gentleman who ran the shop appeared, wearing a gray wool vest and puffing a thin cigar. He started unlocking the door.

"Hello, hello," I said, approaching.

He removed the key and turned his head. He recognized me and nodded.

"How're you?" he said.

"Fine, thank you. I've come to buy back my Proust."

"Certainly, as you wish," he said.

We entered the shop. It had a high ceiling, tall windows, and was full of light. The old fellow stepped behind the counter, used a key and removed my Proust from a display case and then started writing a ticket. I took out my wallet. He used a calculator, then wrote down the number and pushed the ticket toward me. The total with tax was $1,234.32.

"What's this?" I said.

"The cost of the book," he said.

"But . . ." I trailed off.

"Certainly you know a book dealer must charge more for his acquisitions than he's paid for them," he said.

"Yes, of course."

Squinting one eye, he relit his cigar, then shook out the match and tossed it on the oiled wood floor.

"I don't know why you sold the book," he said, "but despite its poor condition, it's quite a jewel, and I can't let it go for any less than this. I thought you must be quite fond of it, so I charged three hundred less than I had planned."

"That's very kind, thank you."

"So is this within your range?" he asked.

"I'm afraid not."

"Well, I'm terribly sorry," he said.

"I am too," I said.

Back at home that afternoon, I answered a help wanted ad for a lawn service, and started work the next morning. I spent an hour unsuccessfully trying to navigate a zero-radius-turn mower, and then my boss, a small, skulking man in gray work clothes who was quietly drunk by 10:00 that morning, pulled me off the mower and gave me a string trimmer; this I managed to use successfully the rest of the day.

The next morning, though, my back was frozen stiff. When I called my boss to tell him I couldn't work that day, he fired me.

I finally found two part-time jobs and held them for six weeks. I was dishwasher on the evening shift at an Italian restaurant, and a helper at a tree nursery in the morning. When I finally got the paycheck that put me over the top, I sped to Pittsburgh the next morning and again met the dealer at his door, an almost exact repeat of the previous scene except for one detail: this time when he recognized me, he shook his head.

"I'm sorry, but I sold it three days ago," he said.

I almost melted where I stood. My heart was literally a stone in my chest. He opened the door and I followed him in.

"I know it might seem irregular," I said, "but would you mind helping me contact the buyer?"

"I'm sorry, I can't do that. There's the question of privacy."

"Yes, of course. Well, would you mind contacting the buyer yourself and saying that the previous owner of the book would like to buy it back."

He considered this. "I'm sorry," he said, "but I'm afraid I can't do that either. The man who bought it is my best customer. He has one of the largest private collections in the state. He's quite eccentric, though. Nearly insane, really. I can't risk putting him off in any way, because my sales to him account for almost ten percent of my total each year. I hope you understand."

And that was that. Eventually I bought a paperback of *Swann's Way* in French and finished the task I'd set myself of reading it in the original.

As for the nuns, they got their new roof, and I continued my friendship with them until their various eccentricities became more than I could bear. It would be unkind to go through a laundry list of them, but as an example, I discovered that when buying bread Mariel liked to take off the twist tie and open the bag and sniff the loaf.

Now, if I were writing this story as fiction, I would leave out the part where Mariel sniffs the bread. Given what we actually saw of her, that detail seems out of character. Also, does it seem believable that a character would go to the lengths I did to make up for a drunken lie? Not really. In fact, even I can't believe I did it. So I would either make the character less scrupulous, or I would give him more motivation for making good on his word—for instance, there could be something terrible in his past that drove him.

Assignment: Look back at the story you've worked on for lessons 1–2 and find at least ten places where you can add new details—step outside the box you usually trap yourself in.

Linda Trane's First Affair Ends

I break up with Wendell. A few days later, though, I drive to his neighborhood and park down the street from his house. He has a stone birdbath in the front yard, gray with a nondescript bowl. There's no shrubbery in the yard, only empty flower beds on either side of the front stoop, their landscape timbers dark, soft, rotting.

I watch the house for an hour. Around noon, Wendell emerges and gets in his blue Buick. The car is new and still has the price sticker on a back window. He pulls out and I follow him. He goes first to a CVS drugstore. I pull in behind him and park a few spaces down from his car. A couple of minutes after he gets out, I decide to go inside, too. I'm already wearing a head scarf, and I put on a pair of sunglasses.

I spot him in one of the food aisles. He's standing behind a shopping cart, reading the label on a can of nuts. I go to the cosmetics aisle because I figure he won't go there. He puts the can of nuts in the shelf of the cart and then goes down the aisle, picking out can after can of food—soup, stew, deviled ham—what an idiot, I think, buys his canned food at a drugstore. Finally he pushes on to the personal hygiene aisle. He starts taking the tops off stick deodorants and smelling them. Then he drops one of the tops. It clatters to the floor. He steps away from the cart, searching. He pulls his pant legs up at the knees and bends over, which takes a good four or five seconds. He raises up again, his face flushed.

I'm getting tired of standing. My back hurts. But he's not through yet. After choosing a store-brand deodorant, he goes to the aisle where they have the plastic dinnerware, the kind you use when you eat on the patio. He puts a stack of green plastic plates in the cart. Then bowls and cups. He goes next to a display of elastic bandages and starts examining boxes. I've had all I can take. I leave the store, go back to the car and wait.

Fifteen minutes later he comes out. He loads his trunk with plastic shopping bags, then leaves the cart in the parking space next to his and we're off again. He drives several blocks down one street, then pulls into a strip club called Gals Galore. The building is new and the parking lot asphalt is shiny and black, its yellow paint brilliant and crisp in the bright afternoon sun. Wendell parks facing the building and I park a little up from him, backing into the space so I can watch him. He doesn't get out, though. He just sits in the car and stares at the building. Five minutes pass. Finally he starts the car but right away kills the engine. He keeps staring at the building. Once he ducks his head to look up through the windshield like he sees something in the sky.

Another car pulls into the parking lot, a white Camry with tinted windows. Two women get out. One is tall and brunette, one petite and blond. Both wear jeans and tank tops and carry long tennis duffel bags. They're headed toward the front door, but they stop at Wendell's car. He rolls down his window. It looks like they all know each other. The women are laughing. Wendell's arm slides out the window and around the brunette's waist. He leaves his hand there, then, after a quick pat, pulls his arm back inside. The women set their duffels on the ground and lean into his window. They talk a couple of minutes. Then Wendell starts his car. Laughing, the little blond reaches inside and grabs his shoulder. Then both strippers step back from the car and pick up their duffels. They wave.

He goes to get a haircut. The barbershop is in a strip mall and has plate glass windows, a lighted barber's pole spinning next to the door. I park right next to the main aisle, a perfect view. Wendell takes a seat to wait his turn. I can see the back of his head, his shoulders. He picks up a magazine, but right away he seems to join a conversation and suddenly the man in the barber chair lifts his hand from under the apron and points a finger at him. The next thing I know Wendell comes outside, grinning.

Next he goes to the library. I follow him into the parking lot, but this time I don't stop. I pull on through the lot and start back toward his house.

His neighborhood is all brick ranches and split levels, chain-link fences and yard furniture. Some of the houses are immaculate, some are doing a slow dive—Wendell's is somewhere in between. He has a small ranch and his driveway has a large crack with tufts of grass growing in it. I pull in to the driveway, then get out and stroll through his yard and around his house. The roof and gutters could use some work.

A woman is in the backyard of the house on the right, on her hands and knees digging with a hand spade around some rosebushes. A Coke can sits nearby and when she finishes digging, she picks up the can and pours a liquid that obviously isn't soda into the hole. She looks around sixty, energetic and fit. I go up to the chain-link fence and introduce myself.

Maud Gonne Roberts, she says, getting to her feet and approaching the fence. She pulls off a canvas glove and we shake.

Are you a friend of his? she asks nodding at Wendell's house.

Yes, I say.

She nods. If you're looking for him, I think he left about an hour ago, she says.

All right, thank you, I say. I guess I'll just wait. I smile. Your name sounds familiar for some reason, I say.

Yes, well, not many get the connection, she says. I've got the same name, Maud Gonne, as a woman who jilted the poet W. B. Yeats. My grandfather actually knew her. She was an Irish nationalist and he was too. He sent my father over here when he was eleven to live with an uncle. If I'd been a boy my father was going to name me after my grandfather, but he got a girl instead and did this. I was always called by both names in the family, and even though I don't especially like it, I'm so used to it now it seems I can't stop using it.

That's interesting, I say.

I suppose, she says. You'd think I would've gotten around to reading some of the man's poetry by now, but I haven't.

There's always things like that, I say.

Yes.

She nods, gives a little smile, and then gets down on her hands and knees and starts digging again. Would you like to come over here and sit down while you wait? she asks, motioning toward a lawn chair with her spade.

Sure, I say.

You can just walk around the fence, she says.

Okay, I say.

I walk down the fence, enter her driveway, and walk back. I sit down in the lawn chair a few feet behind her.

Beautiful day, I say.

Yes, she says, still digging.

Have you and Wendell been neighbors long? I ask.

I've lived here twenty-seven years. My late husband and I built this house, she says. She nods toward Wendell's house. He moved in four years ago, she says.

I see.

How long have you two been acquainted? she asks.

Not long, I say.

If you don't mind my asking, she says, what does he do for a living? I never see him leave at a regular time. He told me he's a writer, but when I asked him the names of his books he just said he had two novels in progress. That was right after he moved in.

I don't really know what he does, I said.

I see. You two just starting to date? she says.

Something like that, I say.

She digs for a moment without saying anything, then stops. She stands up and faces me, wipes her brow with the back of her glove. She says, You know, I should probably keep my mouth shut, but I'm not going to.

What'd you mean? I ask.

Oh, it's probably nothing. I'm probably just a silly old woman. But I'd watch my step if I were you. That's all I'm saying.

What is it? I say.

Well, he's in and out a lot. Doesn't keep regular hours. Plus I see all manner of people coming and going at that house. Don't get me wrong, he's friendly enough when you see him, but there's something odd there. I used to think he was selling drugs, but I don't think that's the case now. I've caught him in more than a lie or two, though, and that's not a good sign.

Like what? I ask.

Well, when he first moved in he told me he'd been in the Gulf War, then just a couple of months ago we were talking and he said he'd been in the air force back in the eighties. Once he actually told me he made the Olympic archery team, but said it was the year the games were in Moscow and he missed his chance because of the boycott. He went on a rant about Jimmy Carter. He doesn't strike me as an athlete though, not even an archer. I've seen him try to do things in the yard.

I see, I say.

Yes, well, it's none of my beeswax, I know that, she says.

No, thank you, I say. I'll keep all that in mind.

Then I hear a car on the street. I look up, afraid it's Wendell, but it's not. I knew it was risky coming here, but now it strikes me just how much so.

You know, now that I think about it, I guess I better go, I say. I'll just catch him another time.

I've offended you, she says.

No, not all, I say. I've just got another commitment and I don't have time to wait any longer.

We say our good-byes and I walk down to the end of her drive, then into Wendell's front yard. I stop at his birdbath and stand in front of it a moment. Then I start pushing the bowl off the stand—it's heavy and difficult to move—but finally it slides off and lands in the grass with a dull thud. Then I push over the stand.

Famous Writers School
P.O. Box 1181
Fayette WV 32111
June 3, 200—

Linda Trane,
   I'm writing to inform you that I am canceling your participation in this course. I don't know what you're doing, but if I receive any more correspondence from you or have even the slightest inkling that you've been to my house or are following me, I will contact the police immediately. Understand, this is not an empty threat. I wrenched my back returning my birdbath to its former state, and it is only my hope that this matter can fade away peacefully that keeps me from going to the police now. I don't know how you discovered my address, but just remember that Mrs. Roberts—despite her catty vitriol and old-woman gossip—is still a witness to your skulking, so it will be easy to prove your vandalism.
   Enclosed you will find a prorated refund of $147.50.
   Wendell Newton

Dan Federman

Lesson 3

Dear Mr. Newton,
   If I had known you were a fan of Proust, I never would've made a joke about him—sorry about that. Also, please know I respect your opinions. I recently found an old copy of *Upward Spiral* in a used bookstore, the one where the whole issue was taken up with your novella, *The First and the Last*, and I sat in the bookstore and read it and really liked it, especially the part where the woman rips apart the pearl necklace while the man watches, sipping a cup of coffee. I think we might just inadvertently be at cross-purposes here. What I really want out of this course is some page-by-page editorial advice, some cleanup

work before I try to find an agent, and not necessarily suggestions about how I should rethink my whole approach to writing fiction. I think you and I simply disagree on what good fiction does, and if that's the case, let me say again that I *do* respect your opinion, and I hope that you can respect mine.

I think I might have a solution to our situation. What if, instead of writing me letters about my work, you just send back the pages with edits? I'm sure I would benefit greatly from seeing your suggestions. I'm also sending a few more pages than usual this time. I hope that's okay.

Oh, by the way, I've been meaning to ask if you might have any ideas about a title for my novel. I don't have one yet, so I'd appreciate any insight you have.

Again, sorry about the Proust thing.

14

My car was gone. I guess because there was nothing else I could do about it I searched the pasture entrance for a clue to what happened. The blue hound sat on the shoulder a few yards away, watching me. The entrance was dirt and gravel and the gate was set back from the fence like a bay window. I found my faint tire tracks in the dust and also some bent blades of grass—I was a regular little G-man. Then I started feeling sick again, and I bent over and started dry heaving.

While I was bent over, I saw something blue in the grass around the creosote post where the gate was hinged. When I finally stopped retching I went over there and took a look. It was a poker chip with the name of a casino on it, the Northern Belle, a boat anchored in the river near Cincinnati. I'd been there once on a business trip, long enough to get a free drink and lose $5 in a slot machine. I pocketed the chip, spit a couple of times to clear my mouth, and started down the road. The hound got up and followed me. I really couldn't believe this dog. He seemed like a dog in a movie, one of those that has a constant voice-over of its thoughts so that by the end you wished you'd stayed home and read some Nietzsche.

I tried to figure out what significance the poker chip could have, but then I realized I was acting like a squeamish detective in a squeamish novel, who solves little Freudian mysteries in hotels and manor houses that have clocks that strike but no bathrooms and everyone just sits there holding it for three days until a couple of them confess just so they can go to jail and take a piss. I knew who took my car and why; the poker chip was just a coincidence.

I started thinking about the time I had visited that casino. There was a company convention in Cincinnati and I was one of the best salesmen in the state that year, so I had to go. The fact that I was so good at something I hated so much made me want to go to the garage at 3:00 A.M. and start the car and sit in it eating a bag of potato chips. I asked Joan if she wanted to go to the convention, but she didn't. That was probably just as well. If she had gone everything and everyone would've been disappointing to her in some slight but troublesome way, and by the third day she would've been staying in bed all day with a bag of red licorice and five or six magazines, complaining about everything, the television on just loud enough to be audible but not understood. Joan was a complainer, and any subject would do. A few weeks ago while we were driving home from an ice cream parlor, she said her pistachio ice cream should have more nuts. She said the pistachio ice cream she used to get had plenty of nuts, but they didn't make it like that anymore because there weren't any dairies left that were family-owned, they'd all gone corporate and the bottom line was all they cared about.

—The suffering of late capitalism, I said.

—Funny, she said.

We rode in silence a moment.

—Why do you always say things like that? she said. Things that don't really mean anything?

—I don't know, I said.

—Well, I wish you wouldn't do it, she said.

—Well, maybe I should learn French like you, I said. Then if I said things that don't mean anything it wouldn't seem so strange.

—See? she said. That's the kind of thing I'm talking about.

15

I walked for twenty minutes and didn't come to one house, wasn't passed by one car. It seemed like one of those dreams where you never get where you're going. The hound still followed me. The land had flattened out, the valley was wider and the hills less severe, but other than that there wasn't much to say about where I was. It was just a crappy deserted road.

Then I rounded a blind curve and came upon a snake sunning itself in the road. I almost stepped on it. A noise escaped my throat and I jumped back. The snake seemed to eye me and it flicked its tongue twice. I didn't know what kind of snake it was. It didn't have rattles, but it was around three feet long and as thick as a man's wrist, brown with a darker pattern on its back. There was some open road on either side of it, but even if I walked on the shoulder I didn't feel comfortable passing it.

I looked over my shoulder: the hound was a few yards behind me, sitting there panting. I still had the stick I'd found in the woods, so I shouted and smacked the road with it, making hollow whacks. The snake didn't move. Then a boy's voice yelled, Hey! and I nearly jumped out of my shoes.

—Hey! I yelled back. I looked all around but didn't see anyone.

—Stay right there! he said.

—Where are you? I said.

—Right here! and then there was the crack of a rifle followed by the whine of a bullet and a low splat. I looked at the snake. Its head was gone, but its body was still jerking, seeping blood onto the road.

Suddenly the hound trotted by me. He stopped at the snake and then with a quick snap it was in his mouth. He shook his head, growling, the snake's body whipping. Then he trotted by me again, the snake dragging the ground on both sides of him.

16

—Just got this rifle, the kid called out, loping sideways down the hill to my left. He leaped over a narrow gully at the bottom and approached the fence, where the hound waited for him with the snake. He slung the rifle over his shoulder, lifted the top two strands of barbed wire and stepped through the opening. He petted the dog's head, then came over to me. He swung the rifle off his shoulder and turned it this way and that, smiling.

—I paid for this mowing yards, he said.

I hesitated before answering.

—Yeah, well, it's nice, I said.

—You can make good money in town, he said. They're too lazy to mow their own yards.

He looked eighteen or so and was built like a marathon runner. He wore a red T-shirt faded almost to pink, jeans, and stiff clean white tennis shoes. His hair and sideburns would've been about right in 1975.

—So where'd you find my dog? he said.

—He's yours? I said.

—Yeah. His name's Buck.

—He was at a cabin up the road, I said. He started following me.

—That's Uncle Fee's place, he said. Then he gave a low whistle.
Come here, Buck, he said.

The hound picked up the snake and carried it over.

—You ever eat snake? he said.

—No.

—I ate it twice, he said.

He swung the rifle off his shoulder and started fooling with the
bolt, examining the action.

—Fee Yates is your uncle? I said.

—Yeah, he said. He helps me get to town. He reshouldered the
rifle, then smiled at me. He's got three of those Korean medals, he
said.

—You live at the cabin? I said

—I used to, after my dad went away, he said. But now I just stay
with Uncle Fee sometimes. The rest of the time I stay with my sister. But Buck stays with Uncle Fee after we've been on a run for
coons and he's too tired to walk home.

I asked him where the nearest house was.

—Long ways, he said.

—How long?

His expression turned perplexed, frustrated. Finally he pointed
at the hill he had just come down.

—My sister lives four valleys over that way, he said. Takes about
an hour to get there from here. I come over here and hunt on Uncle
Joe's land a lot, though. He don't mind.

—Joe Brockton's your uncle too? I said.

—Yeah, he said.

—Are your Uncle Fee and Uncle Joe brothers? I asked.

—No, he said. Uncle Fee was my mom's brother. She died a
long time ago, before Dad went away. She got sick before I can
remember.

17

A car approached, coming from the same direction I had. Its engine was missing badly and from a distance it sounded like a child's cap gun firing. The kid and I moved to the shoulder and he used the rifle barrel to toss the snake out of the road and into the grass. The car came closer and closer and then rounded the curve with a terrific noise: it was a yellow Chevy Vega, going slowly, no more than twenty. As it passed Fee grinned at me through the open passenger window, so close I could smell his chewing tobacco. The car stopped a few yards past us, then with a metallic grind went into reverse and backed toward us, whining, and jolted to a stop. Fee was still grinning.

—Hey, Uncle Fee, the kid said.

—Hey now, Tommy.

All I could see of Fluke from my angle was his tattooed arm draped over the steering wheel.

—Who's your friend? Fee said, grinning at me.

—I dunno, Tommy said. We just met.

—Well, whoever he is, he holds his liquor pretty good, Fee said.

—That fucking bitch, Fluke muttered.

—What'd you mean? Tommy said.

—Nothing, Fee said. You want a ride?

—I gotta pack this snake, Tommy said. Buck needs to go too.

—That feeb ain't bringin' a snake in my car, Fluke said.

—A dead snake ain't gonna hurt nothin', Fee said.

Tommy picked up the snake with the barrel of his rifle and let it hang there in view. He was grinning.

—See? The damn thing's bleeding, Fluke said.

—A little blood would be an improvement in here, Fee said. He opened the door. Let's throw her in the hatchback, Tommy, he said.

Fluke started to object, but then he just sputtered and spit out a string of meaningless obscenities.

18

Fee got out and pulled the seat forward and motioned for me to get in the back. I did, squeezing in behind Fluke's seat, my legs jutting out on both sides. At my feet there was a softball-sized hole in the floorboard. Fee lifted the hatchback and threw in the rifle and the snake, then they decided Tommy would get in the back too and Buck would lie across our laps. Tommy threw his leg in, but my right leg was taking up too much room and he couldn't get the rest of the way in and sit down. He kept pushing against my leg but there was nowhere I could move it. Fluke started cursing again, low and meaningless.

—You ride up here, Fee said to me. I'll ride in back.

I got out, Tommy got in, and then Fee and I were left standing at the door.

—Now don't you try to get away again, he said. Remember, I'll be right behind you, and he patted the front of his overalls.

I started backing away from the car.

—Now why would you want to do that when you could get a ride, he said.

—I know you haven't got that pistol, I said. You left it at the cabin.

—You don't know what I got, he said.

—Yeah, well, you're going to have to show me, I said.

He grinned. He said, Hey Tommy? Can I hold your rifle while we're a riding?

—Yeah, Tommy said.

—Now you can either make me get that rifle, Fee said, or believe me when I say I don't need it.

—Get it, I said.

He went around to the hatchback and undid the elastic tie-down that held it in place and got out the rifle. Then he got in the back and laid it on the floorboard and sat there grinning at me. Tommy whistled and Buck jumped in on their laps, and then I sat down in the passenger seat and closed the door. It was stiff and hard to pull.

—Doesn't anybody ever drive on this damn road? I muttered.

—Not since the four lane came in, Fee said. Now when I was a boy, this was the road from Cincinnati to Cleveland, but the Lord didn't see fit to leave it that way.

19

The car had no rearview mirror. There was a gaping hole in the dash where the heater and radio should've been. A small digital clock was stuck by a magnet to the dash above the hole and it said four-seventeen. It had been ten-thirty when my car broke down. I wondered if the clock was working and watched it to see if the numerals changed; they did.

As soon as we were in motion, Fee made one of his noises and quieted the hound. Then he and Tommy started discussing deer hunting that coming fall. Fluke drove without talking, a cigarette slanting across his chin. His head barely topped the steering wheel, and he looked like a child operating a bulldozer.

The speedometer didn't work, but I could tell the car never got above twenty-five. Then we started up a long steep hill and it seemed as if the car suspended motion for an instant and then gathered itself and continued, slower and louder.

I looked into the backseat.

—Where's my car? I said.

—We're gettin' it fixed for you, Fee said.

—That's right, Fluke said. Fixed.

Then I asked what they wanted with me; I wanted to see if their story matched up with Melinda's. It did. Fee told me about the truck.

—Hey, I could drive the truck, Tommy said.

—Maybe next time, Fee said. We've already promised this feller.

—But I could do it, Tommy said.

—I know you could, Fee said. One of these days we're gonna let you.

—I don't never get to drive, Tommy said.

—You will, don't worry, Fee said.

Tommy didn't say anything for a moment.

—But Fluke's driving, he said, and I'm bigger than him.

Fee laughed. Well, you got me there, he said.

—Fuck a duck! Fluke said and smacked the top of the steering wheel. Bring that dick-smellin' dog into my car and a damn snake to boot and expect me to take lip from a feeb! His face was almost purple. He tried to accelerate the car but we were still on the hill and when he jammed his foot down on the gas pedal the engine just whined.

—Just settle down now, Fee said.

—By God if I will, Fluke said.

No one said anything for a moment.

—I could drive, Tommy said darkly.

20

We turned onto a wide two-lane road I'd never driven before and suddenly houses appeared, one every twenty or thirty yards. Cars passed regularly going in the other direction, and after a while we had a line of traffic backed up behind us. A couple of horns blew. Fluke cursed and stuck his arm out the window and angrily waved them around. The vehicle right behind us, a dark green pickup with tinted windows, tried to pass but had to back off because of oncoming traffic. Finally Fluke pulled into the gravel parking lot of a little church and fifteen or twenty cars went by. As I watched them, I realized Fee and Fluke might not be as stupid as they seemed. If they were moving a lot of pot they were smart to drive such a crummy car. But if that was true, I didn't understand why Melinda would've been stealing cigarettes.

I asked them where we were going.

—Taking the feeb home, Fluke said.

—That's just about enough of that, Fee said.

—Why Tommy don't mind, Fluke said. Do you, Tommy? Hell, I'd trade places with Tommy in two shakes. I'm jealous of him. He gets that check for being a feeb, and then makes all that extra mowing for them rich bitches. They even give you a tip sometimes, don't they Tommy? Let you watch them change panties through the window.

Fluke grinned at me.

—He got caught once standing there like that, with his mouth hanging open and his drawers around his ankles. Didn't have no idea what to do with himself, though.

—I said to stop it, Fee said.

Tommy hadn't spoken since being refused the chance to drive. He was staring out his window with a blank expression.

—All right, I'll stop, Fluke said. But you make him understand he don't say shit when he's around me.

—He'll speak or he won't as the Lord pleases, Fee said. The Lord made him as he is for a reason.

—Yeah, somebody's got to watch them fat bitches change drawers, Fluke said. Their husbands ain't got the stomach for it no more.

We entered a long straight stretch of road, new-looking houses bunched together on both sides. Two cars passed us, one after the other.

—You know, maybe I been wrong, Fluke said. Maybe we should let him drive tomorrow night. Since he's got the Lord on his side and all.

Tommy leaned up between the seats.

—Really? he said.

—Sure, Fluke said.

—Fluke, Fee said, you're gonna get your mouth shut for good one of these days, and it's gonna seem so peaceful people'll think Christ has done come back and got things straightened out and gone home again.

Then a school bus came into view fifty yards ahead. It was slowing, its lights blinking. Fee leaned up.

—Don't get any ideas now, he said.

—I want to ride with Carrie, Tommy said.

—You know she can't let you, Fee said. You couldn't bring Buck and the snake on the bus anyway.

Then I remembered that Carrie drove a school bus. I wondered how Tommy knew her, but I quickly put it together that they shared an uncle, Brockton—I'd been so preoccupied I hadn't made the connection. They were at least cousins, and, if Fee was her uncle, too, they were brother and sister.

The bus stopped and the stop sign beneath the driver's window popped out. A few seconds later we were stopped in front of it. The door wasn't all the way open, and no children were coming out yet. The bus faced the afternoon sun and had a glare on its windshield that hid its interior. The Vega idled, gasping. We kept waiting.

—What the fuck, Fluke said.

Tommy leaned up between the seats.

—So I can drive tomorrow, right? he said.

Fluke jerked around.

—I wouldn't let you drive a fucking tricycle I found in the fucking trash, he said.

Tommy's face fell. He sat back. Then children started coming off the bus. Suddenly Tommy started punching the back of Fluke's seat. Fluke jerked around again.

—What kind of feeb shit you pullin' now? he said.

—Go Buck, Tommy said.

21

The hound sprang, its feet scrabbling for purchase, its teeth closing on Fluke's nose. Fluke let out a womanish scream and his foot slipped off the clutch and the car lurched forward and the engine died—the children passing in front of the car squealed and jumped back. The hound had its front paws between the seats. Fee made one of his sounds but it had no effect on the dog and Fluke started punching its nose, but it hung on to him.

I opened the door and jumped out and ran around the front of the car to the door of the school bus, which had just closed; the last children to get off were staring back at me. I looked through the door's narrow windows and the driver was Carrie, wearing that same little yellow dress. I started beating on the door. A look of astonishment came onto her face. She opened the door and I hopped up on the first step.

—What're you doing here? she said. What happened?

—I'll explain, I said. Just go.

22

She shut the door and we started moving. As we passed the Vega, Fee was just getting out. She shooed two girls out of the seat behind her and I sat down and leaned over the chrome rail and told her what had happened. As I did, though, I had second thoughts: I didn't know if she might be in on this business, too, since her uncle was, so I told her everything except the part about Brockton. I wanted to see what her reaction was.

—That's wild, she said. I almost can't believe it.

I watched her face but her expression betrayed nothing. The bus was hot and her forehead and cheeks had a sheen of perspiration.

—Yeah, you can imagine how I feel, I said.

She put on the blinkers and started braking. A boy of six or seven with a green backpack walked past me; he stood holding the rail next to the steps and stared at me. I smiled, but he didn't smile back, and then I gave myself the once over: my shoes were dusty, my khaki slacks were rumpled and dark here and there with sweat, my light blue shirt was untucked and drenched in all the right places, and suddenly I became aware of my own smell—in the last six hours I'd walked seven or eight miles, puked a few times, had sex on a moldy couch, and was still sweating out a moonshine drunk. I ducked my head and looked in the rearview mirror and what I saw would've sent Mother Theresa screaming in the other direction.

The boy got off and we started moving again. I asked Carrie why the bus was running in summer.

—Summer school for some and an enrichment program for the others. There's just two routes operating for the whole county.

—Must take a while to do yours, I said.

—Almost two hours, she said.

We rode without talking for a moment, the kids chattering behind us.

—They're following us, she said and pointed to the mirror over the right front wheel. I looked in it and saw the small distorted image of the Vega. It was now creating puffs of thick dark exhaust smoke that hung over it like cloud. It looked like a car being chased by a thunderstorm.

—You know Tommy's my brother, she said.

—I thought he might be, but I wasn't sure if Fee was your uncle too.

—Yes, he is, but he and I don't have much to do with each other, not if I can help it. I haven't been around him much since my dad owned the dealership.

—I thought your uncle and dad had owned the dealership together, I said.

—That's what a lot of people thought, she said. But my dad actually owned the dealership outright and Joe worked for him. Dad let people think Joe was a partner to save his feelings. Joe never could make a go of much of anything, and he always resented my dad because he could. Dad was always bailing him out, propping him up. Then when Dad died, Joe bought the dealership from the estate.

—Tommy said Fee is your mother's brother, I said.

—That's right, she said. She got sick not long after Tommy was born. He never knew her, really.

I shook my head. Keeping all this straight is like trying to keep Britney Spears in clean socks, I said.

She gave me a funny look.

—Sorry, I shouldn't have said that, I said. Don't pay any attention to me.

—No, it's okay, she said. I like people who are almost funny.

I checked the side mirror. The Vega was no longer in sight. Carrie put on the blinkers and we stopped again. Two boys who looked like they'd left the navy to go to high school and a fat girl wearing tight jeans got off. As the door was closing, I heard the roar of the Vega and saw it approaching in the mirror.

—Is there any way you can speed up? I said.

—When I'm empty, she said. On the way back.

—Okay, I said.

—What're you going to do? she said. Go to the police?

I looked at her before answering, but still her face told me nothing. If she was in on this business she was one stone cold liar.

—No, I don't think so, I said. They said the sheriff was part of the deal and I believe them. What I really need is to get out of town. But like I said, I don't have any money, no credit cards, nothing. Fee knows where I live now, he knows about my family. I'm not sure I can just walk away and go home. I mean, I could tell the state police what's happened and they might arrest them, but they'd probably get out on bail, and even if they didn't, they'd have friends, and the only real evidence against them is my word. Get rid of me, you get rid of the problem.

—This all sounds like stuff that happens in movies, she said.

—Yeah, so where do you think they get their ideas?

—Who? she laughed. The criminals or the movies?

—What's the difference? I said.

23

Carrie made her last stop, letting off a shy-looking little girl in a dirty blue dress at the head of a dirt road. No house was in sight. When she opened the door the sound of the Vega approaching was loud. The girl stepped off the bus.

—See you in the morning, Macy, Carrie said.

The girl kept standing in the doorway. I did good on my test, she said.

—What'd you get? Carrie asked.

—Eighty-eight.

—That's great, Carrie said.

The girl threw up a wave and then took off running up the road.

—Hey now! Fee yelled behind us. In the mirror I saw him coming around the open door of the Vega.

Carrie yanked the door shut and we roared off.

—Where do you turn around? I asked.

—I don't, she said. I make a loop.

She sped up and soon we were doing forty. I got up and walked to the back of the bus and looked out the window. The Vega was quickly losing ground. For a while it looked like it was stretching away from us, and then like it was standing still, and then it was gone. I walked back to the front of the bus. Carrie was smoking a cigarette. I bummed one from her and lit it with her paisley lighter. It was a long thin cigarette with a gold filter and it tasted like air freshener. I sat in the seat behind her, leaning on the rail, my lips only the right kind of smile away from her ear.

—Well, at last we're alone, I said.

She paused before answering.

—Yeah, no one but us and our rings, she said.

—That's easy enough to fix, I said.

She threw her cigarette out the window and pointed to the large doorless glove box above the steps. Could you get my phone out of my purse? she asked.

I stood up and stepped over to the glove box.

—This is turning out to be easier than I thought, I said.

—Just smoke your sissy cigarette, she said.

—What I'd like to do is take a shower, I said.

—I'm working on that, she said.

I handed her the phone and sat down again. She scrolled through some numbers and then hit one and a few seconds later she was talking. She told whoever it was she was going to be late, that she had to go back to the dealership to do some letters and then she was stopping at Tracy's. There were two "all rights, all rights," and then an "I love you" so dead it would've made Byron enter a monastery. Then she turned off the phone and handed it to me to put back in the purse. I did, then sat down again and waited for her to explain what the plan was, but she didn't.

—Your husband, I presume, I said.

She nodded.

—What's he doing home this time of day? I said.

—It's after five o'clock, she said.

—Oh, right. So what's he do anyway? I said.

—He watches television, she said.

24

We rode for a while without talking. I started thinking Fee and Fluke might follow us back to the county garage so it might not be a good idea for me to go back there. I told her that. She nodded, but didn't say anything. I asked her what she had planned.

—I'm taking you to my friend Tracy's house, she said. You'll be fine there until you figure out what you're going to do.

—Aren't you going to let her know we're coming?

—We're good enough friends I don't have to, she said. And she's not home right now, she's at work. I've got a key.

A minute or two later we were in town. Marsburg still looked like towns did in 1970, there wasn't a franchise in sight and all the businesses were downtown. We had to stop at the town's one traffic light. To our left was a hardware store flanked by a dress shop and a small department store; to our right was a pool hall flanked by a law office and a drugstore. Sidewalk traffic was light. Then I saw a white duck waddling down the sidewalk to our right. He stopped, pecked at something on the ground, then went on.

—Over there's a duck, I said.

—Yeah, that's Mailer, she said. He lives in the pool hall.

The people who passed the duck didn't pay it any attention. I was glad they didn't. This didn't seem like one of those cute deals where they put a ribbon around the duck's neck and take pictures of it for the weekly newspaper, it was more like the duck could've walked into a voting booth and they would've closed the curtain behind it and waited. You had to like that.

25

We passed the dealership, which was at the far end of town, and I saw Brockton out among the tractors, talking to two old men in overalls and baseball caps. He looked up at the bus as we passed—I wondered if he saw me. Then we made a left which put us on a street from a Nancy Drew novel. Old trees sat at perfect intervals in the front yards of old brick homes with porches that looked like nice places to rock yourself to death. My own house was in a three-year-old suburb and looked like it was three-quarters garage; I could mow my yard in ten minutes and everytime I stepped out my front door it seemed like the sun was right in my eyes.

Carrie made a right, and then we were on a street that was nice, but not quite as nice as the first one. The houses were smaller and less well kept, though the trees were still old and pretty. She drove the bus to the end of the street and parked it in front of an empty grass lot across from a small church. She turned off the engine.

—Okay, she said. Here we go.

We got out and walked back up the street. The sidewalk had a lot of mismatched concrete and we walked over some pictures a kid had drawn with several colors of chalk—they made me think of my daughter Katie because she liked to do that, too, and then I started thinking of the child we had on the way. We didn't know if it was a boy or a girl and we wouldn't until it was born. We'd had all the tests, but like we'd done with Katie, we asked not to be told the baby's sex. Joan and I both hated that kind of modern antsy-ness. We hadn't bought a video camera and taped every move Katie made, either, the way our friends did with their children. The wedding chapel where we'd been married videotaped all their ceremonies as a matter of course and when they tried to sell us a tape, Joan got angry that they had taped ours without telling us and demanded they erase the tape in front of her, refusing to leave until they did. I had really loved her at that moment, watching her threaten a skinny guy with a comb-over and too many rings. My girl. She knew the difference and wasn't afraid to tell you about it.

—Here we go, Carrie said.

She turned up the sidewalk of a house built in a style I had always liked, mission or something like that, the kind of house that always made me think of 1930s Los Angeles. One and a half stories, tan stucco with dark green shutters that actually worked, a slate roof, and a deep, dark front porch that ran the width of the house; we took three steps up and entered the cool shade of the porch. A bicycle hung on ceiling hooks at one end and at the other an unpainted wood swing was suspended on shiny new chains. While she looked for the key in her purse, Carrie asked me to get the mail out of the black box next to the door: a cheap notions catalog, three junk offers, an electric bill. She used the key and we went inside. I laid the mail on a little round table just inside the door.

—Let me get you set up here, and then I've got to go, she said. I'll call Tracy, of course, and let her know you're here.

She led me through a cool dark hallway into a bedroom. She went straight to the closet, standing in the space between it and an unmade bed with yellow sheets. She slid open the closet and start-ing pushing clothes around.

—Your friend, I said. You're sure she won't mind?

—No, not after the husbands she's had.

I smiled at that, and she pulled out a white terrycloth robe and threw it on the bed.

—Anyway, I can usually tell about people, she said, and I'm pretty sure you're all right. I think you'd let a mosquito bite you three times before you even thought about slapping it. Then she pointed to a door across the room.

—That's the bathroom, she said. Why don't you go ahead and take your shower? If you'll throw your clothes out, I'll get them started washing.

I thanked her, then picked up the robe and went into the bath-room and closed the door and started undressing. The bathroom looked like it had been decorated by a woman who had had two marriages and was determined not to have a third. You couldn't take a breath without making lace flutter.

I cracked the door and held out my shirt, pants and socks. She took the clothes.

—All right, she said.

I thanked her again and closed the door. I figured out the shower, turned on the water and pulled the curtain. There were seven bottles of hair products and four different bars of soap on the tub's rim. I closed my eyes and ducked my head under the water. As I cooled off, I started feeling a little drunk again.

The water pressure suddenly got weaker and I knew Carrie must've started the washer. That was the way with the plumbing in a lot of these old houses.

A couple of minutes later, I was soaping my chest when I heard the bathroom door open with a creak that would've been at home in any number of bad movies.

—Carrie? I said.

No answer. The shower curtain had about six layers and was opaque. I felt a little silly, but I was afraid to pull it back and take a look. It had been that kind of day. If my day had been a movie, Sylvester Stallone would've quit halfway through filming and gone home to suck the thumb of any woman who'd let him.

—Carrie? I said again, louder.

Still no answer.

I was thinking about turning off the water when the curtain whipped back and Carrie said, Boo! I jumped back and lost my footing and as I was falling I saw she was naked. I landed on my tailbone. Despite the pain, I kept looking at her. She knelt beside the tub.

—I'm so sorry, she said.

—It's all right, I said, grimacing and smiling at the same time.

With her holding my arm, I stood up.

—So what's the plan? I asked.

She stepped over the edge of the tub and into my arms. She looked up at me. The water was hitting us.

—I don't know, but I'm dirty too, she said.

26

We had our fun in the shower, and then Carrie had to leave to get the bus back. She said she'd call Tracy and let her know I was there, and then she'd come back later. After she left I washed my underwear in the bathroom sink, then went into the bedroom and put on the robe, which hit me where a miniskirt hit a hooker. The closet was still open and I looked in it; from the looks of her clothes Tracy wasn't a heavy woman.

I found the washer and dryer, which were on a porch off the kitchen, and put my clothes in the dryer. Then I found coffee in a kitchen cabinet and started a pot brewing. I felt like getting something in my stomach, but I didn't see a refrigerator; finally I found it in the walk-in pantry between the kitchen and the dining room. The refrigerator sat against the back wall, with shelves floor to ceiling on either side of it. I pulled the string on the overhead light. The shelves were stocked like they were in a Bulgarian convenience store, cans of stewed tomatoes, hominy, kidney beans, a jar of pimentos and a box of Cream of Wheat, nothing I wanted to eat. The refrigerator was old and short with rounded corners, and the door was covered with photos held by magnets. The photos indicated I was in the house of a very good-looking woman—small, olive-skinned, with long black hair and bright dark eyes. In one photo she was on a boat dock holding up a small fish, in one on a ski slope standing next to a guy with a face as empty as a belt buckle, in one she was at somebody's graduation, and in four or five shots she was at parties. Then I saw one that made me take a closer look. I pulled it out from under the magnet and held it up. It looked like she was standing in a bass boat with Melinda, Fee's daughter. The picture was taken from a distance, a stretch of shimmering lake separated the boat from the camera, and the woman I thought was Melinda didn't look at all scruffy, her hair was done up and her clothes were L. L. Bean. I wasn't a hundred percent certain, but it looked like her. She had the red hair, pale blue eyes and matching sets of freckles on the cheeks.

I put the photo back on the refrigerator and opened the door. There wasn't much in there but she did have a package of American cheese slices, so I took four of those, then found a loaf of bread and made a couple of sandwiches and ate them with a cup of coffee. Dying for a cigarette, I nursed another cup and thought about what my next move should be. I needed to call work and tell them about the car, and I needed to call Joan to tell her I wouldn't be coming home.

There was a sunburst clock over the sink and it said six-seventeen. Joan would be expecting me home in about ten minutes.

I found the telephone in the living room. The furniture in there was dime-store modern and I sat down on a black vinyl couch with tubular chrome legs and dialed a collect call to Joan. A moment later, she was on.

—Doug? she said. What's going on?

I told her I'd had a breakdown and it might take a day or two to get an alternator here in Podunk and that I'd be back as soon as I could. When I finished, she didn't answer. I could hear the television playing in the background.

—Yes, well, we've got problems here. The air conditioner's on the blink again.

—It's still under warranty, I said. Just call Schmeils and have him come out.

—I know to call Schmeils, she said. I've already done that. The problem is I called him at ten this morning and he still hasn't shown up. I've called back four times and the last time all I got was the answering machine because the office has closed for the day. I don't think he's coming. I think we're going to have to sleep in this hotbox tonight.

—Well, I'm sorry, I said.

—Katie's sick from the heat, she said. She's got a headache. She's in her room right now with a washcloth over her face. I've got a fan going on her, with a bowl of ice set up in front of it.

—Forget about the warranty, I said. Call someone else. We'll pay for it.

—I've been trying to call you the last three hours to see if that's what you wanted to do. I've left four messages. Haven't you gotten them?

—No service here.

—Then what's your number at the motel? Wait a minute, where's a pencil, dammit.

—Actually, I don't have a phone in the room, I said.

—What?

—I'm calling from a pay phone in the lobby.

—Are you trying to tell me there's still a motel in America that doesn't have phones in the rooms?

—Yes. You don't know the towns I visit, Joan.

—I don't believe you, she said. You just don't want to have to deal with this. With me. Where are you really? Are you in a bar or something?

—Okay, you've caught me. I confess. I've gotten drunk this afternoon and slept with two women, but not at the same time. Give me credit for that, anyway. One of them had just gotten out of jail and one of them was driving a school bus and picked me up off the road. Now I'm at the house of another one, but I haven't met her yet.

—Ha-ha, she said drily.

—If you want to call someone else, just call them, I said.

—I just dread it, she said. You know how they can be with women. They make the estimate sky high if there's not a man standing there who looks like he knows something about it.

—Well, if you don't want to call, I'll be home in a day or so and I'll take care of it then.

—And what am I supposed to do until then?

—Well, you'll just have to open the windows, I said.

27

After we hung up, I called the office's 800 number and got through to Drommel, my sales manager. He wasn't happy with the situation, either. The problem was we were forty percent under quota that quarter and we hadn't met quota for the last two quarters. With farm subsidy programs up in the air and real estate developers buying farmland like it was bubble gum, the mostly small to midsize farms in our sales area weren't buying new equipment. Drommel wanted every salesman on the road six days a week, because if we didn't meet quota this quarter he knew his job would probably go to someone else and he'd be back out here hawking manure spreaders like the rest of us.

—Where's the car? he asked. He had a voice like an alarm clock.

I made up the name of a garage and told him, then thought that was a mistake because I'd have to produce a receipt, but then I realized he'd never see it anyway.

—If it's not ready by noon tomorrow, don't stay there. Get a cab or something and go to the nearest rental car place.

—I'll try, I said. I don't know if there's a cab stand here.

—Well, just get back, he said. Figure it out. You're not on the fucking moon.

—All right, I said.

—And we're having a meeting Sunday, he said. Two o'clock at the office.

—Sunday? I said. What's it about?

—Angie Dickinson's panties, he said. Just be here.

I took a deep breath and looked around the room. It had plenty of windows and was cool and shady because of the deep front porch.

—I'm probably not going to be at the meeting, I said.

—Why not? he said.

—Because I'm quitting, I said.

—Stop pissing around, he said. I don't have time for it.

—Neither do I, I said. I'm serious.

—Are you drunk? he said.

—Yeah, a little, I said.

—Then why don't you think about it before you open your mouth again, he said.

—And why don't you go back to the Mamet play you crawled out of? I said.

—What's a Mamet play? he said.

—Nothing. Forget it. It's just a figure of speech, I said.

—Yeah, well, what's it mean?

—I don't know.

He paused. I could hear his brain searching and coming up empty. No one had talked to him like this since the last time he'd dreamed about Raquel Welch.

—Didn't I hear your wife's pregnant? he said.

—Yeah. So?

—Bad time to quit a job, unless you've got another one lined up.

—You're right about that, I said.

There was a short silence, and then he started laughing.

—What's so funny? I said.

He didn't answer. He kept laughing.

—Hey, I said. What's funny?

—So you think you're the only one? he said.

—What'd you mean?

—I mean drink one for me, he said. I'll see you when I see you.

28

I found her liquor in one of the kitchen cabinets. She had more liquor than food, which was one reason to like her. I pulled out a bottle of Maker's Mark and poured two fingers in a glass with a chipped and fading hand of playing cards painted on it, a full house, jacks and threes. I took a good drink, then looked at the glass and thought about the corporate process that would've gone into choosing the hand to go on the side of the glass. Probably took at least a month.

I carried my drink back to the living room and sat down on the couch. I took a couple more sips, then set the glass on the chrome and glass end table, next to a kayaking magazine. I closed my eyes and kept them that way for a while. The adrenaline that had kept me going the last several hours was wearing off, my head felt like it was clearing, and suddenly I was very tired. I thought about the things that had happened that afternoon and most of them didn't make sense. I could accept that getting hooked up with Fee was just bad luck, as was my car going on the blink. Those were unlucky coincidences, just as meeting the school bus was a lucky one. What started to seem strange was the fact that Carrie brought me here. Women, in my experience, didn't dump strange men at another woman's house, especially without asking. In fact, it was the kind of thing they wouldn't even think of doing, but I'd been so addled I hadn't seen that until now. And then she had slept with me after exchanging maybe three hundred words total, and that didn't make sense, either. There was also that picture on the refrigerator. If that *was* Melinda, I didn't know what could be going on. I went to the pantry and took the picture down and carried it back to the living room, switched on the lamp next to the couch and held the picture under it. The woman looked like she was from a different world than the woman I'd seen that afternoon, but I was still pretty certain it was Melinda. The eyes, even from a distance, were hers.

Of course, though, the biggest red flag in my mind was the fact that Carrie was both Fee and Brockton's niece, and with most people I'd known, blood usually won out.

I started thinking this house wasn't a good place for me to be. I figured there was at least an even chance that Carrie had left me here so that Fee and Fluke or Brockton could come get me without any trouble, and she had probably slept with me to make me feel safe, to keep me put. It probably hadn't meant anymore to her than putting a stick of Juicy Fruit in her mouth.

I checked my clothes in the dryer. They were dry enough, so I took them to the bedroom and changed, then started searching for money, a pistol, anything that might help me. I looked through all her dresser drawers and the shelves in the closet, then opened the drawer in the nightstand and found a snub-nosed .38 with a full cylinder.

I went out to the kitchen and searched for a cookie jar savings account or a change bank, but had no luck. It was now seven-forty-five, an hour before dark. I decided to wait until dark to leave.

I went back to the bedroom and lay down, the pistol at my side. I decided my best chance was to walk to Lindsey, the next town over. I'd been there many times because it had a dealership. It was about fifteen miles away and I could easily be there by daybreak. I'd find the law and tell them my story.

I caught myself nodding off and sat up against the headboard. I couldn't risk sleeping. Then I looked at her alarm clock, a silver and black thing with lots of tiny buttons. I figured out the alarm, then set it to go off the next minute. It worked, so I set it to go off in thirty minutes and laid down again.

Famous Writers School
P.O. Box 1181
Fayette WV 32111
June 8, 200—

Dan,

Color me red, because I'm deeply embarrassed. My whole approach to your work has been misguided, and my advice to you has been wrong. I've been suggesting you temper the action in your novel when actually I should have been suggesting you make it even more raucous. For instance, why wait for the narrator and Carrie to have sex until they get to the friend's house? Wouldn't it be more interesting to let them indulge themselves on the school bus parked alongside the road? No need to let all the kids off first, either, and don't be shy about writing the sex. Those scenes need to be on the page in full detail. No need in this day and age to follow the old-fashioned examples of Faulkner, Woolf, and others who had that kind of action take place offstage.

Also, I think the story could use at least one more idiot and at least one more short, comically inept man. You seem to do those kinds of characters very well.

As for your request for line edits, your skills with language and scene making are far beyond the stage where they need *my* correction.

You mention trying to find an agent. I would rewrite the novel per the suggestions above—tiny changes, really—and then try to get excerpts of it published in magazines such as *Swank* and *Club*. It's possible an agent will spot it and give you a call, and if not, at least publication in those magazines will give you instant credibility and will also introduce your novel to the demographic it will likely be marketed to.

Funny you should ask about titles. I *have* been tossing around a few ideas. What do you think about *Undress, My Lovely* or maybe *The Member Monologues*?

And please, don't worry about our disagreement over Proust. Despite the fact that his work is still being read decades after his death, I can still understand how you might find him nothing but a fey and mannered darling of the professors.

Sincerely yours,
Wendell Newton

Famous Writers School
P.O. Box 1181
Fayette WV 32111
June 10, 200—

Dear Rio,
I'm just dropping you a note to see if everything is all right,
since I haven't heard from you for a while. Did lesson 3 arrive
safely in the mail? I thought maybe it hadn't since you haven't
sent your response yet, and before you've always been so
prompt. I hope the writer's block you mentioned hasn't per-
sisted, but if it has, don't let it get you down. That happens to
the best of us, and it's just part of the process. I mean, look at
Hemingway. His career spanned forty years and how many novels did he write? Six? He obviously suffered long periods of
artistic impotence. Or take Katherine Anne Porter, who spent
twenty-five years finishing *Ship of Fools*. I know she couldn't
have been writing every day.

Are you Catholic? I was afraid maybe I had offended you in
lesson 3 with my story about the nuns. If I did, I guess my only
defense is that nuns are people, too, subject to the same foibles as
the rest of us. But I meant no disrespect. I'm a lapsed Catholic
myself.

I hope I'm not out of line in saying this, but I sensed a certain
malaise in the conclusion of your last communication, and I fear
that in my letter back to you I wasn't sensitive enough to it. I
have your last lesson here in front of me, and I see where you
wrote that you wanted "an ordinary life." Now, far be it from me
to tell anyone what to want, but I consider the path you've cho-
sen to be a courageous one. To be an artist (a singer AND a
writer, no less), you've walked away from a secure future full of
pedants and footnotes. You might not exactly fit in at the church
social or at PTA, but just imagine a world without artists—it
would be a utilitarian hell. I'm afraid that's where we're headed
in this country where even the churches are starting to follow
the Wal-Mart megamodel. Don't get me wrong, I think capital-

ism works. But when it robs people of their humanity, as it does now in this country, it becomes a pestilence. A better model are the newly capitalist economies of Eastern Europe. Vibrant shopkeepers and other entrepreneurs jostle vigorously for fair advantage in their *own* businesses, while here in America we beg for the right to lick the corporate manna off the ground.

Anyway, I hope you are doing well and I hope it's not too long before I see more of your wonderful prose.

All the best,
Wendell

Lesson 4

Make It Mean Something

When I was still living in the small house in town, a new neighbor moved in one summer, a twenty-eight-year-old stewardess named Maud Gonne. Until I told her, she had no idea she shared a name with the Irish actress and revolutionary the poet W. B. Yeats was so enamored of. I met her one afternoon when she was sunbathing in the backyard—but more on that later.

Her house was a small brick ranch and its previous owner had been an elderly widow who grew champion rosebushes. When Maud moved in, Mrs. Tripplehorn had been dead for a year, and in her absence I had tended the rosebushes. The only time anyone from the estate had been to the house was the day when Mrs. Tripplehorn's three daughters came and ransacked the place, their husbands standing around drinking beer with a radio playing loudly in a pickup truck. Several children ran around the yard and the daughters, wine coolers in hand, divvied up Mrs. Tripplehorn's possessions, but then an argument about a television broke out. The sisters yelled at one another, one of them holding the small television under her arm. I watched from a window. One of the husbands finally stalked off and started the pickup truck. He raced the engine several times, but didn't leave.

I then thought about the rosebushes and wondered if they were going to haul them off, too. I went to my guest bedroom, which had a window with a view of them, and opened the blinds. A boy and girl who both looked eight or nine were playing around them, and an overweight golden retriever was digging a hole right in front of one of them. The girl was squeezed between two bushes, crouched down and making noises like a monkey, and the boy was beating them with a broom. Pink and red petals were scattering in small explosions.

I rushed out to the backyard. The children saw me coming and stopped what they were doing. They both looked small for their age, underfed. The dog stopped digging and looked up, his tail wagging.

"You don't want to hurt those," I said.

"Dad said it was all right," the boy said, then grinned and started whacking the bushes again. I started climbing the fence, and the boy dropped the broom and ran toward the front of the house shouting, "Dad!"

I landed on the other side and started examining the bushes. The girl slid out from between them and watched me. Her knees were dirty. I smiled at her. The dog approached, his head lowered submissively, and I petted him.

"Hey," a man said sharply.

I looked up and saw him approaching, his hand on the boy's shoulder. He was small and wiry and had such a long, thrusting stride it was comical. He wore jeans and a black T-shirt and had a faded red heart tattoo on his right arm.

"What's going on here?" he said.

I explained the boy had been hitting the rosebushes.

"So?" he said. "I told him he could do it."

"I'm not sure if you're aware of this, but these roses are—"

"Yeah, yeah, I know, she won the county fair. So what?"

"Well, they meant a lot to Mrs. Tripplehorn," I said.

The dog resumed work on his hole in front of one of the rose-bushes.

"They sure as hell did," the father said. "She spent more on them than she did on us. On her grandkids." He kept looking at me. "I guess you know she left all her money to the dog and cat society, and when the house sells, that goes to them too." He waved at the children. "What kind of grandmother is that?" he said.

I shrugged.

"They're up there right now arguing about a damn black-and-white TV." He shook his head. "As far as I'm concerned, my kids can beat the hell out of these bushes."

The boy gave me a defiant look and picked up the broom. The dog looked up from the hole he was digging, then trotted off toward the house.

"Would you be willing to sell them?" I said.

A calculating look came into the man's eyes.

"How much?" he said.

"I'll give you forty."

"Are you kidding? She won the fair with these bushes."

Then there was a shrill scream from the front yard, but it didn't faze him. His gaze never left me. The boy reached back with the broom, but before he could swing it, the father pulled it out of his hands.

"Dad!" the boy whined.

"Is it my turn?" the girl asked.

The father grinned. "If this fellow don't buy them, I might not just let you hit them. I might let you set fire to them."

"*Awe*some," the boy said.

"I don't want to," the girl said. "They're pretty."

"Scaredy-cat," the boy said and punched her on the shoulder.

"Dad!" she said. "He called me scaredy-cat."

"Well, sounds like he's right. You said you don't want to help us start the fire."

The girl pouted and kicked the ground.

"If you're gonna be like that, then just go up there and help your mother load towels."

After a moment's hesitation, she stalked off. From the rolled-up sleeve of his T-shirt, he pulled a pack of cigarettes with a butane lighter stuck behind the cellophane and lit one.

"Why don't you go see if you can find a can of gas?" he said to the boy. "Look in the back of the truck."

The boy ran off. The father grinned at me, the cigarette hanging in the corner of his mouth.

"I could go sixty," I said.

He thought about that, then shook his head.

"Between sixty and a fire, I think I'd rather see a fire."

The boy came running back, carrying a small rusty red-and-yellow gas can.

"Splash it all over those things," the father said.

"I'll give you seventy," I said.

He took a puff from his cigarette and smiled.

"Deal," he said.

"Aw, Dad."

He pointed the cigarette at the boy. "Don't you tell anyone we sold them, not your mother or Uncle Tad or anybody. Do you understand?"

The boy nodded. "Can I have a dollar?" he asked.

"No."

All right, let's stop here. Why have I told you this story about the rosebushes? The opening of the lesson described the first meeting between me and a pretty neighbor, but why did I leave that? Well, I did it because something important is getting ready to happen with those rosebushes, and in the episode just described, you see that they had meaning for me. The poet T. S. Eliot coined a term, *objective correlative*, and it means that you invest objects or settings or events with emotional meaning, and in this story, the rosebushes are the objective correlative. So let's go back to that first meeting in the backyard, and see how the rosebushes figure in:

"Welcome to the neighborhood," I said to my sunbathing neighbor.

"Nice to meet you," she said. "I'm Maud Gonne."

I smiled. "I guess you must get tired of people commenting about your name," I said.

She looked puzzled. "What'd you mean?"

I explained about Yeats and Maud Gonne.

"Well, huh, I didn't know that," she said, settling her sunglasses back on her nose.

We continued to chat. She told me she was a stewardess, divorced, with a boy ten and a girl fifteen. Eventually I mentioned the rosebushes, told her I'd been tending them and could keep doing it if she liked.

"I wouldn't want to put you to any trouble," she said.

"It's no trouble," I said. "I enjoy it."

"Well, that's probably a good idea," she said. "I'm sure they wouldn't do too well with me taking care of them. I don't know a thing about flowers."

Then neither of us said anything.

"You know, I got in pretty late last night from a flight," she said, "and I came out here thinking I could catch forty winks."

"Certainly. Nice to meet you," I said.

"Same to you."

That evening around six, I was in her yard, on my hands and knees in front of the rosebushes weeding with a hand trowel, when I heard her sliding glass door open behind me.

"Hey," she said.

I looked over my shoulder and said hello. She looked as if she had just stepped out of the shower. Her hair was wet and combed back, and she wore fringed denim shorts and a man's white tank top undershirt.

"Thanks for doing that," she said.

"It's no problem."

"All right, well, talk to you later."

"Okay."

I went back to weeding, and a moment later muted rock music started playing inside her house. Almost immediately, though, it shut off and the sliding door opened again. She was in the doorway with a glass of iced tea.

"I thought you might want something," she said.

I stood up and brushed my hands on my jeans. "Looks good. Thanks."

"Say, you don't like chicken livers, do you?" she asked. "I'm making some for supper. Breading and deep frying them."

"That's exactly how I like them," I said.

"Great. Come on in."

I followed her inside. She didn't have the house put together yet and boxes were everywhere. I sat down at the kitchen table, which was covered with cookbooks and an unassembled aquarium. She started rolling chicken livers in meal and dropping them into a deep fryer. The oil sizzled and popped.

"Do you have pet fish?" I asked.

"Not yet, but my son's been asking for some, so I bought that for him." She paused. "Say, what kind of salad dressing do you like?"

"Anything's fine."

"How about Russian?"

"That's fine," I said, though that was about the only salad dressing I didn't like.

"I've got some ranch too," she said.

"Well, okay, I think I will have that."

We ate chicken livers smothered in ketchup and a lettuce and tomato salad. She had to turn in early because she had an early flight, so I left right after dinner. For the next three days, I didn't see anything of her, except for her headlights sweeping through my bedroom window as she came in at night. Then late Friday afternoon, as I sat working at my desk, I heard her car pull in, and then heard not one but three doors slam. A few minutes later, the phone rang.

"Hey, what're you doing?" she said.

"Nothing much," I said.

"You wouldn't want to come over, would you?"

"More chicken livers to get rid of?" I said.

"Hot dogs," she laughed. "My son and daughter are with me, and my son's got this board game he wants to play that he says isn't any fun with just two. Of course his sister wouldn't play it if she had a gun at her head, so you wouldn't be interested, would you?"

"Sure."

"Okay, give us about an hour. Barry's got some homework I want him to do first."

"Anything you want me to bring?"

"Have you got any mustard?" she said. "I think I'm out."

An hour later, mustard in hand, I rang her bell. After a long wait—during which I heard some muted yelling—the teenage daughter answered. She was a small, not-quite-as-pretty version of her mother. She gave me a disgusted look, then stomped back down the hallway and slammed her room door behind her.

I went in. The house was still messy. I smelled hot dogs boiling. In the kitchen, Maud was at the stove, smiling.

"Hey," she said.

"Here's the mustard," I said.

"Thanks," she said.

I sat at the kitchen table while she cooked. She had on black bike shorts and her hair was in a ponytail. She set the table and then called Barry from his room. He was a handsome, sullen-looking boy wearing a gold stud earring and a black T-shirt with the name of a band on it. When Maud introduced me, he barely nodded.

"Can I eat in my room?" he asked.

"No, we're eating in here," she said.

He jerked out a chair and threw himself into it. Maud gave me an I'm-sorry look, then laid out hot dogs, chili, slaw, baked beans, and chips. Apparently it wasn't even at question whether the daughter would join us.

During the meal, Maud and I kept trying to draw Barry into our conversation, but he never replied with more than a nod or a shrug. After dinner, he set up his game on the living room floor. I helped Maud with the dishes, then the three of us sat cross-legged around the board and Barry explained the rules in a disinterested monotone. It was a role-playing game called Search for Callas and I took the identity of a monk turned warrior. I caught on pretty quickly, but Maud had more trouble. On her third turn she made a particularly bad play that allowed Barry's character to invade her cavern lair.

"God, that was so dumb," Barry said.

Maud shrugged and gave a little smile, but I could see the hurt in her eyes. It was my turn and I picked up the dice.

"Enon," I said in the deep voice I'd been using for my character when trying to joke with Barry, "a strong wizard always shows respect for his opponents."

Barry rolled his eyes and didn't respond, but Maud gave me an appreciative look and patted my knee.

We played until midnight. The daughter never came out of her room again, and when we quit, Barry went to his room without saying good night. Maud saw me to the door.

"Thanks a lot," she said. "You really made things easy." She shook her head. "I don't know. This has all been hard on him."

"He'll come out of it," I said.

"I hope so, but I don't know." She looked out the door. When she looked back, her eyes were moist. "Sometimes I think both of them would be better off if they could just stay with their father all the time. He's so much more. . . oh, I don't know," and she broke off and shook her head. She looked like she was going to cry, but then quickly composed herself. "Anyway, really, thanks for coming over," she said.

"Sure, I enjoyed it. Maybe we can do it again," I said.

"For sure," she said.

Then there was an awkward pause. I didn't know whether or not to lean in for a kiss.

"Oh, your mustard," she said.

"Yes, I almost forgot," I said.

For the next week she left early and got in late each day, and I didn't see her. That Friday night, though, as I lay in bed, I saw her headlights lights sweep through my room. More than one car door slammed, and I figured she had her children again. I thought it likely we'd have another get-together the next night.

The next morning, I decided to take a well-deserved break from writing. I showered and put a load of laundry in the dryer, then went out to check the oil on the Dart. As I was raising the hood, I heard the storm door slam at Maud's house. I looked up, expecting to see her, but instead a tall man in a blue-and-white striped robe was going down her sidewalk. He picked up the newspaper and started back, examining the front page.

I wrote fiercely that day. Early in the afternoon the doorbell rang, but I didn't answer it. At dusk I smelled a barbecue fire next door. I went to the guest bedroom and looked at her backyard: a shiny new barbecue grill was smoking, and the tall man, dressed like a Kennedy on vacation, was playing catch with Barry.

That night, after her house finally went dark, I threw a trowel and a ten-pound bag of fertilizer into her yard and vaulted over the fence. I got down on my hands and knees in front of the rosebushes and dug until I exposed the root structure of one of them, then filled the hole with fertilizer and covered it with dirt. I did the same thing to each rosebush.

It took a few days for the rosebushes to start dying, but over the next several days they became bare gray skeletons. Maud didn't seem to notice, or if she did she didn't say anything. A couple of weeks later, she asked me over for dinner and a game night with Barry, but I thanked her and declined, saying I had too much work.

Assignment: I didn't kill the rosebushes until they had meaning. If I had killed them without having gone to such lengths to save them earlier, my act would've just seemed like a prank; however, since it was obvious I cared about them, my act expressed the depth of my anger. Look at the story you've been working on and pick some object in it, such as a bicycle or a spatula, that you wouldn't normally consider important, and invest it with meaning. Show the character using it, cursing it, praising it, protecting it. Make it mean something.

Linda Trane Says Fuck You

I park in Wendell's neighborhood, then wait until he leaves in his Buick. He still hasn't taken the price sticker off the window. I just can't believe I slept with a guy like that. I get out and walk to his house. I put on Isotoner gloves as I go—it's May, so they look stupid. On the front stoop I lift the mat. He doesn't keep a spare key there anymore. However, I have two skeleton keys. One big and one small. A man I went to high school with is a locksmith. We're having a drink next Thursday.

Wendell's house is poorly furnished. I sit on his old couch covered in scratchy brown material with a horse-and-coach pattern. There's no coffee table, no end tables. Just a cheap floor lamp and a Navajo rug. There's a large television on a stand that sways to one side. A small round table with nothing on it is against the wall to my left, flanked by curtained windows on each side. Some plank and block bookshelves rise for five tiers against the wall opposite the table. Nothing hanging on the walls except one photo over the couch, a framed, poster-size black and white of Wendell. He's standing on the steps of an official-looking building, a city hall maybe, wearing a dark sport jacket, a white shirt, a thin dark tie. He looks like a 1960s FBI agent and is much thinner than he is now.

The room has a monkish quality. It is completely silent except for the occasional passing car or faraway door slam. Then the refrigerator starts humming in the kitchen. I get up. First, I go to his bedroom, which has a mattress and box springs on the floor. He's using a quilt for a cover and there's a milk crate beside the bed with a dark green towel draped over it, a small lamp, a digital alarm clock, and a paperback book on it. The front cover of the book has been torn off, but I turn a couple of pages and discover it's a novel by James Lee Burke. Wendell has made notes in the margins and underlined several passages. I pull out the bookmark and place it a quarter-inch ahead of where it had been. Then I slide open the closet door and poke around. Nothing but clothes and shoes.

The next bedroom is completely bare except for a rolltop desk and an office chair. The desk is locked. I peek in the third bedroom, which is being used for storage and is stacked with boxes. The bathroom at the end of the hall is utilitarian and smells of disinfectant. He's using beach towels instead of bath towels. I pull one off the rack and leave it on the floor, then pull back the shower curtain. He uses Suave green apple shampoo and has a shaving mirror hanging from the shower head. The bar of soap is thin as paper. The tub is beige and spotless. I turn on the water and leave it running, then think to look in the medicine chest—that's what everyone does, isn't it? I open the mirrored door and examine the shelves. No prescriptions, nothing embarrassing.

The kitchen is nothing to remark, except he has an old perk coffeepot sitting on an eye of the stove. I turn on the other three eyes to the warm setting, then go back to the second bedroom to explore the desk. I fiddle the small skeleton key in the lock, then feel it click and I slide up the cover. A stack of typed manuscript pages is on the left, a small electric typewriter is in the middle, and on the right is a small book with a plain, dark blue cloth cover. I pick it up and flip through the pages—it's a journal. I put it in my bag. Then I pick up a fountain pen, the one of lesson 2 fame, I suppose. It doesn't look like any kind of heirloom, but more like something he bought last week. I put it in my bag too. Then I look through the manuscript pages. The first sheet says they are by someone named Dan Federman. Wendell has made several marks on them. He's changing the names of the characters and making other edits, too. A log cabin has become a pool house, for instance.

Then I look through all the pigeonholes. It's mostly junk, but then I find a ledger sheet drawn on a piece of typing paper, the columns and lines hand-ruled in pencil. It has April written at the top and I see this is Wendell's record of income and expenses for his writing school business. I count seventeen current students, this Dan Federman among them. After paying for postage, supplies, and advertising, Wendell has cleared almost thirty-two hundred dollars—I wonder how he handles his taxes. I fold the sheet and put it in my bag, then put a piece of paper in the typewriter. Its cord is folded behind it and I pull it out and plug it in behind the desk. The typewriter hums. The carriage jerks and returns to the left. I type the following:

I THINK I LOVE YOU

I leave the paper in the carriage, the typewriter running, the desk open.

Wendell has some Diet Pepsi in the refrigerator and I decide to get one before I leave. In the kitchen, I glance out the window over the sink. I see the same old woman I saw last time, tending her rosebushes.

When I get home it's almost time for me to pick up the children at school so I tell Nancy what I want for supper, hide the journal in the basement in a box of Christmas decorations, and then go to the school. Sally has dance that afternoon, Bart soccer. By the time I get them home, Nancy is gone and has left dinner on the stove and my husband is home, watching the stock market channel and having a beer, wearing running shorts and a tank top, his bare feet propped on the ottoman. He almost never dresses like that after work. I ask him about it.

Thought I might take a walk later, he says, then sips his beer.

At the dinner table, he says, That Nancy is a heckuva cook. We really ought to try to keep her.

I nod.

She told me she needs next Thursday off, he says. Is that okay with you?

I guess, I say. Did she say why?

No, he says.

I like her cookies, Bart says and Sally nods enthusiastically, chewing.

Well, we're lucky to have her, my husband says.

Yes, I say, it's always good when you can find a housekeeper who looks like she was born with a pool cue in her hand.

Hey, my husband says.

What's a cue? Bart says.

Neither my husband nor I answer. We're staring at each other across the table.

What is it? Bart says.

I start eating again.

It's the stick you use when you play pool, my husband says.

Oh, Bart says.

I hate potatoes, Sally says.

Later that night, after my husband's asleep. I slip out of bed and go down to the basement to retrieve the journal. I sit on a stool at the wet bar with a bourbon and Coke. The journal entries are dated. They go back a couple of months. I start reading:

April 10

Lately it seems I find myself either avoiding mirrors entirely or looking in them all the time. I'm not sure why.

April 11

I could do the business just as easily from Prague as I can from here, and if I didn't like it there, I could just move back. While I'm gone, I could rent the house.

April 13

Need to research the popularity of mystery novels in Eastern Europe.

April 16
The woman in Pittsburgh seems like a possibility. I'd feel better if I could see a picture, though.

April 18
Sometimes I wish I'd gone to law school when I had the chance.

April 21
Need to watch Vertigo again.

April 24
There were moments during Father and Mother's visit when it seemed as if a clock were ticking loudly in the background, filling our silences, though I have no such clock. As usual, I felt like a pennyboy sitting there with them and as often as I could I excused myself to the kitchen. Lunch was a disaster. The coq au vin was fine, but its reception was not. I finally asked Father if he'd be happier if I pressed it into a small meatloaf shape and served it with some ketchup on top. He said yes. After lunch, they stayed another two hours. To make matters worse, the whole time they were here I couldn't stop thinking about the woman from Pittsburgh and how my hopes for her are probably nothing more than pipe dreams. The near impossibility of human connection just crushes the heart.

  After lunch, when we had settled back down in the living room, the phone rang. It was Honoria making one of her infrequent calls. She was in Colorado trying to organize slaughterhouse workers into a union. When I told her I had to go because my parents were there, she insisted on speaking to Mother, so I handed over the phone and it sounded like they had a wonderful conversation; during it, my father glanced at me once, then spent the rest of the time staring out the window. I finally went to the kitchen and turned up a bottle of Chivas three times. After Mother got off the phone, I had to endure the it's-a-shame-you-two-couldn't-stay-married-she's-such-a-nice-person-you-both-are conversation.

May 1
I wish I had the time and energy to learn French.

May 6
According to Henry, my record will make it nearly impossible to get a visa. This is a terrible blow.

May 7
Burned all the old photos today. Fire almost got unruly.

May 8
The Hammett books have proven to have a rough, tight grace that I am sure I can transfer to my own milieus.

May 10
I don't know what'll happen if I don't get to see the novel in its entirety. His writing is sloppy, sure, but his plotting is crucial to the project.

May 11
You wonder how something like Bonanza stayed on so long.

May 14
I've lost seven pounds, but am in utter misery.

May 15
I wonder what this Linda Trane looks like? For some reason I always imagine women like her being pretty. I suppose she's had an affair with someone and now she's transferring her obsession to me. In many ways, the little I know of her reminds me of both Honoria and Lana. Is this

the sort of woman I attract? Oh well. The whole damn thing is pretty disconcerting, but I have to admit I find the attention flattering.

May 16
Make the Fluke character a violinist.

Famous Writers School
P.O. Box 1181
Fayette WV 32111
June 11, 200—

Ms. Trane,
I have filed an incident report with the police. They have been to my house and Mrs. Roberts has given them a description of you. Though according to her you wore a scarf, dark glasses, and some "godawful kind of shift," she was still able to give the police enough detail that we have a good idea of your appearance. You are, she said, "an average-size woman with a slightly plump build, a heart-shaped face, and brown hair." This description has been given to all the residents of my neighborhood, and they're on the look out for you if come back; the police say that if there's any more difficulty, I can take steps to require the workers at the Mail, Etc. where you have your post office box to reveal your identity, and the officers said this investigation would be turned over to a detective if you contact me or trespass on my property one more time. They suggested I write you first, though, and let you know all this and see if that solves the problem. So I am doing so. I am willing to let this go if you will return my journal and my business records and simply leave me alone. However, if you should continue your harassment, I think you should know that I am now carrying a weapon.
If I don't receive my journal and ledger sheet within two weeks I will take the needed steps to discover your identity and secure their return.
Wendell Newton

Rio Jordan

Dear Wendell,

Sorry I haven't been in touch these last few weeks—we had such a good correspondence going there before I fell off the face of the earth. Thanks for going ahead and sending me lesson 4 and also for the nice note—and no, your talking about the nuns didn't offend me! It's just been crazy here. I don't even know where to start. I made the mistake of getting involved with a guy who works at one of the clubs where I sing, a bartender named Jerry. He's twenty-five, lifts weights, has a Prince Valiant haircut and a master's in biology. He bitches constantly about how a master's doesn't mean anything anymore, and his favorite thing to say is that nowadays a master's "won't even get you on the radio." I have no idea what that means. The way I got mixed up with him was so DUMB. One day a few weeks ago I was just feeling like I couldn't put one foot in front of the other, like I had made a HUGE mistake quitting my dissertation, throwing over all those years of work. I mean, everyday I slept till noon in an apartment with bugs and a window air conditioner, and I imagined in a few years I was going to be a hag wearing too much makeup and a tight dress who couldn't open her mouth without smoke coming out. I just lay in bed all day that day, thinking about that, drinking Diet Coke and smoking. Then I finally got up and started getting ready for my gig that night. My first show was at ten and I fixed up a lot more than I usually did. I did my makeup like I was getting married, painted my nails, and put on a red flapper dress and a strand of pearls and pearl earrings that I inherited from my great-grandmother and had only worn three times before: at each of my graduations and my wedding. I felt like I looked better that night than I ever had. I didn't want to forget what I looked like, so I set up a camera on my dresser and took some pictures. I've included one of them because I thought you might get a kick out of it—I could've gone trick-or-treating as Zelda Fitzgerald!

When I got to the club it was still early and not too crowded, but every head turned when I walked in, and some of the women looked ready to kill me. I sat down at the bar and Jerry came over. He's a phone book shy of six feet and has that cartoony look weightlifters get.

"Boy, you look great," he said. "What's the occasion?"

"Nothing," I said. "Just felt like fixing up. I'll have a rum and Coke." I snapped open my bag and took out my cigarettes.

"Super duper," he said, which is what he says instead of *okay*.

I sang that night like never before, which was miraculous because I had smoked almost three packs that day. Between shows people tried to buy me drinks but I didn't want their drinks or their praise—I knew what I had done, and I didn't need anyone to tell me. My second show went long because I just didn't want to stop. Hal my piano player didn't mind because the snifter on top of his piano had filled up with fives, tens and twenties. I sang right up to fifteen minutes before closing instead of stopping an hour before like usual, and when I finished my last song the applause just kept going. I motioned to Hal, who turned on his bench and used his hands to swing around his bad leg and bowed sitting down.

After the applause finally ended, I nodded at the snifter. "Two, three hundred dollars in there," I said.

Hal looked at it, filled to the brim with bills, and nodded.

"You keep it," I said.

"What? You crazy?" he said.

I shrugged and smiled, then stepped off the stage and made my way to the bar, fending off congratulations. I sat down on a stool near the lift-up pass through. Jerry saw me and nodded, and as soon as he could brought over a rum and Coke.

"You want some peanuts?" he asked.

Sometimes after the last show I'd sit there with a drink and a bowl of peanuts. I could tell he wasn't going to say anything about my singing; he didn't understand it had been anything special. He didn't have enough ear to know.

"No, thanks. I think I'm going to go have breakfast," I said.

"Oh, okay."

"You want to go?"

He looked surprised. He and I had never hung out before.

"Where you going?" he said.

"Home," I said.

It happened that night, and every night for two weeks before I broke it off. After the night I told him I wanted to slow down and take a break from seeing each other, he showed up at my door at seven the next morning. I'd had a gig at a different bar the night before and hadn't slept yet. I wouldn't let him in. I left the door chained and we talked through the opening. He was drunk and crying and I felt like a worthless whore, so the conversation didn't last long. When I shut the door he start pounding on it, then beating on it with what turned out to be some kind of big hook, something used in marine biology—I didn't find that out, though, until after I called the police and they came and arrested him.

Two days after that, Rob, my ex, called. He said as soon as Jerry had gotten out of jail he had called him and delivered some threats. He then said he wanted to meet at a restaurant and talk. I asked him about his girlfriend Alma.

"She's out of the picture completely," he said. "I mean, she still calls sometimes, and I've caught her following me in the car, too, but I've got no interest in her. She's nuts."

So we met. He seemed like the old Rob and we laughed a lot. Over the next couple of weeks I guess we got back together in a way. I thought there might still be something there because he seemed like the same fun guy he'd been before he lost all his money—his 401K, a small sum he'd inherited from an uncle, everything—in a stock scam. I don't understand much about it, but it had something to do with a fake tech company that was supposed to be starting up in Florida, and he lost almost 50,000 dollars. He changed a lot after that.

Jerry kept calling me and Rob knew it, but it didn't seem to bother him. Then one Sunday afternoon the phone rang while I was in the shower and Rob answered. When I came out, he was sitting on the bed, staring at the floor, the phone in his lap. I started getting dressed. We were going to a movie.

"Who called?" I said.

"Your fuck buddy," he said.

I gave him a long look, then stepped into my skirt and zipped up.

"Don't be like this, Rob," I said.

"Like what?" he said.

"I'm not going out if you're going to be like this," I said. "I'm not getting in the car with you."

"Then don't," he said and tossed the phone on the bed. "Call the fuck buddy. He'll go. I'm sure he's got the price of a movie. That's about all it costs to get in there nowadays, isn't it?"

"Rob," I said.

"He said he was coming over, so you won't even have to call him."

"What?"

He nodded.

"What'd you say to him?"

"Yeah, automatically it's my fault. Jerry the frog expert couldn't do anything wrong."

Then he bent over and lifted his trouser leg; he had a hunting knife strapped to his calf. He lifted the knife out of its sheath.

"What in God's name," I said.

He held the knife above his lap and turned it back and forth. The metal looked new, shiny and brilliant.

"I got this a couple of days ago," he said.

Seeing that knife just exhausted me. I plopped down on the bed beside him.

"I was in Wal-Mart and walked by the counter where they had them," he said. "You said this joker had that big fishhook, and I just had a gut feeling one of these might be a good idea. I guess I was right, because he said he was coming over here to kick my ass."

He was now holding the knife loosely in his palm, looking down at it; I reached over and grabbed it.

"Hey," he said.

I stood up and started toward the bathroom, then pivoted in midstride and pointed the knife at him.

"I want you to leave before Jerry gets here," I said.

I went into the bathroom and locked the door, then sat down on the edge of the tub. The back of my skirt got wet but I didn't care. I laid the knife between my feet on the bathmat. I looked at it a moment, then started crying.

Soon Rob was at the door. "Rio?" he said. "Come on, come out of there."

"No," I said.

He tried another minute or two to convince me to come out and when I wouldn't, he started beating on the door and cursing. I didn't respond, though, and finally he quit. Then he said in a low sweet voice, "Rio? I love you."

"Oh God," I muttered. I leaned up and turned on both the hot and cold water in the sink, then reached behind me and turned on the water in the tub.

"All right," he said in a loud voice. "I'll leave, but I want my knife."

"I'll give it to you later," I said. "Just go before he gets here."

"I'm not leaving without it," he said. "I need it for protection."

"I'm not opening the door," I said. "I don't trust you. You tried to hit Alma at the club."

"Yeah, and do you know why? Because she was talking about you. Saying she was going to beat you up. I knew what we had done was a crummy trick anyway, coming in and ambushing you like that, but you just stood up there and sang, so classy and so beautiful, and she just kept putting you down, until finally I just about wanted to kill her."

"Is that why she had a black eye the next time I saw her?" I said.

"No, that happened a different way," he said. "It was an accident. I don't want to talk about it."

I turned off the water in the sink and the tub, then went to the door.

"Rob?" I said.

"Yes, honey?"

"How did we turn into this?" I said. "Into an episode of *Cops*?"

"I don't know," he said.

"You're certified in counseling, for chrissakes," I said.

"I know," he said.

Then he tried to get me to leave with him, to go to the movie before Jerry showed up. So much time had already passed, I was thinking Jerry had been probably been bluffing, which sounded more like him anyway. Then I heard pounding on the front door.

"Just don't answer it," I said.

"All right, but will you at least come out of the bathroom?" he said.

"No," I said.

"I can't believe this," he said. "What is it, you think I'm going to stab you?"

The pounding got louder, more insistent.

"I just don't want to be in the same room with you, me and a knife," I said.

"If you don't come out, I'm going to answer the door," he said.

"Rob, please," I said.

He didn't answer. I waited. Maybe thirty seconds passed. Then the pounding on the front door stopped.

"Rob?" I called out.

Then I heard him shouting. Something crashed and it sounded like someone banged into a wall. I went to the door, unlocked it and opened it enough to see out. Down the hall I saw Rob and Alma standing nose to nose in the living room shouting at each other. Alma was jabbing a finger at him. She was wearing a blue police uniform and had her hair up in a bun. She had one hand resting on her pistol like she might pull it at any moment.

I shut the door and locked it again. I didn't know what to do, so I turned on the water in the sink and tub again, then sat down and put my hands over my ears and closed my eyes. I was so scared. I kept expecting to hear a gunshot, and I was afraid she would shoot through the door. I don't know how much time passed. When I did finally lower my hands I didn't hear anything. I turned off the water, and then I heard the sound of traffic on the street. That meant my front door was open; you couldn't hear traffic unless it was open. Somewhere faraway a dog was barking. I picked up the knife and opened the door and walked out, holding the knife in front of me. The bedroom hadn't been disturbed, and the door to the hallway was still open. I went out there and into the living room and found it an absolute wreck. My mission chair had been overturned onto the coffee table and broken its glass top and the chairback still sat in the table's metal frame. My CD tower had been knocked over and cracked jewel cases were everywhere, magazines and books were scattered, and a vase of wildflowers had been knocked off the dining table and the vase broken. The sheetrock had been punctured in a couple of spots. In the kitchen, there were some broken dishes on the floor and the butcher's cart had been overturned.

I closed and locked the front door, then got the broom out of the pantry and started sweeping up the kitchen. Near the refrigerator, I found a pool of blood the size of a saucer.

I didn't hear from Rob for four days. Then he called and said he and Alma were getting back together. He kept saying he was sorry, but he never offered to pay for the damages. I told him that this was the last time I wanted to speak to him for the rest of my life, and that if there was ever another incident with Alma, I was calling the police. He made a joke about that, about Alma being a cop.

I thought about getting a lawyer and making them both pay for the damages but decided it wasn't worth it. I pawned the hunting knife for fifteen dollars.

I know at this point it sounds pretty hollow, but I'm ready to take another stab at this course, so be looking for my first lesson. But I just wanted to write you first and let you know what's been happening and why you hadn't heard from me.

Talk to you later,

R.

Famous Writers School
P.O. Box 1181
Fayette WV 32111
June 16, 200—

Dear Rio,
Good to hear from you again. Sounds like you've had quite a time, and I'm sorry to hear it; however, I'm happy you felt you could tell me what's been happening, and thanks for the photo. It's a very flattering picture and I can see why you were able to have a modeling career. I haven't enclosed one in return because I've not had one taken recently. I'm not really much of a camera bug. In fact, I don't even own one.

Fate, it seems, has us on parallel tracks. I've recently had two situations that closely mimic your current ordeal in many respects. Most recently, a woman taking my course has become obsessed with me. Twice she has come to my house while I've been gone, and the last time she broke in and pilfered my journal, my heirloom fountain pen, and some business records. And what's strange is that this has happened when I, too, was feeling especially low, just as you were. I've been feeling as if maybe I should just leave America. I just feel ill about the whole direction the country is taking. When I hear our politicians talk, whether they're on the right or the left, I find myself wishing I were reading some Nietzsche instead. They seem about as adequate to their task as a child driving a bulldozer. Literature is dead too. All we have are squeamish writers writing squeamish novels about little Freudian mysteries in upper-middle-class houses that have clocks that strike but no bathrooms. If Mother Theresa were still alive to see us, I think she'd go screaming in the other direction.

I've been considering giving Prague a look-see. Do you know anything about the city? I've read it's a wonderful place, cosmopolitan and cheap. From what I know, it sounds like a place well suited to your own artistic pursuits. Apparently American standards are all the rage, and the Czech recording industry is still mostly a grassroots affair, with studios the size of the old Motown and Sun Records. Quality still matters more than the singer's haircut.

In the other situation, I, like you, got involved with someone on the spur of the moment, a woman who, like your bartender, turned out to be unstable. It started last summer and ended just a few months ago, on Valentine's Day. There was an awful scene in a Burger King restaurant—the police were called, though no one was arrested. I met this woman at a street fair while looking at a display of beeswax candles. We had coffee that day, and then saw each other for four months before she told me she was married. I had thought it strange we always met at midday, but she explained that by telling me she was a nurse who worked the second shift. I also didn't quite understand how a nurse could drive a new BMW, but it didn't seem too much of a red flag in this age in which so many people leave so much of their paychecks in the driveway. She explained not having me over to her place by telling me that her mother and an adult brother lived with her and that they both drew disability checks and drank heavily. She wasn't wearing her wedding band the day I met her—I suppose she was trolling for an affair even then. However, as it turned out, she has two children and her husband owns four dry cleaners and three Hardees franchises. When she told me about him, I didn't break up with her right away. We kept seeing each other for three more months. I had already fallen for her, so I found it hard to just break it off. Even before I found out she was married she seemed a little nutty, but her idiosyncrasies were merely endearing to me, not troublesome: for instance, she sometimes wore sunglasses inside the house and refused to explain why. She was an attractive iconoclast, and since I have not taken the usual middle-class route in my own life, I often find myself being quite forgiving of foibles others might find intolerable; however, when I did finally break with her, I discovered that calling Lana an iconoclast was like calling Joyce a good little writer. She called me at all hours, sometimes threatening, sometimes pleading. In her softer moods she sent gifts and love letters. She wanted back with me, but she kept refusing to break up with her husband, and she left me alone only after I threatened to expose our affair to him.

Oh well, I suppose we'll both work out whatever karma is afflicting us soon enough. I'll hope for you that you have no more trouble from your ex-husband or the bench-pressing bartender, and you hope for me that my stalker finds someone more interesting to follow. Whatever happens, though, it's good to have someone you can discuss things with. Thanks for listening.

All the best,
W.

Dan Federman

Lesson 4

Dear Mr. Newton,

I didn't appreciate the tone of your last letter, and I'm not going to put up with paying $295 and getting treated like that. I know we disagree about some things, but that's no reason to take the attitude you have with me. I'm going ahead and sending you another installment of my novel, and I want you to either reply to it in a reasonable fashion or send my $295 back. If you don't do one or the other, I'm going to contact *Writing Life* and tell them I haven't had a satisfactory experience with your course and that I don't think they should allow you to advertise with them. I will also send them a copy of your last letter. I wonder what they'd think about your comments? They have such a large circulation, I know you wouldn't want to lose the privilege of advertising in their pages.

Please understand, I don't relish this kind of disagreement. I didn't sign up for this course so I could have a pissing match. All I want is some feedback on my novel. I understand very well by now that you don't like the type of fiction I do; fair enough. But

I've paid good money for your course, and I expect the service and expertise you promised.

29

When I woke up the room was dark. I heard low voices in the next room, women's voices. I couldn't make out what they were saying. For a moment I thought I was home, that I had come awake in my own bed and Joan was in the next room with the television on, but then I realized my bedroom didn't have this many windows, the bedspread was too soft and fluffy to be one of ours, and suddenly I remembered where I was and that I wasn't supposed to be here, I was supposed to have left at dark, and I looked over at the alarm clock wondering why it had failed me. It said nine-thirty-two and I had a terrible sinking feeling.

I remembered the pistol and felt around on the bed for it, but couldn't find it; I switched on the lamp but still couldn't find it, then thought maybe I had knocked it off on the floor, but when I checked it wasn't down there, either. That meant the women I heard talking—Tracy and Carrie, I guessed—had probably come in and taken it. I sat up on the edge of the bed. One of the windows was open. I figured I could pop out the screen without making too much noise and leave that way. I decided I'd be just about as well off walking through the night to Lindsey without a pistol as I would've been with one.

The women laughed, and then I heard one of them clomp-clomping across the hardwood floor in what sounded like boots—the other one's voice rose to follow her, and I could tell it was Carrie talking though I couldn't make out what she said. I got off the bed and stepped lightly to the door. It was a four-panel door, solid wood, and I put my ear against it. I heard Carrie say:

—and I'm never going to King's Island again.

—Bobo's taking me to a dinner theater in Sandusky this summer. He said we'd make a weekend of it.

—That'll be fun, Carrie said.

—Yeah.

—You're so lucky with him, Carrie said.

—I guess.

—Have you got any more coolers?

—No, that was the last one.

—You want to go get some more?

—Sure, if you want to.

I heard the sound of boots again—their rhythm made you think of cheap jewelry. They kept getting louder, and then they stopped and someone was on the other side of the door. I heard a click at my waist and looked down. The door had an old-fashioned knob with a keyhole. The boots moved away. I gave the knob a try as slowly and quietly as I could. It wouldn't turn.

—Let's go, the other woman said.

—I don't think you needed to do that, Carrie said.

—If he hadn't messed this place up, I wouldn't have, she said.

I didn't understand that, but let it go and considered whether I should wait until they left and go out through the window or let them know I was awake and see what they did. I decided if they knew I was awake and still left me locked up, I could always get out through the window. I reached down and rattled the knob, then knocked on the door.

—Hey, I said. What's going on? Let me out of here.

—Doug, Carrie said. Hold on.

A moment later, the lock clicked and the door swung open and Carrie was standing there smiling. She was wearing dressy blue shorts and a yellow halter. I had seen all of her that afternoon but the outfit made her look even better.

—What'd you say, sleepyhead? she said and reached up and pushed some of my hair back in place.

—Not much, I said.

The other woman, the one I had seen in the photos on the refrigerator, was standing at the end of the hallway. She wasn't smiling. She was dressed about like she had sounded, fifty dollars of jewelry you couldn't take your eyes off of, faded jeans with a plain white blouse tucked into them, and black suede boots that almost reached her knees. Carrie turned around and looked at her.

—Tracy, this is Doug, she said.

I nodded and said hello, and she nodded back without speaking. I thanked her for letting me stay there.

—Crashing here was fine, she said, but messing with my stuff wasn't cool.

—Your pistol, I said. I know. But I felt like I needed something—

—The pistol? Tracy said. What about the pistol?

—I got your pistol out of the nightstand before I went to sleep. I just wanted some protection. I figured you came in and took it while I was asleep, because when I woke up it was gone.

—We didn't take the pistol, Carrie said.

—Well, I couldn't find it, I said.

Tracy flung her arm out and waved behind her.

—Are you saying you didn't do this? she said.

Carrie and I went down the hall to the living room. It wasn't trashed so much as rearranged. Furniture had been moved. The television now sat in a narrow space between the couch and the wall; the easy chair faced the kitchen doorway. One end table with a lamp on it was in the middle of the room, the lamp's electrical cord trailing behind it, all the photos and paintings on the walls were hung upside down, the coffee table was sitting top down, legs up in the air, but with the magazines that had been on it earlier fanned out neatly on its underside and the small brass vase that had been there earlier sitting next to them. It was deadpan chaos. Alice In Wonderland stuff.

—When I went to sleep it wasn't like this, I said.

—The kitchen's the same way, Tracy said.

—I promise you, I didn't do it, I said.

—Carrie said she was sure you hadn't, Tracy said. That's the only reason you got to keep sleeping. That and she said you'd had a helluva day.

—Someone else had to be here, I said.

—Did you have the door locked? Tracy asked.

—I locked it when I left, Carrie said.

—And I didn't touch it, I said. I took a shower, made some coffee and then went to sleep. I set the alarm, but it didn't go off. Or at least I don't think it did. Maybe I turned it off without knowing. I don't know.

—So you're saying my pistol is gone, Tracy said.

—I think. I couldn't find it.

She shook her head, then went clomp-clomping angrily past us down the hall to the bedroom and started looking around, flinging things.

—This is like a Hitchcock movie, I said.

—Yeah, sort of like *Vertigo*, Carrie said.

—I always thought that was one his crappier ones, I said.

—Yeah, me too, she said.

I rubbed the small of her back. Then a drawer slammed loudly in the bedroom.

—I found it, Tracy called. She came to the bedroom doorway, the pistol hanging at her side. It was in the nightstand, she said, and then held up a piece of paper. It had this taped to it, she said.

We went down the hall. The paper was a sheet from a pharmaceutical company notepad with the name of a drug I didn't recognize printed in pink across the top, and beneath that written in pencil in neat capital letters was, LET SLEEPING DOGS LIE.

—What the hell does that mean? I said.

—That's what I'd like to know, Tracy said.

—This is weird, I said.

—Jeez, you oughta be a profiler, Tracy said.

I gave her a dry look, then said:

—I can't imagine why any of the people I've dealt with today would've come in here and left this instead of just grabbing me, but I'm getting ready to leave, so don't worry. That should be the end of this for you.

—Where're you going? Carrie said.

I started to tell her I was walking to Lindsey, but the thought of Brockton and Fee and the photo of Tracy and Melinda stopped me.

—It doesn't make any difference, I said.

—Well, *how*'re you going? Carrie said. You don't have a car.

—Don't worry about it, I said. I made arrangements this afternoon. But thanks for all your help. You too, I said, looking at Tracy. She still had the pistol hanging at her side.

—You can't just take off walking in the middle of the night, Carrie said.

I shrugged.

—I can give you a ride anywhere you need to go, Carrie said.

—You've given him enough rides today, Tracy said drily.

Carrie gave her a drop dead look.

—That's not even close to funny, she said.

—No, it's close, I said.

Tracy put on a fake smile.

—I can't tell whether you're the straight man or the funny man, she said.

—I'm both, I said. The last of a dying breed.

—What the hell does that mean? she asked.

Then the phone started ringing. Tracy went to the living room and answered. After saying hello she listened for at least a minute. Then she said, Yeah, I've got it. Hold on. She carried the phone back to us, her hand over the mouthpiece.

—It's Bobo, she said. He's drunk. He's the one who did all this, and she jerked her thumb over her shoulder. He wants me to put him on speakerphone because he wants to talk to all of us. I think we better do it. He said he's outside in his Escalade with a rifle.

—For real? Carrie said.

Tracy nodded.

—He said he can see our shadows through the curtains. He said if we turned off the lights tonight, he was just going to assume we were in here screwing and start shooting up the place.

—Just call the police, I said.

Tracy shook her head, then started back to the living room and we followed. Carrie and I sat on the floor in front of the couch, out of the line of sight of the windows. She told me that besides being Tracy's boyfriend, Bobo owned the insurance agency where Tracy worked. She said he'd been on the wagon for several months and that when he wasn't drinking he was the nicest guy you'd ever want to meet. Then Tracy gave us a look that said be quiet and punched a button on the handset and suddenly the song "Dream Weaver" came over the phone's base unit. Hearing it was funny. I smiled and Carrie giggled, and Tracy rolled her eyes. The song was just ending and a T Rex song started up right after it. Tracy came over and sat down next to us on the floor. She pulled off a boot. She was wearing white athletic socks.

—Okay, we're here, she said. You're on.

For a moment nothing happened. Tracy pulled off her sock—her toenails were painted a dark red—and then she started pulling off the other boot. Suddenly the volume of the music lowered and a man cleared his throat.

—You know, he said, I'm a good-natured guy.

He didn't say anything else. We waited, glancing at each other. His voice sounded small town southern, wrong for Ohio, and it had the practiced friendliness of a salesman, which was what I sounded like half the time.

—Yes, I know that, Tracy finally said.

—I don't think you do, he said.

—But I *do*, Tracy said. Why do you keep going on about that?

He ignored her question.

—Doug, buddy, you there? he said.

I paused.

—Yes.

—So did you find my note?

—Yes.

—Guess I shouldn't've done that, he said. That right there will get you put in jail.

Then there was some kind of unidentifiable noise in the background. It sounded like a scuffle of some kind.

—What's going on out there? Tracy said. Is someone with you?

—My girl don't know this, he said, but I came by this afternoon to drop off a gift. A little surprise something I was going to leave on her pillow for her. Had a nice card and everything.

—That was sweet, Carrie said.

Tracy rolled her eyes. Then she hugged her knees to her chest and stretched all ten of her toes off the floor so that you could see the bones underneath the skin of her feet.

—But I found a man on her bed, he said. All splayed out, and an alarm clock going off.

—I told you why he was here, Tracy said.

—Yeah, that's a good strategy, he said. Make the lie so crazy you don't believe anyone would make it up.

—What was the gift? Carrie asked.

He didn't say anything for a moment.

—An engagement ring, he said.

Tracy and Carrie gave each other a look. Carrie had an aston-ished expression, while Tracy's eyes were narrowed like she was de-ciding whether the price of a blouse was cheap enough.

—Weren't you going to ask me in person? she said.

He didn't answer right away.

—It had a diamond so big, he said.

—Bobo? Carrie said.

—Yes?

—I *swear* Tracy's telling the truth. I brought Doug here. He's my friend, not hers. He's in some trouble, and I didn't know what else to do.

—I'm not marrying a man who won't ask me face-to-face, Tracy said.

—So that's the deal breaker, is it? he said.

—Just hang up the phone and get in here, Tracy said.

—No, he said, I think I'm going to stay put. I've got everything I need right here.

—Dammit, Bobo, she said.

—No, I'm gonna sit here and watch the house, he said. If the lights go out I'll know where I stand. But if the lights stay on, I'll know you want to be with me.

—That's crazy, Tracy said. We could be in here screwing like rabbits either way.

—True, he said. Maybe it doesn't make sense. But let's just call it a test.

—You're going to help me put this house back together tomor-row, Tracy said.

He didn't answer. The volume on his radio went back up, and the song playing was something by Duran Duran.

30

Tracy got up, turned off the speakerphone, and started talking to Bobo on the handset. She went into the bedroom and closed the door. Carrie stood up and asked me if I was hungry, and I told her I was starved. We went into the kitchen and I sat down at the table while she went into the pantry to look in the refrigerator. She came back carrying a package of frozen pork chops. She unwrapped it and put the chops on a plate and put them in the microwave to defrost, found a bag of potatoes under the sink, and then turned on the oven for biscuits.

—My uncle asked about you when I got back to the dealership, she said. He said someone who came in told him they'd seen you broken down on Thirty-two. He asked if I'd seen you and I told him no.

—Thanks.

She got a paring knife out of a drawer and started peeling potatoes. She was at the counter, her back to me. The backs of her legs were the smoothest things I'd ever seen.

—So how does a married woman get away with staying out so late? I said.

—I stay over here pretty often, she said. Bill doesn't care. He doesn't come home a lot of nights, either.

—A modern marriage, I said.

—I guess you could call it that.

—Sounds like you're not too crazy about it.

She shrugged.

—Then why stay in it? You don't have any kids, right?

She didn't answer. She finished peeling a potato and let a long curlicue shaving drop into the sink. Then she picked up another potato and asked me if I wanted a drink.

—I guess not, I said. I've probably had enough today.

She smiled over her shoulder.

—You going to make a girl drink scotch alone? she said.

I grinned.

—You didn't say you were having scotch, I said.

While I was pouring the scotch into two of the glasses with playing cards on them, I asked her about the photo I'd seen of Melinda and Tracy on the refrigerator. I told her I'd met Melinda that afternoon at Fee's cabin, something I hadn't mentioned the first time I told her the story.

—Melinda didn't used to be like she is now, she said. She used to have a job, a husband, everything.

—You're kidding, I said.

—No, she said. She was in the same class with Tracy, a couple of years ahead of me. She'd come to school smelling to high heaven because she didn't have anywhere to take a bath, or an easy way to wash her clothes, but she worked like a dog, stayed in the library all the time.

I carried her drink over and set it on the counter, then stood there next to her and leaned back against the sink. She looked beautiful, cooking like that. A couple of gossamer wisps of hair hung over her forehead, which had a sheen of perspiration from standing next to the stove, where she had two eyes warming. She stopped slicing potatoes, smiled at me, took a sip of her drink, then set it down and started slicing again.

—So what happened to her? I asked.

—I don't know exactly. Tracy was the one who was friends with her, not me. I stayed away from her because of Fee. You see, after my dad died, Fee went to court to be made Tommy's guardian. I was seventeen, Tommy was ten, and they gave Fee custody—he wasn't nearly as messed up as he is now, plus he had Uncle Joe's support. I guess the judge figured if the dead man's brother wanted Fee to have custody, it must be the right thing.

—That must've hurt.

—Yep, it did. As for Melinda, I know she got arrested for possession of meth a couple of years ago and got sent through drug court. She did have a job at a bank and was married to a decent guy, but look at her now. I guess she must be back on the meth because she's gone down really fast. She used to be so pretty.

She poured Mazola oil into a skillet, then started dropping potato discs in it. The pork chops were already frying in another skillet. When she had the skillet full, she pulled the tab on some frozen biscuits and whacked the tube with a spoon and the dough sprang out of the seam and filled the air with a yeasty smell.

—Does Melinda's mother still live around here? I asked.

She shook her head.

—As soon as Melinda finished high school, she left. She was a nurse.

—Fee didn't strike me as a guy who'd be married to a nurse, I said.

—He used to be different than he is now, she said. He used to have a house here in town and be big in Kiwanis and all that kind of stuff, a deacon in the church where all the movers and shakers go. He was a war hero or something, then came back here and even though he didn't have a penny, he got a loan to open up a hardware store because no banker wanted word to get around that he'd turned down the big medal winner. He got married to his first wife, and then after a couple of years he opened up a second store over in Lindsey and let his wife's brother run it. Apparently the brother-in-law started stealing, and Fee fired him. His wife couldn't believe her brother had done anything wrong, though, and one night she and Fee had a big argument about it and she left the house in their car. She broadsided some drunk that didn't have his lights on, got thrown through the windshield and killed.

—So Fee lost it after his wife got killed? I asked.

—Not really. He kept the stores going. Started drinking some, I think, but not enough to mess him up. But it was after she got killed that he got big in church. He got so caught up in it that every Monday morning he'd go to the church office to argue with the preacher about what he'd said in his sermon the day before. Fee got real involved in the end-of-the-world thing, my dad said, and that's when they stopped being as good a friends as they had been. Fee thought the preacher should be talking more about that stuff. You know, warning people, getting them ready. My dad said one time they were supposed to play cards, and when he showed up, the table in the back of Fee's store where they always played, the chairs around it, each one of them had some clothes in it, a shirt, pants and underwear, and a pair of shoes and a pair of socks was on the floor in front of it. Him and the other guys were standing there saying what the hell, when Fee stepped out of the shadows holding a fifth of whiskey and told them that was what the tribulation was going to be like, poof, you're gone, so they better start thinking about that instead of poker. My dad told Fee he guessed that meant everyone in heaven was going to be naked, so he guessed he *would* start living right because he'd hate to miss that. Fee said, Eton Brockton, you're going to hell, and then ran him out. The next day Fee apologized, but my dad said their friendship was never quite the same, and Fee just kept getting stranger and stranger. Then he married Susannah, Melinda's mom, and that's what *really* ruined him in this town. People'll put up with a lot, but they won't put up with a man almost forty marrying a girl seventeen.

—Yeah, if he just could've waited another year, I said.

She smiled over her shoulder, then took the skillet with the pork chops off the stove and forked the chops onto a platter that already had the fried potatoes on it, then lowered the heat on the burner and put the skillet back on it and poured some flour and milk she'd already mixed into the grease and started stirring.

—You like your gravy thick or thin? she asked.

—Either way's fine, I said.

—Okay, she said.

—How'd Fee get her to marry him? I asked.

—I don't know, she said. They could've been in love for all I know. Or it could be she just used him, her family was dirt poor and she was working for him at the store here in town. She was attractive, but she wasn't going to win any contests either—before the drugs, Melinda was a lot prettier than her. Her parents signed for her and they got married her senior year in high school, and the next year Fee sent her off to college. She came home on the weekends and sometimes he went up there to visit. Her first year back here after college she got pregnant and had Melinda, and then she left him, and in the divorce Fee had to sell the stores, the house, all of it. The judge wasn't too sympathetic about a grown man having married a girl that young. People around here were so happy they just about couldn't stand it. The men had all been jealous of him, even though they pretended to be as offended as their women, and the women, well, I don't know what the women were. I mean, I know what they were, I just don't know what to call it.

—Outraged?

—No, that's not it, exactly, she said. It was more like a dog had hiked its leg over their dollhouse.

She put the platter of chops and potatoes on the table, then a bowl of gravy and a plate of biscuits. I don't think I'd seen a meal that looked or smelled better since last Thanksgiving dinner, which had been good only because I had convinced Joan to go out instead of cooking at home.

—Here's pepper for the gravy, she said. I didn't put any in because I wasn't sure how much you'd want. What'd you want to drink?

Before I answered, I found myself wishing this was my house and she was my wife, that I lived in Marsburg, and that tomorrow wouldn't come.

—Some milk, if she's got enough that it doesn't take it all, I said.

She brought me a glass of milk, then sat down across from me and picked up a potato disc and took a dainty bite of it. I started eating. The food tasted good the way food tasted good when I was a kid, when you didn't think about what you were eating, whether it'd kill you or not, when it wasn't unusual to see people lighting cigarettes in the middle of meals.

—This is great, I said. You ought to go into business. I've never had better gravy than this.

A proud smile came onto her face.

—You're not going to have a plate? I said.

She shook her head.

—You eat it all, she said. You're going to need your energy.

I started to ask her what she meant, but the look in her eyes answered my question.

31

While Carrie was washing the dishes Tracy walked into the kitchen wearing a short blue satin night robe. She put the phone back in the base set, then sat down across from me at the kitchen table and pulled a hairbrush out of a pocket of the robe and started brushing her hair, her head leaned to one side.

—Sorry about earlier, she said and gave me a sheepish smile. I hope you can understand. Fucking Bobo.

—Sure, I said. No problem.

—Isn't he going to come in? Carrie asked.

—No, Tracy said. He said he feels too embarrassed now. He said he's going to stay in the Escalade all night as penance for being a dumb ass. He said it'll prove to me that he's sorry.

—Have you looked to see if he's actually even out there? Carrie asked.

—Yeah, I saw the Escalade parked on the street. I made him turn on the rooflight so I could make sure it was him. He did, then waved and held up a beer can.

—I swear, the people who end up with money, Carrie said.

She finished wiping down the sink and hung the rag over the faucet, then sat down in the chair next to mine. Underneath the table she put a hand on my knee. Tracy smiled.

—I see that, she said.

—But Mom, we're in love, Carrie said.

—That's fine, but when you're in my house, you live by my rules, Tracy said.

—So that means he sleeps in your room? Carrie said.

They started laughing. The exchange sounded to me like a riff on something they'd done before, and that they were laughing about that as much as anything. That deflated and then irked me.

—But it's a moot point, isn't it? Tracy said. Our knight in shining armor here says he's leaving. Knights always leave before the party starts, don't they? Then all you've got left are the fat earls and scrawny pages.

—And sometimes the fat earls don't even come in. They stay outside in their Cadillacs, Carrie said.

—Ow, good one, Tracy said.

—Like shooting fish in a barrel, Carrie said.

Tracy put her elbows on the table, interlocked her fingers and rested her chin on them, and smiled at me like she was having her senior picture taken.

—Aren't you going to say anything? she said.

—Uh, could I have permission to go to the bathroom? I said.

Carrie laughed, and Tracy put on a pout.

—I can see this conversation is going nowhere, Tracy said.

—Where do you think most of them go, I said.

—That's so easy, she said.

Carrie yawned and squeezed my knee at the same time.

—I'm getting sleepy, she said.

—That makes two of us, and it's not the hour, I said.

—Uh-oh, him's upset, Tracy said.

If someone had bet me a dollar I wouldn't do it I would've reached across the table and slapped her. Her kind of bright young thing made me want to stick knitting needles in my eyes. Then suddenly my daughter came to mind, and Joan, too, and I felt like I had a dirty film on my skin and the weak glare of the kitchen fluorescents took on an evil, flaccid quality in my mind. But before I could tell Tracy what I thought of her and walk out, and then go to Bobo's Escalade and tell him to start using a grown-up name, and then start walking through the night to Lindsey, Carrie squeezed my knee again and said:

—You're going to stay, okay?

And her voice was so childlike, trying to be innocent and sincere and not quite making it, which was even more heartbreaking than if she actually had been innocent and sincere, that I said:

—Okay.

32

Carrie and I shared the guest bedroom and as soon as we turned in we made love again. I didn't really feel like it, but she wanted to and not doing it would've been awkward. Afterward she curled up next to me and went right to sleep, but I couldn't drop off. I'd had the long nap earlier, and I was still wired from the day I'd had. I lay with my hands behind my head and stared at the dimly lit walls. There was a streetlight outside the windows and a breeze was swaying the branches of a big tree and the wall next to the bed was a shifting mess of shadows, a moving Rorschach test. I thought about everything that had happened that day. In a weird way it had been great. Usually I thought about women all the time, and today things had happened that I had only dreamed about before; however, what surprised me is I didn't feel elated or even satisfied. It was like I had wanted a million dollars, and on the first morning I finally had the money, I woke up and didn't feel any different.

Carrie had one leg thrown outside the covers, her foot hanging over the side of the bed. I watched her a moment, then started paying attention to her breathing, which was soft and regular. I decided it wasn't all bad being there with her, even if it wasn't what I expected it to be. I started wondering about her life, how she'd gotten hooked up with her husband, why she hadn't been able to answer when I asked why she stayed with him. For some reason I started thinking about her wedding, wondering if she'd had a big one, maybe Brockton had thrown a real shindig for his niece, doing the job for his dead brother. Then I started thinking about my wife again, feeling guilty. Joan wasn't a bad person, and despite the fact I was in bed with another woman, I didn't think I was either. Neither of us was any more petty, selfish or unreasonable than the usual run of human. She was a good high school French teacher and I was a good tractor salesman, we were both good parents, if we saw a turtle crossing the road we stopped the car and carried it to the other side. In fact, that's how Katie got her first pet, a turtle named Mr. Tripps she kept in her room in an aquarium filled with rocks and plants and a bowl of water buried in dirt like a swimming pool. The problem with Joan and me was that we had nothing in common. We didn't really like spending time together and we didn't have good conversations. The first year or two we did, but now we didn't, and I didn't know why or how the change had happened. I thought about the promise I'd made myself earlier in the day, that if I lived I was going to divorce her, but now that a lot of the danger was gone, I doubted I'd keep it. I figured Joan had probably thought about leaving me, too, but I was glad we were both smart enough not to talk too much about our problems—if we had, the fragile truce we lived under would've collapsed. Talking probably wouldn't have done much good anyway. My uncle has a friend who's a marriage counselor, and at a party once the guy told me that in twenty-some years of seeing clients only two couples had ended up staying together, that by the time people came to him they really just wanted to be reassured it was okay to break up.

I wondered if Joan had managed to get the air conditioning fixed. I hoped she had.

The clock said a quarter after twelve. That got me thinking about what I was going to do in the morning, because this fantasy of pork chops and pretty women was going to end at dawn. I still didn't really trust Carrie and I didn't think I wanted to get into a car with her driving—I didn't have any evidence to base my suspicion on, just my ignorance and caution and the fact it was her relatives I could get into trouble. I thought about getting up right then and walking to Lindsey; I could make it by dawn if I left right away. Then I thought of Bobo—it didn't seem likely he'd have any connection to Brockton or Fee, and he might be sorry enough for what he'd done to give me a ride even though he didn't know me. I sat up and gently pushed away the covers, then swung my legs over the side of the bed. I looked over my shoulder at Carrie. She hadn't stirred. I stood up and walked over to the chair where I had left my clothes and put on everything but my shoes, then went to the windows and lifted a corner of the blinds and looked out: a white Escalade was parked in front of the house.

33

Then I heard furniture sliding across the floor in the living room—
we hadn't moved anything back into place before going to bed. I
turned from the window and as I did the television came on loudly,
but the volume quickly lowered. Carrie didn't wake up. I went to
the door, stood there a moment, then turned the knob slowly and
eased out into the hallway and shut the door behind me.

Tracy was in the living room on the couch, wearing the blue
robe, her feet propped on the coffee table, which she had set right
side up. She was holding one of the leftover pork chops at her
mouth like a drumstick. She had scooted the couch around just
enough that she could sit on it and see the television, a big flat
screen model on the floor two feet in front of her. When I walked
in she looked up.

—Hey, she said. Hope I didn't wake you.

—No, I was awake.

She held out the pork chop.

—Last one, she said. Want a bite?

—No thanks.

I stood in the middle of the floor, not sure where to sit. The easy
chair was still facing the kitchen, and if I sat down on the end of
the couch opposite her I'd be blocking her view of the television.
She curled a finger at me and took her feet off the coffee table and
scooted over.

—Come on, I won't bite, she said.

I sat down half a cushion away from her, the only place I could
without blocking her view. She nodded at the television.

—This is pretty good, she said.

—What're they selling? I asked. I couldn't tell because they were
in the part of the infomercial where the man and woman were sitting on stools behind a kitchen counter spread with food, talking.

—A machine that'll cook two whole chickens at once in under forty minutes. It's the size of a bread box, though, and I don't see how they get them both in there. Must use small chickens.

—Who needs two whole chickens at once, anyway? I said.

—That's what I was thinking, she said.

We watched for a couple of minutes. She finished the pork chop and licked her fingers clean. The machine did look kind of interesting. Now they were making beef jerky in it.

—I guess Carrie's asleep, she said.

—Yeah.

—You know, I think she really likes you, she said.

—Well, one would hope, I said.

—No, I mean it, she said. I've seen her get to know a lot of guys, and she's different with you.

—A lot of guys, huh?

She smiled.

—Aren't jealous already, are you?

—As long as I'm one of the first hundred, I'm okay.

—The first hundred? she said.

—Bad joke, I said.

—You got that right, she said, then popped off the couch and stepped around my feet and headed toward the kitchen.

—Want a drink? she asked.

—Thanks, yeah. But no booze. Any kind of soda would be fine.

She brought back a can of orange soda and a can of beer, handed me the soda and sat down again, curling her legs under her. We both popped the tops on our cans, looking at the television. They were showing a close-up of a beef roast cooking.

—You usually up this late? I said.

—Usually, she said.

I waited, but she didn't go on, and I couldn't think of anything else to say. She kept looking at the television. Then suddenly she reached down with her foot and pushed the power button on the television with her big toe and turned it off. She looked at the blank screen a moment, then took a drink of her beer, then turned to me.

—Well, she said, what are we going to do now?

34

We started talking. She told me about her divorce, and I told her about fantasizing about one. She had a son eight years old who lived with his father in Cleveland; she had him three weeks every summer and some holidays. She had lived in Marsburg all her life except for four years of college and a year after that in Cleveland. She'd moved back after her divorce, she said, and she was guilty about leaving her son, but she'd done it for him, she said, because she thought it'd be less confusing and traumatic if she weren't around, her ex had a new wife who was good to her son and she didn't want to make him constantly deal with split loyalties. Something about her explanation sounded tinny and canned like she just didn't want the tether of a child and had made up this self-martyring story to cover herself. I started disliking her for that, but then realized I didn't really know shit from shinola. Truth was, I was tired of my own responsibilities. In some ways I had probably been happier the last fourteen or fifteen hours being chased by drug dealers than I had in seven years of going to work and mowing the yard and paying for dance lessons.

She got up and got another soda for me, my second, and a beer for herself, her fourth. When she sat back down I asked her why she thought Carrie stayed with her husband.

—You know, I don't know, she said. I can't tell you how many times I've tried to get her to leave him. He's just a jerk. Lays around all day, stays out all night. He's not even that good-looking. I think she just feels sorry for him, and despite what you might think, Carrie's actually pretty loyal.

I chuckled.

—It's true, she said. I mean, I can see how you'd think different, but she's not usually like this.

—I thought you said you'd seen her with a lot of guys.

—Well, yeah, but duh, I've known her since she was six.

—So she's never had another man here in your house?

—One, she said, and he didn't get to go in there, and she nodded toward the bedroom.

—Hey, I knew I was going to be special someday.

She laughed, then looked at me a little too long from up under her eyelids.

—It's kind of dumb of me to even ask about her husband, I said. I'll probably never see her again after tomorrow.

—You never know, she said.

I shook my head.

—I'm married, she's married, we've gotten off to a fast start, and her uncle wants to kill me, I said. I'd say that's a pretty good recipe for relationship disaster.

—But you've had fun, haven't you? she said.

—Can't deny that, I said.

She smiled and stood up.

—I'm empty, she said, waving the beer can back and forth.

She went into the kitchen and came back with two beers and put one of them down on the coffee table in front of me.

—In case you change your mind, she said.

She sat down and curled her legs under her again and either because she was drunk or trying to tease me or both, she left the flap of her robe open at the bottom and I could see the inside of one of her thighs all the way up to the seam of her blue cotton panties.

She caught me looking and waved a finger. I looked away, embarrassed, but when I looked back she hadn't covered herself.

—Well, it's almost three, I said.

—What's that got to do with anything? she said.

—I don't know.

—So stick to the subject, she said.

—And what's that?

—I don't know, she said. You tell me. It's three in the morning and you're sitting on a couch with a woman drinking her fifth beer.

—Yeah, well, I guess Freud was right, I said.

—About what? she giggled.

—Everything, I said.

Then I had an idea. I decided to ask her about Joe and Eton Brockton, see if she knew if what Fee had told me about them was true, that Eton had been sleeping with Joe's wife. So I did that, and also told her a lot of what had happened to me that day. When I finished she was grinning.

—Are you trying to play detective? she said.

—Kind of.

—Want me to call you Sam Spade?

—If you want to.

—You know, I think you'd be better off just minding your own business, she said, paused, and then let out a silly drunken laugh. That's what they always say, isn't it? she said. In the movies?

—Yeah.

—Well, it's good advice. I don't think you should worry about anything except just having a little more fun here in old Marsburg and then going home.

She leered at me again. I wanted to reach out and tear her flimsy robe open, but finally I turned from her and leaned forward for my soda on the coffee table.

—All right, she said and I heard the suspension of breath while she took another drink. I lifted my soda and took a drink myself, then sat back again.

Suddenly there was a knock at the front door.

Famous Writers School
P.O. Box 1181
Fayette WV 32111
June 18, 200—

Dear Dan,

I want to congratulate you on the fine work you've done here. I think the novel is coming along swimmingly, and I have no suggestions for improvement—just keep up the good work. Actually, I've been toying with the idea of asking you if you'd offer first serial rights for the book to *Upward Spiral*. You think about it, and I will too. Maybe we can do business. There'd be no payment, of course (as I'm sure you know, there rarely is with the kind of small magazine I run); however, there'd be the satisfaction of publication, and magazines like *Upward Spiral* are the kinds of venues where promising young writers such as you often get their starts. In fact, I'd like to publish the whole novel in *Upward Spiral*. I know this would probably take at least two and maybe even three issues, but I'd be proud to publish such fine work in our pages. As you probably know, serial publication of novels has a long and storied history. For instance, Conrad's island tale *Victory* was the only one of his novels that was a financial success during his lifetime, and it first gained attention during serial publication. Also, just about everything Dickens wrote came out serially, and he was so popular people would wait at the docks in New York for the ships carrying the magazines with his new chapters. And, believe it or not, sections of *Ulysses* first saw the light of day in a literary magazine, at a time when the "big boy" publishers wouldn't touch the novel with a ten-foot pole.

How long do you think the novel will end up being? I figure at the rate we're going, I probably won't get to see the whole thing before the course is over, so I was wondering—partly as an amends for my rude behavior, but mostly because I'm interested in the story—if you'd be willing to let me act as reader for you on the whole book? There'd be no charge, of course.

Let's put our disagreements behind us, what do you say? If you still feel the need to contact *Writing Life*, though, I completely understand and you would be completely within your rights. You've just been in the wrong place at the wrong time, I'm afraid, and for that I apologize. You see, recently I have become absolutely sickened by this country, and you've just happened to catch some of my stray bullets. I think if I explain my position, you'll understand.

I believe you'll agree with me when I say we've become a libertine culture. On the surface, this might make me sound like a latter-day Elmer Gantry, but let's look at the facts: we've become a nation in which the sex industry has twice the revenue of the steel industry, and you can't turn on the television without seeing a commercial for a sex pill—are all these millions of dollars of pills being sold out of "medical necessity"? I think not. Yet the country blithely accepts these soft porn interludes as our children sit in front of the television drinking their fifth soda of the day and eating Pop Tarts for supper while their parents, still baffled about why the Ritalin isn't working, sit behind them in recliners and think about trading for bigger SUVs. Even what seems good and decent really isn't: all of the WTO protesters with their floppy haircuts and peasant skirts couldn't tell you the difference between macro- and microeconomics if they had a gun at their heads, and I seriously doubt there's many of them who, when it comes down to it, won't take their degrees to IBM or some such place. We're dying on the vine, my friend. Yet what can we do? Where can we go? Unlike Huck Finn, we can't "light out for the west" when circumstances become intolerable. There is no more 'west', because it has now become the world's largest, dirtiest megalopolis. I've been thinking the answer might now lie to the east, in the former satellite countries of the Soviet Union—open, growing, newly vibrant places not unlike California in the 1950s, I imagine, where one has an opportunity to be in on the ground floor of something great. Australia is also a possibility, though its immigration laws are more draconian. I digress, I suppose, but I feel you deserve the legitimate explanation for my unprofessional behavior, and, as I said earlier, if you still feel the need to contact *Writing Life*, I certainly understand, but I also promise you, there won't be any more trouble in our future correspondence.

You know, what the heck, I think I *will* offer payment for first serial rights to your novel. This is the first time *Upward Spiral* has done such a thing, but how does $100 sound?

I look forward to your answer and to your next installment!

Best wishes,
Wendell

Lesson 5

What Comes First, Plot or Character?

When I was in the military, I spent a month traveling with the brigadier general I was assigned to. The trip was called a "fact-finding mission," but in reality it was designed for the general to spend time with his young German mistress. She was in her early thirties, had played volleyball professionally, and was now a club coach in Düsseldorf. The general was fifty-seven and sprinting from death. I spent most of my time in his service scurrying around D.C. looking for this or that vitamin supplement, or allowing him to batter me in squash, or waiting for him in a government car outside a clothing store. While I worked for him he lost nineteen pounds, had hair plugs installed that looked as if they might start bleeding at any moment, and spent a good part of every working day on the telephone to Düsseldorf. His wife was a loud, bossy woman who called me several times each day. Part of my job was to satisfy her every whim, and I soon learned she liked her lobster from Maine and her tickets front row center.

One morning I dropped off the general for an early morning meeting, then went back to the office and began opening the mail; however, before I realized what I had done, I tore open a manila envelope from Düsseldorf—the standing order was that only *he* opened mail from *there*—and out spilled several nude photos of his girlfriend.

I knew I was in a pickle. If I put the photos back in the envelope and resealed it, he'd know I'd seen them and go berserk; if I just threw them away, which seemed the better option, he would still eventually ask if we received a package from Düsseldorf and then treat me with suspicion when I said we hadn't; he was insanely jealous of the woman and called Germany at all hours of the day and night to see if she were home. Shuffling through the photos, I could see why: if one could look past the scatology he saw an exceedingly beautiful woman, tall, with long dark hair, fair skin, strong hips and a small, high bust.

The photos were black-and-white and I stared at them absent-mindedly, deciding what to do. Then the telephone rang. I picked up the receiver and gave our standard office greeting.

It was the general's wife. She wanted to speak to him and I told her he was in a meeting. Her voice had tears in it, which wasn't uncommon.

"Do you know anything about this trip to Germany?" she asked.

"No, Mrs. —, the general hasn't mentioned it."

"Well, he said you were going with him. Of course I'm not invited."

"I'm sorry, ma'am," I said, but inside I was elated. I had never been to Europe.

"Will you do me a favor, Wendell?" she asked, sniffling.

"Certainly, ma'am."

"Will you call me if you two go over there, to keep me updated on what's going on?"

"I will if I can, ma'am. I don't know anything about the trip yet, so there might be things I can't talk about."

"Why? Security?" she guffawed. "They wouldn't let my husband near anything that really mattered—you think I don't know that? He can't light a candle without burning his finger." She paused. "I think he's going to see that Austrian maid we had when we were over there. I had my suspicions, you know."

"I'm sorry to hear that, ma'am."

"Then give me a report on everything that happens," she said.

"Ma'am, I'm sorry, but like I said—"

"I'll say you made a pass at me," she said.

I rested my forehead on my fist and closed my eyes.

"You tried to grab me when you were over here last Thursday bringing the steaks," she said. "How's that sound?"

I opened my eyes and stared at the green blotter.

"Mrs. —, please. I don't think the general would believe that."

"Why? Aren't I good enough?"

"No, ma'am, it's just that. . . I don't know, he just knows I would never do that. I mean, despite the fact you're attractive, ma'am."

"Don't try to butter me up," she said.

"No, ma'am."

"You *will* tell me what's happening, or you *will* be up for court martial," she said.

"Yes, ma'am."

"All right then," she said, "here's what I want from the drugstore. Have you got a pencil?"

"Yes, ma'am."

All right, let's stop here. Our character has been presented with a difficult situation—how would you, as a writer, decide what he'll do next? Many new writers often ask if they should first decide what's going to happen and then create characters to carry out the action, and the answer to that is *no*. Plot, or the story's dramatic action, should *always* grow out of character, not the other way around, unless, of course, you want to write the kinds of stories that start with a young woman's favorite horse getting sick and end twelve pages later with her marriage to a virile country vet.

We all know the story of *Hamlet*—an idealistic and thoughtful young man has to determine if his father was murdered by his uncle and if his mother was in on it. However, what if Hamlet had not been "idealistic and thoughtful," but instead "practical and decisive"? Then he might've secretly murdered his uncle as quickly as possible, taken the throne, married Ophelia, held sway over his mother, conquered Norway, and had a lifetime of encounters with courtesans. And they'd still be cleaning a statue of him in a Copenhagen park today.

Our young attaché is not unlike Hamlet. He is twenty-four, idealistic, trapped by the corruption of his elders, and he must quickly decide on a course of action. On the one hand, duty requires loyalty to his superior, and on the other, a threat from Potiphar's wife could prove ruinous. He also has the photos to deal with. So let's see what he does, paying close attention to how character drives plot:

After I hung up, I sat there awhile, staring at the list Mrs.— had given me:
- Leggs pantyhose XL (kind in egg)
- toothpicks (round)
- 2 citronella candles, orange
- 25 ft. garden hose

I put the list in my pocket, then double-checked the envelope the photos had come in to make sure there wasn't a letter. I picked out a photo at random, one in which the woman's face was hidden behind a Japanese fan, and put it back into the envelope. The other photos I put in a different manila envelope, then took it into the inner office and put it on the general's desk. The photo I was keeping I took out to my Dodge Dart, then new and shiny, and stored it in the trunk.

I picked up the general from his meeting. On the ride back to the Pentagon, he stared out his window in the backseat and didn't say a word, which was unusual.

"Did the meeting go all right, sir?" I asked.

"Just more of the motherlovin' same up there at State," he said, shaking his head.

Back at the Pentagon, he went straight into his office and closed the door. I sat down at my desk. Two minutes later, his voice boomed out:

"Newton! Get in here!"

I got up and went into his office, a studied innocence on my face. The photos were nowhere in sight. He gestured at the door with one finger as if he were trying to toss something disgusting off it. "Close that motherlovin' door," he said. I did.

"You've got a big problem, son," he said.

"Sir?"

"Don't give me that. You get cute with me, I'll have your ass in Beirut by Saturday."

He was sitting forward in his leather chair, his face tight and red.

"I'm sorry, sir," I said. "I'm not sure I understand what's wrong."

Then the telephone rang. I stepped to the side of the desk and answered it. It was his wife. She wanted to know why I hadn't brought her things yet.

"I'm sorry, Mrs.—," I said. "I had to get the general from his meeting."

"Put him on," she said.

I held out the receiver. "Sir, your—"

"I know," he said, grabbing the phone.

He swiveled his chair so his back was to me, then said little more than yes and no during the conversation. When he finished, he swiveled around and slammed the phone back in the cradle. He glared at me.

"You opened my personal mail," he said.

"Yessir," I said. "I'm very sorry. It was a mistake. I didn't notice the return address."

"Got an eyeful, did you?" he said.

"Well, there is one problem, sir," I said. "One of the photographs is missing, along with the envelope they all arrived in."

"What?" he said.

"Yessir, and earlier this morning Mrs. — called about your trip to West Germany. She said—" and I told him about our conversation.

When I finished, he fixed me with a fake smile and said:

"You know, son, this could work out for both of us." Then he outlined a plan in which I accompanied him to Europe and had most of my time free to travel, all on his expense account. The only stipulations were that I call his wife every day with a credible lie about his whereabouts and that I return the missing photo and envelope. I told him I could do the first, but the second I wasn't sure about.

"Why not?" he asked.

I said I thought I could return the photo and envelope if he'd get me diplomatic credentials to visit Poland, Yugoslavia, and Czechoslovakia, which were then still behind the Iron Curtain. He shook his head.

"No way," he said. "Not enough time."

"I know those things can be expedited, sir," I said.

"If there's good enough reason," he said. "But I couldn't sell this as a rush job."

"I see, sir," I said.

"What's over there anyway?" he said. "Nothing but tank factories and bad sausage."

"I don't know, sir, I guess it's just that those countries have been off-limits for so long, there's something of the attraction of the unknown about them. Also, the Slavic cultures are so much older than ours that there's something that seems elemental about them."

He looked at me like I was crazy. During that silence, I realized that if I gave him the photo before I was discharged, he could have me transferred to Greenland if he wanted. So I spoke up and said I supposed I could do without the travel to Eastern Europe, if I could wait to give him the photo back when my discharge was in process, seven months from then. He agreed.

A few weeks later, his mistress met us as we left the gates of the Frankfort airbase. She spoke passable English and was even more beautiful in person. On the cab ride to the hotel, she made conversation with me about our flight and the local sights I should see. The general looked furious. He stared out his window, tight-lipped.

Over the next month I toured Germany, Austria, and France, and saw many interesting literary sights: the house where Balzac wrote his last work and then died a consumptive death; a Vienna public garden where a young Thomas Mann burned the pages of an unfinished novella, for which act he was arrested and briefly jailed; and Sartre's favorite bar, now a dress shop. However, my favorite episode of the whole trip was my last afternoon in Germany. I spent it sitting on a bench across the street from a stark concrete and barbed wire section of the Berlin Wall, enjoying a Fanta and thinking about the mysterious world that wall hid. After a while a man sat down at the other end of the bench. He was forty or forty-five, clean-cut, and from the look of his dress working class. We exchanged nods, and a couple of minutes passed uneventfully. When I glanced over at him again, though, he was crying. I almost got up and left, but he wiped his eyes with his hand and looked at me. I asked him if he spoke English. He nodded.

"Is there something wrong?" I asked.

"No," he said with a perfect British accent, "and I apologize for disturbing you."

"You haven't bothered me."

"I'm just homesick," he said.

It turned out he was from Budapest. He had studied in England for three years and then participated in the 1956 uprising in Hungary. He managed to escape the country after the rebellion was crushed. He been an architect in his own country, but because of licensing regulations couldn't practice and now worked as a carpenter.

I told him I had wanted to try to visit Eastern Europe on my trip but that it had been impossible.

"West Europe is nice, but the East is twice as good. No, three times," he laughed.

"Yes, well, it's my dream to see it one day," I said. "I guess the world will have to change a lot for that to happen, though."

"Yes, a great deal." He paused. "So how did you come to care about my home? Most Americans, they see it as a boring place."

"I read several books when I was in high school," I said. "Our study hall was in the library and the teacher didn't try to control us, so it was always pretty raucous. I used to—"

"Raucous?" he interrupted.

"Wild. Out of control," I said.

He nodded, and I went on.

"Anyway, I was slight and studious as a young man, so in the study hall I'd get picked on by the older students. I started sneaking away from my table and hiding in the stacks to avoid them. The first day I did that, by chance I went to the section that held the books on Slavic history. At random I picked out a history of Czechoslovakia and sat down on the floor and started reading it. All I'd heard was that these people wanted to drop atom bombs on us, but here was this lively people with such an interesting culture. Everyday during study hall I went back and sat on the floor and read a book about Eastern Europe."

After a few more pleasantries, he said he had to get back to work and left.

I sat there a good while longer, indulging my bittersweet reverie about being so close to my dream but yet so far. Finally, though, a young couple sat down right next to me and started kissing. At first I wasn't sure what to do, but when the girl's leg started squirming against mine, I got up and left.

Assignment: Because it ends well, this story is a comedy. Our character handles a difficult situation in a way that creates union for the general and his mistress and preserves union for the general and his wife. Because he was cool-headed, things turned out well. However, if he had been rash and panicky, we could've had a court martial for him and a divorce for the general, which would've made the story a tragedy. Comedies end in union, tragedies in separation. With that in mind, look at the story you've been writing and decide if what you have is a comedy or a tragedy. As an exercise, if you think you've got a comedy, make it a tragedy, and likewise, if you've got a tragedy, make it a comedy. Change the characters accordingly.

Linda Trane Would Go

May 20
I have a mole on my left shoulder. It's roughly a quarter-inch in diameter but I can't tell if its shape is irregular or not. Just what exactly is the regular shape of a mole? I can't tell if it's growing either, since I just noticed it last week. It looks almost exactly like the mole Honoria had on her back right before she left me the first time. They removed hers right away.

I need to learn about the Internet. Then I could thoroughly research things such as moles instead of waking up at three in the morning and looking at my shoulder in the mirror until daybreak.

Don't worry, Wendell, everything will be all right. Probably.

May 22
Rio. Rio, Rio, Rio.

Wendell is chasing some whore. He hasn't seen her, but he just can't stop thinking about her. She must be a real slut in her letters. Wendell is such a poet when it comes to sluts. That's quite an ode, saying her name four times.

May 23
I think the mole is getting darker, but I'm not sure.

Look at it with a flashlight, Wendell.

May 24
Romance and sex have been so completely deified that we now bank almost our entire sense of well-being on them. Although I

can rail against this and its various manifestations—pornogra-
phy available at the touch of a button, $30,000 weddings—I
still can't stop thinking about women all the time. Even though
I've never seen Rio I think about her constantly. So what, if
when I do see her, her stomach pooches out? Why should that
bother me? Why do I insist on beauty? With Lana beauty cer-
tainly mattered, because despite our problems, I loved her greatly.
I still do; I can't deny it. When I look at the picture I took of her
that day we spent at the lake and see her eyes squinting prettily
against the sunlight, her wet hair, her straight smile and the
point of her little chin, the womanly curves of her figure, a feel-
ing comes over me that wipes away all strikes against her. I even
forget my guilt about her children.

Wendell. Pobre cito.

My husband is having an affair with the housekeeper. Nancy is
twenty-four and has a boy six years old she brings over to play with
my children. Nancy was a foster child who got pregnant her last
year in high school, and now she's going to school to be a certified
nursing assistant. She is a hard kind of pretty that will look the
same at fifty as it does now, the type of woman who could be seven
months pregnant and hide it with an apron.

I haven't caught her with my husband yet, but I don't need to.
When something is going on, you just know.

I call up our last housekeeper, an Ecuadorian who quit because
of the long bus ride to our house. After some chitchat, I ask if she
can she get me in contact with someone who sells forged visas.

No, she says.

Emilia, I swear, I don't want to get you into any trouble. I've just
got a friend who needs some papers.

Sorry, she says.

I'd be willing to pay for just a phone number, I say.

Okay, hold, thank you, she says.

She puts down the phone. I hear a conversation in Spanish. A moment later, she comes back on and tells me to meet her at a bodega in her neighborhood tomorrow afternoon.

Can't you just give it to me now? I say. I promise I'll mail the money.

Yes, she says. One hundred.

Okay, a hundred. I'll mail a hundred.

No, no thank you. We will meet.

The next afternoon in front of the bodega, some loitering old men eyeing us, Emilia gives me a phone number on a slip of paper and I give her a hundred dollar bill. As soon as she has the money, she nods and walks off without another word. The old men are sitting on kitchen chairs and one of them says something loudly in Spanish and they all laugh, looking at me.

In the car on the way back home, I call the number. A man answers.

Yeah? he says.

I tell him I need to buy a visa for Czechoslovakia.

So?

I heard you were the person to call.

You heard wrong.

Well, do you know anyone who could help me?

Nope.

I could pay you if you did, I say.

In the background the volume on a television rises and falls.

Five hundred, he says.

For a phone number? I say. I pull into my driveway, up to the garage door, and sit there with the engine running.

Like I said, he says.

All right, all right. How'd you want to arrange it?

He gives me the address of a bar near the bus station and tells me to meet him the next day at 12:30.

How will I know you? I ask.

Don't worry about that, he says. I guarantee I'll know you. Just hearing you talk, I can tell you'll stick out like a sore thumb in this place.

The next day, I arrive at the bar and sit down at a table. It's a shotgun room and half the stools at the bar are occupied, but no one's having a conversation. There's no television and the bar is unnaturally quiet. I'm the only woman in the place. There's only one other person at a table, a young man wearing a UPS uniform, short pants version. He's got a stack of sandwiches in front of him, eating like he's on a Japanese game show.

The bartender takes my order from behind the bar, then hands the beer to one of the men on the stools, who hands it to me and takes my money without meeting my eyes. Then the man in the UPS uniform looks up, wipes his mouth with the back of his hand, and motions me over.

I go to his table. He nods at the chair across from him, then starts eating again.

My mom owns this place, he says.

It's nice, I say.

It's a hole, he says. But that's the best kind of bar to own. Low overhead and dedicated customers.

He has a shred of lettuce hanging on his chin. It bobs up and down with his chewing.

So how much do you want this visa? he asks.

I really want it, I say.

Yeah, but how bad? he says.

I let out a sigh.

With every fiber of my being, I say in a tired voice. Is that enough?

He takes the last bite of a sandwich that has nothing but baloney and mayonnaise, then picks up another that has only ham and mayonnaise, the mayonnaise leaking out the sides. Two more sandwiches are on the plate, but both of them are stacked high with fillings. The man couldn't weigh more than a hundred and fifty. His looks are a little ratty.

Trouble is, this just don't make sense, he says. Someone like you goes through regular channels.

I've got a friend who might have trouble getting a visa, I say.

Yeah, but places like Czechoslovakia are begging for Americans, he says. They want the dollars. You could kill someone on the plane going over there and they'd still let you in.

Then a swinging door at the back of the room opens and an enormous woman comes out. She looks pained by the effort of walking and as she gets close, her labored breathing becomes audible. She wears a colorful housedress that hangs to just below her knees and terrycloth house shoes. Her ankles are like grapefruits.

Hey Mom, the man says.

She beams at me, thinking her boy has a new friend.

I'm Nancy, Joe's mother, she says.

Lana, I say.

Pleased to meet you. Would you like a sandwich?

No, thank you.

We've got soup too, she says.

I've already eaten.

Well, all right, she says. If you change your mind, let me know.

Thank you.

Would you like any more, honey? she says.

No thanks, Mom. They're good.

She pats him on the shoulder. Then her hand darts out and plucks the shred of lettuce from his chin. Neither of them acknowledges what she's done. She starts back toward the swinging door.

Mom runs a soup kitchen back there, the man says. Gives the rummies one of these sandwiches and a bowl of soup. That way when they get their checks, they come here to drink them up. When they're broke again, she feeds them till the next check. You gotta know about it by word of mouth, though.

That's nice, I say.

She gets her meat for next to nothing, he says. It's meat you couldn't sell in Indonesia.

I don't answer. He picks up another sandwich.

So your friend, he says. Why don't he come himself?

He doesn't know I'm here, I say.

Why? he says.

What do you care?

Because I got to be careful, he says.

All I'm asking for is a phone number, I say.

He takes a moment to swallow before he answers.

Look, he says, let's get something straight. I can get you into China or I can get you into Switzerland, which, believe it or not, is just about harder than China. I can get you a piece of paper that says it's okay to throw your gum on the sidewalk in Singapore. I got the whole world in my hands, lady, understand? What I said on the phone was just smoke.

I see.

Okay then, he says. So why you doing this?

Well, I guess because I love him, I say.

He keeps staring at me, chewing.

All right, he says. Someone like you don't do something like this for anything less than the fact she thinks she loves someone. So the next question is, Why can't he get his visa the regular way? He got paper out on him?

Paper?

A warrant, he says.

No, I say.

Then what's the problem? he says.

He's got a record, I say.

What'd he do? he asks.

Before I can answer, one of the men at the bar falls off his stool. It topples behind him with a screech and a bang. He lies motionless on his back under the bar for a moment, then starts moving his legs in the air like a bug. The young man watches this as if it's nothing remarkable.

Take him back for a sandwich, he says. Then he raises his eyebrows at me and tells me to go on.

Several years ago, I say, my friend was involved in a stock scam of some kind, a boiler room operation I think it's called. I don't know much about it, but he was convicted on federal charges, then got time served and probation for testifying. He was young, just out of the air force, and said he didn't know what was going on. That might be true and it might not, but it doesn't make any difference to me.

He's not in witness protection? he asks.

No.

He tells me the forged papers will cost $5,000. I can tell he's charging that much because he thinks I can pay it, but I say the price is fine. We arrange our next meeting, where I'm to bring half the money. He looks at his watch.

Okay, he says. Gotta get back to work.

Famous Writers School
P.O. Box 1181
Fayette WV 32111
June 20, 200—

Lana,

Is this you? I can hardly believe it. Are you really getting that visa, and is your husband really having an affair? Are you splitting with him? If you're trying to let me know you want to get back together, that's the first thing I would insist on.

Although I have little doubt this is you, pobre cito, I'll say no more until I'm sure. Call me as soon as you get this.

Until,
Wendell

Rio Jordan

Dear Wendell,

Thanks for calling me this evening, but I couldn't get your number off the answering machine. It's digital, and you know how the sound quality on those things can be. Even if I could've gotten it, I guess I was shy about calling back. I'm not sure why, maybe because you already know so much about me. But yes, I'd love to meet sometime soon—like you, I've enjoyed our correspondence more than any "conversation" I've had in a long time. How's next Thursday sound, say for a late lunch? I thought we could meet somewhere between Fayette and Pittsburgh. I know a nice place in Ostor, near the border, a restaurant that's in a local motel, the WhileAway Inn. It looks like a dump, but the food's fantastic. People up here drive down there all the time and the place even got written up in the paper. Fried chicken is their specialty, and they put six or seven bowls of vegetables on your table, biscuits and cornbread, too. What'd you think? If this sounds good to you, why don't you give me another call? You can usually catch me around noon, when I'm getting up.

In case you're wondering, things here have been going better. Rob actually had the gall to come around again and tell me he'd made a big mistake in getting back with Alma and had already broken up with her again, but I told him to go to hell and apparently he has, because I haven't seen him again. Jerry got out of his legal trouble over trying to break into my apartment by entering a residential psychiatric treatment program, or at least that's what they told me at the bar—that was such a mistake on my part, but I still hope he's okay. You know, I guess I'm finally feeling pretty good again, more like my old self. AND (this is the really big news), I've decided to go back and finish my dissertation. I went by school last week and talked to my old director and he said it shouldn't be any trouble and that he'd help me get a new committee together. I've realized I must've been off my rocker to quit school the way I did. I actually like studying the things I had been, and I'm pretty sure I'll enjoy a teaching career, but I was just suffering from burnout. I mean, I'd just gotten divorced and was going through all that, had just finished my comps, and the thought of taking on a project as big as the dissertation just freaked me out. I'll tell you all about what's been happening and my dissertation too when we get together—I might've already mentioned this, but my research concerned attitudes among troubled adolescents. I guess after hearing me go on, you think I should be part of the study group!

See you soon,
R.

Dan Federman

Lesson 5

Mr. Newton,
    Thanks for offering to publish my novel in *Upward Spiral* and for offering to pay me, but I don't believe that's the route I want

to take. I know that in the past serial publication was common, but I think I'd rather find an agent and then a publisher.

I'm afraid I'm also going to have to say no to you being a reader on the rest of my book. Please don't take offense, but it's obvious you and I don't work well together. I do plan to finish the course since we're well into it and I've already paid my money; however, when the course is over, I think we're going to be done. But just so you'll know, I plan for the novel to be two parts, and you will have read all of part one by the time we finish.

35

The knocking at the door sounded measured and regular, like someone beating with a mallet. Tracy jumped up from the couch and tightened the belt on her robe.

—I'm sure it's Bobo, she said. You better get back to the bedroom.

She hurried into the foyer, out of sight. I stood up and started across the room, then heard the front door open.

—What're you doing here? Tracy said.

—Where's Carrie? a man's voice said.

—Asleep, Tracy said.

I figured it was Carrie's husband, so I sat back down on the couch. A moment later they walked in the room. The man stopped just inside the doorway and Tracy came on in and sat down next to me on the couch.

—This is Doug, a friend of mine, she said.

I nodded at him, and he gave a slight nod back. He looked like he had just left a Lynyrd Skynyrd concert, except for his hair, which was in a spiky gel job—it would've taken a very smart mouse to find its way out of it. He wore a gray service station shirt with the sleeves cut off and frayed shoulders, the name Bill stitched over the pocket.

There were faded indecipherable blue ink tattoos on both his biceps and a leather knife case on his belt. Hollywood couldn't have done a better job of dressing a husband it was okay to cheat on.

—What're you doing here? he said to me.

—What business is it of yours? Tracy said.

—My wife's here, he said.

—Yeah, well, she's here all the time, she said.

He ignored that and nodded over his shoulder.

—And Bobo's asleep out there, he said.

—So? she said.

—So what's up with that? he said.

—You'll have to ask Bobo, she said.

He looked at me again.

—I heard someone was on the bus with Carrie today, he said.

—Doug called and said he was broken down out on Thirty-two, Tracy said. I couldn't come get him, so I called Carrie and asked if she'd mind picking him up on her route.

I was impressed by that lie, how quickly she came up with it. It made me want to spend two weeks in Mexico with her.

—So it was you on the bus, he said.

—Yeah, I said.

He took a pack of Kools out of his shirt pocket and lit one, then kept looking at me, the cigarette hanging from the corner of his mouth. His expression had nothing in it.

—Look, there's really no problem here, I said.

—You ain't from around here, he said. I know every fancypants around here.

—No, he's not, Tracy said. Some of us have friends who haven't spent their entire lives in Marsburg.

Suddenly his head jerked left and right, looking around like he'd been surprised by a sudden noise. It took me a moment to realize it was a twitch.

—So where's Carrie? he said.

—Like I told you, Tracy said. In the bed asleep.

—I guess you two usually get in there together, he said.

Tracy popped off the couch and got up in his face. Her nose was almost touching his cigarette.

—Yeah, we do, she said, her voice low and mean. Carrie likes it even more than me.

His hand darted up like a snake and slapped her—it made a flat, dry sound—and then was back at his side before I could blink, like something from a kung fu movie. He was still without expression. Tracy's head was turned by the blow and she brought it back around slowly. I knew this was where I was supposed to do something. I didn't want to, but I got up and stood right behind her— for a moment the three of us looked like a screwed up conga line—and then I put my hand on her hip and eased her to the side. I heard a metallic click at my waist: a switchblade was hanging in his right hand. I looked up at him. He was squinting through the smoke. Then his hand darted up and at once there was cool air on my left thigh: he had sliced a six-inch gash in my pants leg. I hadn't felt a thing. Tracy let out a yelp, and I took a couple of quick steps back toward the couch. I stuck my hand in the opening. No blood, he hadn't broken the skin.

—Them pants ain't so fancy now, he said.

I looked for something I could use as a weapon but didn't see anything. Tracy had her arms crossed over her stomach. She looked small and scared.

—Next time I might not be so neat about it, he said. I might get sloppy.

—You're both going to have to leave, Tracy said, her voice shaky.

—Look, I didn't do anything with your wife, I said. She just gave me a ride.

He shrugged.

—I don't care if you did, he said.

—Then what do you want? Tracy said.

—I just got some friends that want to see this sumbitch, he said. That's all.

36

Then the bedroom door opened and Carrie was standing there in a long purple football jersey, holding Tracy's .38 at her side.

—Evening, honey, he said.

Carrie didn't speak. She looked flat, defeated. I could see the pistol trembling.

—It was your new girlfriend over there who told me you was gonna be here tonight, he said to me. What'd you think about that?

I looked at Carrie but she wouldn't meet my eyes.

—Is that true? Tracy said.

Her husband chuckled but didn't say anything.

I sat down on the couch. I felt like a fool. I knew I would've been gone long ago, on my way to Lindsey, if these women hadn't been so pretty. I felt like I was getting what I deserved.

—What's going on? Tracy said.

No one answered. Carrie's husband took the cigarette out of his mouth, cupped the hand that was holding the knife and used his palm for an ashtray, then put the ashes in his jeans pocket.

—I want all of you out of here, Tracy said, and I want my gun, too. She started toward Carrie but the husband stepped over and blocked her.

—You know, lizzie, I never have liked you, he said.

Tracy hesitated, then backed away from him. She sat down next to me on the couch. Her expression was both blank and perplexed.

—I don't understand this, she said.

The husband's head jerked left and right. It looked like it was on a swivel.

—Well, Fancypants here got himself into some trouble today. Now he's got you into it too. I guess he's told you all about it.

—He hasn't told me anything, Tracy said.

—Now how do you expect me to believe that, he said, when I just looked through that window over there and saw you sitting here on the couch with him laughing and cutting up, with your legs spread out all nice and wide?

Carrie glanced at me, her eyes flashing jealousy and hurt.

—I didn't tell her anything, I said. Just leave her out of it.

—You don't even know what there is to tell, he said. Fee and Fluke don't even know. But let me tell you, boy, you're into something now. It ain't just some Mexicans gonna buy a couple bales of pot. Brockton's getting it set up for everything in this part of the country to come through here. Coke, meth, you name it. Those Colombians are in on it. They finally figured out one sheriff might be easier to buy off than a whole big city outfit.

Tracy crossed her arms and leaned forward until her face was almost on her knees.

—Oh God, she said. Oh God. She looked up at Carrie. Why did you get me into this?

—Now don't blame her, he said. Brockton just happened to see Fancypants on the school bus and when she got back to the tractor place, he made her tell him about it. Said if she didn't, her brother wasn't going to have such a good time of it. Tommy did something real bad a few years ago, Fancypants, in case you didn't know. State police get word of it and he'd be locked up for good—ain't that right, honey?

He looked over at Carrie and laughed.

37

Suddenly there was an explosion, the whine of a bullet and a sharp chipping noise in the plaster above my head. I ducked. The room turned smoky, and I saw that Carrie had the pistol pointed at her husband. He was looking at me, expressionless. Then he wheeled toward Carrie and started for her, but went only a couple of steps because she tracked him with the pistol, pointing it lower. Tracy screamed and got down on the floor on her hands and knees and scrabbled toward the kitchen.

—You little—he said.

She fired again, stopping him in midsentence. I couldn't see where she had hit him. All I could see was his back, and he didn't move. Then the switchblade dropped out of his hand and hit the hardwood floor with a clatter, and that's when I noticed the blood on his pointed-toe boots. He looked down at his stomach, but didn't grab for it. The blood was coming out lower than that, staining the seat of his jeans. He went to his knees slowly, like a camel sitting down, then reached out and picked up his knife. He looked at it. His head jerked left and right. Then he fell forward and lay with his arms and legs fanned out like he was making a snow angel.

38

Carrie kept the pistol pointed at him. I got up off the couch and walked slowly toward her. She didn't seem to notice me until I had my hand on her arm, gently tugging it down. She let me take the pistol and I put on the safety and stuck it in my pants pocket. Tracy was sobbing in the kitchen.

I wanted to say something to Carrie, but everything that came to mind sounded wrong. A minute passed with us staring at the body, watching blood pool around it.

—That was the only way out of this, I said.

Still looking at the body, she nodded.

Then the front door crashed open and a man carrying a rifle across his chest rushed into the room. He stopped dead in his tracks and looked at the body, then up at us. He looked like a jockey gone to pot and was dressed like he'd just played a round of golf. His eyes were puffy and bloodshot. His head whipped in the direction of the kitchen and Tracy's sobbing.

—Trace? he called out and ran in there.

39

At Bobo's suggestion, we locked the doors and pulled the curtains and blinds shut. He said if he had heard the shots there was a good chance someone else had and they might call the police. He said they'd have trouble knowing where to go, though, so if the house was dark we were probably okay.

The four of us sat down at the kitchen table and I did most of the talking, explaining everything that had happened yesterday. The only light we had was the centerpiece candle and it looked like we were having a séance, with the dead man in the next room visible through the doorway, a dark lump in the floor. No one had touched him yet.

After I finished, Carrie gave us the full story on Tommy. It was pretty awful, but she delivered it without emotion, as if it was a pain she'd had for so long it had quit hurting and just become part of life.

When Tommy was ten, he went deer hunting on the first day of the season with their father and Fee. They didn't sit in tree stands, though, but instead hunted the old-fashioned way by flushing the deer into the open for a shot. Because Tommy's father wanted him to get his first deer, he did the flushing, and Fee stayed back with

Tommy to help him take the shot. What exactly happened next, Carrie said, was a mystery for a long time, but her father ended up getting shot in the back and killed. The police decided it couldn't have been Fee or Tommy since the bullet didn't come from either of their guns, and it was declared a hunting accident involving an unknown shooter.

Then one night a couple of weeks later Tommy came into Carrie's room crying. He told her that Fee had said when grown-up men hunted, they played a game to scare each other, and that he and Fee had circled back until they were behind his father, then Fee gave Tommy a rifle that had been hidden at their new spot and told him it was loaded with blank bullets. Tommy said Fee told him to shoot at his father to scare him, that it was just a game. Tommy took one shot, and when he saw his father jump, he laughed and took another one, the one that killed him, although Tommy had no idea what had happened. He said Fee told him his dad was playing possum, that was part of the game, and now it was time for them to circle back to get their deer. Later they walked out of the woods; Fee told Tommy that his father had arranged to meet them later. Tommy didn't quite understand death, Carrie said, but that night when he came into her room he was still afraid he'd done something wrong since their father had been gone for so long.

She told him that their father had just gone away on a trip. She said she found out later Fee had told Tommy a story to tell the police, one in which they had never circled back or used the new rifle, telling Tommy if he didn't tell the story exactly right, he'd never get to see Carrie again.

Carrie went to her Uncle Joe Brockton with Tommy's story. He said it was just fantasy, so far-fetched no one would believe it, and that he himself didn't. But when Carrie said she was going to the police with it, Brockton told her if she did, there was at least some chance Tommy would spend the rest of his life in a state mental hospital for the criminally insane, and so Carrie, seventeen then, kept her mouth shut.

Joe Brockton was friends with the attorney handling the estate, and the story they told was that the dealership couldn't afford to stay open if Joe had to buy out his brother's estate at full value, the business couldn't bear that much debt, and that Carrie and Tommy would be better off if it was kept in the family. It was an old boy deal, and Brockton got the dealership for pennies on the dollar, with the stipulation that Carrie and Tommy would get a monthly stipend from the business.

That would've been the end of it, Carrie said, and bad enough as it was, but then Fee started trying to get custody of Tommy. Carrie got an attorney and fought him. Again her Uncle Joe offered no help, which baffled her, until one night while the custody battle was still going on, Fee came to see her, dead drunk, crying and wailing. He confessed that her Uncle Joe had hired him to kill her father because he wanted the dealership. He also said Brockton was behind his own move for custody of Tommy. He said Brockton wanted Tommy under his thumb, and that he had the murder weapon, the rifle with both his and Tommy's prints on it, and that Brockton now had them both over a barrel. Carrie said when she asked Fee why he didn't just kill her father himself instead of having Tommy pull the trigger, he started bawling and said he had thought since Tommy wasn't mentally right, he wasn't accountable and there'd be no sin in it, but now he knew that wasn't true, he'd interpreted some verses that told him Tommy was in sin with him equally in the murder. Carrie said she let the baffling self-delusion of that go, and asked him why he would've even considered killing her father in the first place. Fee told her Brockton had promised him a quarter of the dealership, which would've put him back to where he was before he lost everything, but now he himself was backing out of the deal because he couldn't stand the blood that was on his hands, and he was telling her all this for that same reason.

Carrie said when it looked like she might actually keep guardianship, the whole thing blew up. Brockton told her in no uncertain terms that if she did keep it he'd make sure Tommy got charged with murder, and that no one would believe Tommy's cockamamie story about how the shooting happened. Brockton decided he wanted to keep her close, too, which was why he blackmailed her into marrying her husband and also why she worked at the dealership. Brockton made her cook the books, and every now and then she had to mule a load of drugs down to Atlanta or Richmond.

—I don't think I can live through one more day of it, though, she said when she was finished. I think I'd rather be dead.

—Sure, honey, Tracy said. I can't believe you've carried it all this long.

—Okay, Bobo said. The way I see it, we've got three things we need to do.

He had his elbows on the table and his hands steepled under his chin. He looked like he was running a sales meeting.

—One, he said, we've got to get rid of him, and he nodded toward the living room. Two, we've got to get Doug here squared away, and three, we've got to make sure neither Carrie or Tommy ever gets in trouble for any of this.

—We can probably get rid of a body, I said, but I don't know about the rest of it. I think we need to go to the police.

Bobo smiled patiently and shook his head. The flickering shadows of the candle made him look a little menacing.

—Don't worry, he said. I was born to do this kind of thing.

40

Bobo wrapped the body in a bedspread, then taped it up with duct tape, and I filed the numbers off Tracy's thirty-eight, then used a wire brush in the barrel to distort the rifling. We did everything by flashlight. We used bleach to clean up the blood, then Bobo said we should all burn the clothes we were wearing.

—I'm not burning this robe, Tracy said. It cost four hundred dollars and there's not a drop of blood on it.

—And I don't have anything else to put on, I said.

—Don't worry about that, he said. There's a Wal-Mart two shakes from here.

He moved behind Tracy's chair and rubbed her shoulders.

—I'll get you a new robe, honey, he said. Something straight from Japan.

—I don't want anything from Japan, she said.

Then Carrie got up from the table without speaking and went into the bedroom. Bobo sat down and started talking to Tracy, trying to convince her, and I got up and followed Carrie. When I entered the bedroom she was standing at the closet. She pulled the purple jersey over her head and dropped it on the floor, then started looking for something to put on, moving hangers with one hand, holding a flashlight with the other. I sat down behind her on the bed. She pulled out a shorts outfit, then sat down next to me, the clothes in her lap. She set the flashlight on the bed and its beam threw a spotlight on the clothes in the closet in front of us. I put my arm around her. We sat there a long time without talking.

—You know something? she finally said. Even though we've known each other just a little while, I think you're someone I could wake up and see every day.

I started to answer, but she put a hand on the back of my head and pulled me to her and gave me a hard, desperate kiss. When she let go of the embrace, I could see her eyes were moist, full of tears. I kept watching her, waiting for them to fall, but they didn't.

—I don't know why I said that, she said.

—That's all right, I said.

—I can't believe what's happened, she said. I just can't.

—I know, I said.

Then we sat there in silence again. We started staring at the floor, the walls, anywhere but the other's face. There was suddenly a distance between us and I didn't know why. I almost stood up and crossed the room to look out the window, anything to get away, but something kept me on the bed.

Finally she reached over and took my hand. I looked at her then, and she leaned into my shoulder and started crying.

41

She had stopped crying, but we were still sitting like that, her head against my shoulder, when there was a knock on the door.

—Hey, we need to go, Bobo said. Got a lot to do before daylight.

—Be right there, I said.

I slowly pulled away from Carrie. She wiped her eyes with the back of her hand, and I leaned down for my shoes.

—Be careful, she said, her voice flat.

—I will, I said. I started tying a shoe.

—You know, I said, I hate to bring this up, but it'd probably be best if you could go to work tomorrow like everything was normal.

—I know. I will.

I tried to think of something comforting to say about that, but couldn't. I stood up.

—Okay, I'll see you in a little bit. And try not to worry, we're going to take care of everything.

—Like I said, be careful, she said.

I leaned down and gave her a kiss on the forehead, and she managed a brief smile. Then I left, shutting the door behind me. The clock in the living room said it was three-thirty. Tracy was on the couch in front of the wrapped-up body, still in her robe, her arms crossed defiantly. Bobo was holding a flashlight. When he saw me he handed it to Tracy, and then he and I picked up the body. I got the head and he got the feet. He asked to take the feet because that end was easier.

—Got a bad back left over from the military, he said.

Dead weight is always heavy and carrying the body was like carrying one end of a riding lawnmower. Tracy opened the front door, checked the street, then motioned us out. We hurried the body off the porch and across the lawn to the dead man's car, a ten-year-old Grand Am parked on the street, and set it down in front of the driver's door. We crouched there and rested a moment, breathing heavily. Bobo said he'd turn off the dome light before we loaded him, but when he tried the door it was locked. We realized we hadn't gotten the keys.

—Sweet Jesus on a pony, Bobo whispered.

He kneeled over the body and undid some tape and started digging in the opening, then pulled out the keys with a jingle. He opened the door, turned off the dome light, and we loaded the body into the backseat. He handed the keys to me.

—All right, follow me, he said.

—In case we get separated, where are we going?

—You wouldn't know how to get there even if I told you, so just don't lose me.

—Okay.

—It's an old rock quarry, he said. It's harder to find than the end of the rainbow.

42

I followed him through downtown, then just out of town we turned onto an unlined asphalt two-lane that we followed for ten minutes, until we turned off on an uphill dirt road that had sharp S-turns, the grass and brush on both sides of the road higher than the car. It was like driving through a maze. The road was bumpy and the dead man in the backseat thumped up and down when I hit the potholes. This road went for a mile that took almost ten minutes to cover, and ended at a wide gravel clearing next to a small lake. The lake had a high chain-link fence around it on three sides, and on the other a sheer rock face that went up five or six stories. The water was still, black, and streaked with moonlight. Bobo pulled his Escalade around so it was headed back out the road and I pulled in behind him. He left his engine running, got out and took a gas can out of the back and carried it to my window, then leaned against the door like we were two friends who had just happened to see each other in the parking lot.

—This used to be a nice place, he said. A big makeout spot. But now they just come here to buy drugs.

He kept looking at me. I could tell he wanted me to say something.

—Everything changes, I said.

—You got that right, he said.

We got the body out, unwrapped it, and lifted it into the driver's seat. He'd been dead long enough that it was difficult to bend him into position. Then Bobo reached the gas can in the window and slung gas everywhere. The smell of it filled the air. I put the bedspread in a trash bag and stowed it in the Escalade.

We discovered that neither of us had a lighter, so Bobo got a handful of Kleenex from his glove box and lit it with the dash lighter, then threw the flaming bouquet inside the Grand Am. He and I ran to the Escalade, jumped in and took off. Before we made the first turn I looked back and saw the inside of the Grand Am lit up red and orange. I could see the dead man's face as clear as a bell, plastic and peaceful.

43

—I was Marine Recon for eight years, Bobo said.

We were back on the asphalt two-lane, smoking thin cigars with wooden tips he'd taken down from the sun visor.

—You wouldn't believe the places we went, he said. No one knew about it. This was the kind of thing that doesn't make the papers.

—Where were you? I said.

He shrugged. I can't say too much about it, he said.

I nodded and let it go. I wasn't sure what to make of him. He struck me as full of it, but you never know.

—Did you get out because of your back? I asked.

—Nah, I kept that hid from them, he said. I wouldn't give them the satisfaction. I could still be jumping out of airplanes if I had to. I got out because I was just worn down to a nub.

Then there was a muted explosion behind us. From our distance it sounded like a balloon popping in the next room. Neither of us commented on it.

—So what's the deal with you and Carrie? he said.

—I don't know, I said.

—Hey, sorry about all that earlier, he said. I just lost my head.

—No problem, I said.

Bobo's cigar had gone out, so he relit it with the dash lighter.

—Take a look at what I got there in the glove compartment, he said.

I opened the glove box and found a black ring box. I took it out and opened it. The ring it held would've paid my mortgage for two years. The diamond was the size of my knuckle.

—It's a great ring, I said. Tracy should love it.

—If she gets it, he laughed.

I laughed, too, then shut the box and put it back in the glove box.

We rode in silence awhile, smoking the cigars.

You know, you might not believe this, he said, but I've been air-dropped into Taiwan before. Middle of the night.

—Wow, I said.

—Yeah, and when you find yourself in a situation like that, you can ask yourself a lot of questions. Like just how in the hell did I get from being in bed wearing my Superman pajamas to standing on foreign soil with my government's permission to take a life?

—Sure, I can see that, I said.

—But then again, catch yourself on another day, you might not ask yourself anything.

—I can see that, too, I said.

He turned his head and looked at me, the cigar sticking up from the corner of his mouth like FDR's cigarette holder.

—You see, we're all just playing with Monopoly money, he said. There's just some that know it and some that don't.

44

We rode in silence for a long time after that comment. Finally Bobo took his cell phone out of the console bin, punched speed dial, and started telling whoever it was about our situation. Pretty soon we were back on Marsburg's main drag. It was after six now and getting light. A café was open, lit up and already full.

We continued on out of town toward Lindsey. When Bobo finished explaining our circumstances, he listened for a while, answering yes or no every now and then. Then he said good-bye and turned off the phone.

—I think we might have things squared away, he said. That was Chess, my lawyer. He's a Mickey Rourke kind of guy, a jack of all trades, and he's getting right on getting everything ironed out. He's going to meet us at Brockton's later this morning.

—Where are we going now? I said.

—To Wal-Mart get some clothes, he said. Chess suggested we both get rid of what we're wearing. And anyway, you don't want to go into our big meeting with a hole in your pants.

—I guess not, I said.

—Hey, you hungry? he said.

—A little.

—I'm starving, he said. I think I'm going to get a box of Pop-Tarts and some milk at Wal-Mart. What kind of Pop-Tarts you like?

—Any kind, I said.

—Me too, he said.

Then I asked him if he thought Joe Brockton's only motive for killing his brother was getting the dealership. I said Fee had told me that Eton was sleeping with Joe's wife.

—I heard that was true, but I don't know, he said.

—Joe and his wife stayed together, I said.

—Yeah, and they say he treats her like hell. But some people will put up with a lot to keep climbing into bed next to a million dollars.

—I guess so.

He smiled.

—Just look at Tracy, he said.

45

The Wal-Mart in Lindsey was brand-new, one of the superstores. We took a cart from the greeter, a blue-haired lady who seemed to have trouble standing without leaning on something. It turned out she had been Bobo's third grade teacher. It took them a moment to recognize each other, but then they started talking and he told her he now owned an insurance agency over in Marsburg. She put a hand on his arm.

—I knew you'd do well, she said.

—Thank you, Miss Tern.

—Are you married? she asked.

—No ma'am, I'm not.

—Well, it's overrated anyway, she said.

—Yes ma'am, that's what I hear.

After we walked away, he said:

—They go for the Norman Rockwell effect right away, don't they? Always an old person up there giving you your cart. You ever notice, though, they don't give them anywhere to sit down?

That time of the morning the store was almost empty. We went to the men's department and each picked out a package of underwear, then looked through the same circular rack of slacks, me on one side for my size and Bobo on the other for his. Bobo stopped moving hangers and looked at me over the top of the rack.

—I've got an idea, he said. Let's go into the meeting dressed the same.

—Why?

—Because it'll throw them off, he said.

—I don't know.

—Trust me, it'll work, he said.

—It seems a little crazy, I said.

—Yeah, I know, he said. That's the point.

We each ended up getting a pair of gray slacks, a black belt, a white shirt and a thin black tie, a pair of black socks, a pair of black loafers, and an unreconstructed sports jacket made of rough, dark blue material with white specks in it. The jackets looked like they came straight out of the eighties and I was surprised they even had them—they must have been making a comeback. On the way to the register, Bobo stopped at the sunglasses rack, picked out a pair and held them up, his eyebrows raised to ask what I thought. I shook my head.

—You're right, he said. Too much.

He paid for the clothes, a box of chocolate Pop-Tarts and two quarts of milk. On the way out he stopped to talk with Miss Tern again, and before he walked off, he pressed a folded-up hundred dollar bill into her hand. When she realized what she was holding she called for him to come back, but he wouldn't turn around.

We changed clothes in the bathroom of the Shell station across the street, then sat in its parking lot and ate the Pop-Tarts and drank the milk. We looked like either a couple of Mormon missionaries starting to go bad or Quentin Tarantino's houseboys.

Famous Writers School
P.O. Box 1181
Fayette WV 32111
July 1, 200—

Dear Dan,

Carrie's husband and Bobo are both good new characters, and I thought the scene in which Carrie's betrayal was exposed was quite effective, as was the scene of triumphant masculinity in the

Escalade after Doug and Bobo have set the body of the emascu-
lated husband on fire.

I only have one suggestion for improvement. A problem even
excellent detective fiction such as yours can have is unintention-
ally trivializing death, and I thought Carrie's emotional response
to killing her husband was probably a little too flat. Maybe have
her throw a fit. Let her rip apart a necklace or beat on Doug's
chest.

If you'd like to make that revision and send me the chapters
again, I'd be happy to read them. I'd also like to ask you to reconsider my offer to serve as reader on the rest of your novel—
I think you might be surprised at the number of heavy hitters in
the literary world who have private editors. I have a friend who
does that job for some of the biggest names in the business. I'd
tell you who some of his clients are, except that if word ever got
out he'd lose his livelihood. God, the stories he tells. Some of
these writers, you wouldn't even know it was their book if their
fingerprints weren't smeared in chocolate on the manuscript. Of
course, you need nothing close to that level of editing. Your
work's already much more accomplished than that. However,
having a practiced reader with an abiding interest in the success
of the book couldn't hurt, and it won't cost you a penny. Just
think about it.

However, if for some reason you decide not to take my offer,
I'd like to ask one small favor: would you mind sending me a de-
tailed summary of what happens in book two of your novel? I
think I'll go mad if I don't get to see how this story ends.

I look forward to seeing your next work.

Best wishes,
Wendell

Are You Sure, Wendell?

It's Me, Pro: I know the pet name, pobre cito, Wendell used with the married woman he was banging.

It's Me, Con: But she could've told that name to friends. Remember her close friends, Wendell? Jess, Trina, Sallie, and Emma, the one you and Lana had lunch with that day. Remember how Emma called you a "puerile fool" for disagreeing with her politics? I could be her. Or maybe I'm another one of the friends who's just heard the story about lunch. I could be exacting revenge for my friend. Or you could just be a proxy for all the men who have hurt me. You could step around a corner someday and get hit in the face with a baseball bat. Wouldn't that be a surprise?

It's Me, Pro: I know Wendell was in the air force. Only someone who had been close to him would know that.

It's Me, Con: Or, I could've just seen the pictures of him in his blue uniform that are in the upper right-hand drawer of his dresser, underneath the old Christmas cards.

It's Me, Pro: I know Wendell got in trouble right after he left the air force by getting involved in a boiler room scam.

It's Me, Con: Again, I could be one of the friends. Lana could've told me this. It could've been part of the "I'm better off without him" discussion. Or, I could just be a complete stranger, a friend of one of the friends who found out about you in passing, which led me to look for the ad for your writing school business. I was sick of all the lies and cons this world embraces, everything from your little course to Chevy ads, so, to balance the scales, I decided to give you something to worry about.

It's Me, Pro: I acted jealous when I read your journal entry about Rio. I called her a slut.

It's Me, Con: Could just be a red herring. Part of the game.

It's Me, Pro: I know you're obsessed with Eastern Europe. Chances are, if we had a relationship you would've talked about it. I say I'm getting you a forged visa, since you can't get one the regular way.

It's Me, Con: Your journal is full of entries about the glories of Prague. A monkey could figure out you want to go there.

It's Me, Pro: The fact that I'm going to all this trouble to harass you says you must've hurt me. This must be romance gone bad.

It's Me, Con: I could be so troubled that I don't even follow the twisted logic of the jilted lover. I could just be a stranger doing this for kicks.

Famous Writers School
P.O. Box 1181
Fayette WV 32111
July 3, 200—

Dear Lana,

I know this is you now, though I can hardly believe it. I can't put my finger on why I know, but something about your last letter just made me certain. I never knew your feelings were so deep that you would go to these lengths. Now that I see what this whole episode has been about, I'm deeply moved.

Our problems, Lana, were never ones of love or compatibility, but of time and circumstance. Nothing about you bothered me, except the fact you were married and had two children. Otherwise, I loved everything about you and our time together. I loved all that was extravagant or mundane about you, from the sudden fits in restaurants to the way "at home" in some motel kitchen you put diced tomato on microwaved macaroni and cheese. I liked the delicate smell of your makeup as we lay curled together on the motel floor watching the afternoon reruns of home improvement shows. After you left to pick up your children, that smell would linger in my nostrils and with each breath break my heart at your absence. And now, knowing that you might be willing to share an expatriate life in Prague, I feel as if every wild and foolish dream I've ever had is coming true. Two questions, though: were you planning on bringing your children, and do you have a timetable for getting that visa from the forger?

What a wonderful gift the visa will be! I guess time will tell whether it's real or if you're just toying with me, although knowing you as I do, I'm sure it's as substantial as the Rock of Gibraltar. I still have many of the other gifts you gave me. Remember the Pocket Books edition of Chandler's *Farewell, My Lovely* you purchased for me in that used bookstore on our first Saturday trip together? After we laughed about the "From the Library of Richard Nixon" stamp on the inside front cover that caused you to buy the book in the first place, I argued with you about the novel, saying Chandler was vastly overrated and the book overpriced. It's pains me now to recall my own foolishness, and I want to let you know that I've seen the light about Chandler. So thanks again for the book. It's come to be crucial in a couple of matters.

Now, one more thing we must discuss. Since you have my journal, you know that I've been having a pen pal relationship with one of my students, a woman named Rio. Please know that this has developed as an attempt on my part to get past my loss of you. That's all it is and, frankly, it hasn't worked. You're still with me and always will be, even if I never get to see you again. Rio means nothing to me.

My little pobre cito—the fact that you know our pet name is what makes me most certain this is you. Although I have no real doubt, I'll say no more until you call me. Please do as soon as you get this. Or, if you want to just come by the house, that's all right too. I'm still waking up and getting in the shower most days about eleven, if that suits you.

Until,
Wendell

Lesson 6

Subtlety

(I know most of you were expecting a final lesson titled "Putting It All Together." However, from time to time, when the needs of my students change, I adjust the course to meet them. This is one of those times, and from now on "Subtlety" will be lesson 6 of the course. If you would still like to receive the old lesson 6, just send me an SASE and I will send it; if you would also like to do the assignment in the old lesson 6 and get my response, please also include a check or money order for $49.00.)

I was tooling around in my Dodge Dart, going nowhere fast and having fun doing it. I hadn't had a cigarette for three days, though, and that was a long time to stare into the abyss empty-handed, so I decided to give in and buy a pack, but there wasn't a convenience store nearby—in this neighborhood, you would've needed a tank to keep the clerk alive. A laundromat down the street, though, had a cigarette machine. I knew about it because I used to date a Russian woman who washed her clothes there. We were together almost a month, but if she'd spoken English it might not have lasted that long.

I whipped the Dart into the first space I could find, in front of a butcher's shop, five storefronts from the laundromat. I got out and locked the door, then looked up and saw a big Korean in a bloody apron standing in the doorway of the shop, smoking a pipe. He was at least seven feet tall. He had one foot on the pavement and one cocked back against the doorframe, the way a woman will stand if you kiss her right. His eyes followed me as I came around the car. His expression was flat. I gave him a grin and a wink.

"Watch the car," I said.

He didn't speak. His cheeks puffed and smoke rose from the pipe. The tobacco smelled cheap and fruity.

"And put something in that pipe besides Apple Jacks, will you?" I said, walking away.

The laundromat was crowded, steamy, and full of women. The only men were two Latinos in gray factory uniforms and an elderly man so out of place he looked like a dog licking a wedding cake. He wore a dark suit, had a neat moustache and short gray hair, and sat with his chin held up, his hands resting on a cane with an ivory head. An old lady who hadn't smiled since *Maude* went off the air was sitting behind the service counter, her nose in a romance novel with a blinding cover. I approached and put a five on the counter and asked for change. She looked at me like I'd asked her to attend a Ralph Nader rally.

"You washing clothes?" she said.

"Buying cigarettes," I said.

"I can't afford to give change to people who don't use it here," she said. "Bebe don't go to the bank until three."

"Yeah, but I bet she does a good job when she does go," I said.

She gave me a funny look and then the quarters. I fed all of them except one into the machine, then yanked the plunger for the nonfiltered Luckys—if you're going to smoke filters, you might as well drink your whiskey through a nipple too.

I bummed a match from one of the Latinos, then went out on the sidewalk and struck it on the side of the building and lit up. After two puffs I felt human again. I looked down the sidewalk for the big Korean. He was gone. Across the street, a skinny cat was perched on top of a trash can, trying to decide whether to jump in, and just up from him a kid who looked like he'd gotten his driver's license yesterday was buying something through the window of his silver BMW from a younger kid on a banana-seat bicycle.

Welcome to the boomtown.

Then the laudromat door jingled open behind me and I turned around. The elegant old man was there, leaning on his cane.

"Good day, sir," he said.

"The same to you," I said.

"I'm sorry to bother you," he said, "but I was wondering if I might ask a favor."

I asked him what he needed. He wanted to know if I were driving, and I told him I was.

"I need a ride," he said. "My daughter was supposed to pick me up, but she hasn't arrived yet. I fear something may have happened. I could pay you when I get home."

"If you don't mind my asking, what're you doing here anyway? This isn't your neighborhood."

"I was in a cab on my way to the theater," he said, "when I realized I had left home without my wallet. I told the driver, a rough young woman who spoke a Slavic language, that I had just discovered I didn't have my wallet with me, but if she'd drive to my old law offices, I could get her the money I owed her. She apparently didn't understand, though, because she put me out down there." He pointed down the sidewalk. "I walked here to the laundromat and called my daughter, but that was over an hour ago. I don't know why she isn't here. She was miffed at having to miss a class at her health club, but she said she'd be here."

"Some broads are just like that," I muttered.

"Excuse me?" He cocked an ear toward me. "I'm afraid I didn't catch that."

"Nothing," I said. "Forget it. It was a sentiment from a lost world. Sure, I'll give you a ride."

He went back inside and asked the woman at the counter to tell his daughter, if she showed, that he had gotten another ride. Then we walked down to the Dart, with me taking mincing little steps so

I didn't get ahead of him. I got him settled inside, he gave me directions, and we took off. I asked what movie he had been going to see.

"It wasn't a movie, but a play," he said. "The matinee of *Death of a Salesman*."

"Going by yourself?"

He nodded.

"So I take it your wife doesn't like socialist drama?"

"My wife passed away two years ago," he said.

"Oh, sorry," I said. "I saw your ring and figured—"

"No, that's all right," he said.

The street we were on had lots of little groceries with signs in languages other than English, check cashing places that charged twenty percent, and jewelry stores as cluttered and shiny as the inside of a television. Every window was protected by metal bars, and the thick smells of greasy food filled the air. There were stands that sold Mexican or Chinese, pirogues or gyros, and even a guy frying fish over a fire in an old oil drum.

"There aren't many women like my Em anymore," he said.

"I'd say not," I said.

"She laid out my clothes each morning, and if the maid hadn't done a good job shining my shoes, she did them again."

"Sounds like a good wife."

"You know, a moment ago you said something about a lost world," he said.

"It was a joke," I said.

"Yes, but I think something *has* been lost," he said.

We caught a stoplight. On the curb, a hooker gave me her mechanical come-hither routine. She was going for the farm girl look, fringed denim shorts, checkered shirt and a ponytail. I smiled briefly at her and shook my head. Her eyes turned dead and she looked away.

"Men today are too concerned with decorating themselves," the old man said. "They've become the same as women. Dyeing their hair, piercing their ears, all of it. I fully expect the next fad will be male makeup."

"Could be," I said.

I made a left on a yellow light, the car I beat flashing by behind us, a noise like taut wire snapping, his horn giving a fading blare. It had rained that morning and up ahead the clouds in the slowly clearing horizon were a wild mix of colors like a box of crayons that had melted.

"Take my country club, for instance," he said. "Half the members used to keep sailboats, but almost no one does anymore. I taught my son to sail, but his son isn't interested. He only wants to play computer games. Then last year my son sold the boat because he said he was tired of paying the dock fees." He shook his head. "And you know what he did with the money? Took his family to a spa."

I made a right, which gave me a clear view of the freeway exchange in the distance. It looked like an ant farm.

"What kind of effect would it have on a son," he said, "to see his father getting a pedicure while he's got cucumber slices on his eyes? My own father taught me to track deer. One man tracked and then ran the deer toward the other man so he could get a clean shot. We didn't sit in a tree like they do today, waiting until some unsuspecting animal walks beneath them."

"I guess you really had to be in good shape," I said.

He was leaning forward in the seat, staring intently out the windshield, a string of white spittle in the corner of his mouth.

"You know," he said, "I never even made a sandwich until I was forty. Em was in the hospital getting her tubes tied and the maid was sick, so I had to."

I nodded.

"But what does any of it matter now?" he said. "Em's gone, the boat's gone, and they treat me like a humorous artifact at the law practice I founded. My son dreads seeing me and my daughter's a kleptomaniac. I have arrangements with all the stores to pay for whatever she steals."

"Well," I said.

"It all comes to nothing," he said. "Take a blade of grass. You cut it with a mower or tear it out of the ground when you hit a three iron and you don't think twice about it. But what you don't realize until it's too late is that you are that blade of grass. No better and no worse. You die, dry out and rot."

All right, let's stop here. That last speech could just as easily describe everything I just wrote: boring, and no end to it. You can have gorgeous line after gorgeous line, but it all has to amount to something. It has to mean something. True subtlety in fiction requires more than pyrotechnics with language; it requires that every sentence deliver the punch that is appropriate for the story at that particular moment and that leads to its inevitable conclusion. The prose in this lesson is attractive, but empty. There's no story here with delicate shades of meaning and human complexity. You don't want your fiction to be like a puff pastry, take two bites and it loses half its mass. And for that reason, this lesson is over, because there's nothing here for me to finish. Learn from that.

Assignment: Subtlety is at the heart of good fiction, but even great writers need an editor to help them achieve it in their work. For instance, if you didn't have Max Perkins, you wouldn't have F. Scott Fitzgerald; if you didn't have Ezra Pound, you wouldn't have T. S. Eliot. *Subtlety* is defined as "cunningly made," "highly skillful," and "marked by keen insight." Are you certain every sentence in your story satisfies those high standards? Could there be passages that will make editors cringe?

For your final assignment, I want you to go back through your story with a ruthless hand. Cut or revise every sentence that doesn't advance the story; do the same to every sentence that seems awkward or self-conscious. Then, I want you to take the same step *every* writer *always* has to take: I want you to find an editor, a person of some experience who will read your work and give you honest, intelligent feedback on your revisions. You might have to look far and wide to find this person, but keep trying, because you'll never make it unless you do.

Rio Jordan

Lesson 1

Wendell,
Here it is. It's terrible, but it's all I could come up with.
Rio

The Date

Mary met Brad for the first time at a restaurant in the country. It was a blind date and Mary was nervous. Brad knew what she looked like, but she had never seen a picture of him, and he had made a joke about that the only time they talked on the phone.

"I'll be the man in the funny hat," he said.

"Really?" she said. "What kind is it?"

"I'm just kidding," he said. "I don't wear a hat."

"Oh," she said.

When Mary arrived at the restaurant the lunch crowd had cleared out and the place had a vacated, messy look. A teenage boy was going from table to table, loading dishes into a plastic tray. Mary stood just inside the door and looked for Brad, then saw a man in a corner booth staring at her. He waved.

He wasn't bad. His face wouldn't get him in a magazine, but he wouldn't end up in a cartoon, either. His hair was brown and short and looked off-kilter as if he had cut it himself. He had on a dark sport coat, a white shirt and a solid blue tie, and even though he was sitting down Mary could tell he needed to lose twenty pounds.

She approached the table, smiling. He stood up and offered his hand.

"Nice to meet you," he said.

"The same to you," she said.

Mary noticed the top part of his zipper was undone and showing, the way it will when your pants are too tight.

They sat down, and the waitress, a tall young woman with red hair, brought over menus.

"Chicken's the specialty," she said.

"I think that's what I want," he said.

"Yes, chicken's fine," Mary said.

"Two chicken dinners," the waitress said, then took their drink orders and left.

There was a short, uncomfortable silence.

"Did you say you've been here before?" Brad asked.

"Yes, several times," Mary said.

"I think I mentioned this was my first time," he said.

"You did," she said.

Then it was quiet again. Mary looked out the window through the open slats of the blinds. The restaurant's fifties-era neon sign rose up in front of her and the message board on it had black letters that read, WELCOME OPTIMISTS.

"It's been a long time since I've seen one of these," Brad said and started turning a knob on the small jukebox that sat at the end of their table. It was the size of a child's lunchbox.

"Yes, isn't it something?" she said.

They both watched as he flipped through every page of songs. All the selections were country songs twenty or thirty years old.

"Hey, how about this one?" he said. "I haven't heard this one for years."

He was pointing to "Jackson," by Johnny Cash and June Carter Cash.

"Sure," Mary said, though she had never liked country music.

Brad reached down and tried to dig a quarter out of the pocket of his tight jeans; when he finally pulled out the quarter the skin on the back of his hand was red. He dropped the coin and pushed some buttons. The machine made a noise, then started playing a scratchy version of the song:

> *We got married in a fever,*
> *Hotter than a pepper sprout.*
> *We been talkin' 'bout Jackson,*
> *Ever since the fire went out. . .*

Brad tapped his fingers on the table, his time half a beat off, which irritated Mary. While the song was playing, the waitress brought their drinks, two waters and two iced teas. Brad smiled and thanked her, and Mary thought she saw him trying to hold her gaze before she walked off.

The song finished.

"I could just about listen to that again," he said.

"Well, maybe," she said.

"Yeah, one more time, I think," he said.

"Well, okay," she said.

Brad dug in his pocket again, but discovered he didn't have another quarter. He asked Mary for one. She almost couldn't believe it. But she got her purse out and gave him a quarter, and he dropped it into the machine and played the song again.

When it was finished, he said, "So how's your thesis coming along?"

On the phone, Mary had told him she was working on her master's in psychology.

"Pretty well," she said. "I just finished collecting my data."

She started telling him about her project, but then the waitress came with their food. She put down a platter of fried chicken, a plate with biscuits and corn muffins, and bowls of mashed potatoes, gravy, green beans, creamed corn, fried okra, yellow squash, and broccoli-cheese casserole. Brad smiled and thanked her, and this time it was obvious he was trying to get her attention, so obvious that the waitress threw Mary a quick, apologetic glance.

They served themselves, commenting on how good the food looked. Mary started telling him about her thesis again, but as soon as she paused, Brad started talking about a book he was writing, a mystery novel about a rare books dealer who gets caught up in a drug ring in a small town where he's traveled to attend an estate sale. The book dealer is in an unhappy marriage, and while he is in the small town, he starts an affair with the secretary of the auctioneer who is conducting the sale. It turns out the auctioneer is involved in the drug ring too.

To be polite, Mary asked him how the novel ended.

"I'm not sure yet," he said, pouring gravy on everything on his plate, even the okra and squash. "I'm only about halfway through."

Then he started talking about living in Romania. He thought that was the place to be. He had moving there all planned out. He had mentioned something about this on the phone, but Mary hadn't taken it too seriously. She had thought it was just one of those things people say, like "I'd like to go skydiving someday." She thought the whole idea sounded like some college sophomore's escape-from-his-parents fantasy.

He asked Mary if she'd ever considered living in a foreign country.

"No," she said.

Then for the rest of the meal, they didn't talk much. Mary noticed that he ate too fast. He also ate until every bowl was empty and all the chicken and bread were gone. When the waitress came and asked if they wanted dessert, he said he'd like a slice of apple pie with cheese melted on top and ice cream on top of that. It almost made Mary sick.

Again, he tried to catch the waitress's eye.

After she was gone, he said, "I noticed some antique shops downtown. Would you like to go take a look at them after we eat?"

"Maybe," Mary said, then looked at her watch. "Oh, you know, I don't think I can. I've got a meeting with my thesis director this evening."

"This evening?" Brad asked.

"Yes, well, we have some paperwork to get turned into the graduate office right away. In fact," she said, "I guess I really need to leave right now. I can't stay for dessert. I didn't realize it was so late."

"Well, okay, maybe another time," he said.

"Yes," she said.

She opened her purse and took out a ten and laid it on the table.

"That should cover my part," she said.

"How much was it?" he said. "I didn't even look to see what a chicken dinner costs. I hope it's not too much."

"That'll cover it," she said.

She stood up. He started to slide out of the booth, but she held up a hand to stop him.

"That's okay," she said. "I'm fine."

"All right, well, nice to meet you," he said.

"Yes, the same here."

"You wouldn't have any free time this weekend, would you?" he said.

"I'm sorry, but I'm afraid not," she said.

"Well, what about the next?" he said.

"Maybe," she said.

Then she smiled and said good-bye. She went outside, got in her car, and started back toward Philadelphia.

Famous Writers School
P.O. Box 1181
Fayette WV 32111
July 11, 200—

Dear Riordan,

I think it's good you could push through your fears and finally write a draft of something. This time you actually had a continuous flow of narrative and few awkward moments of direct address to the reader. However, your story has a problem that is quite common among hobby writers, and that is using fiction as a vehicle of self-aggrandizement at the expense of the other "characters" in the story, who, more often than not, are nothing but projections of the writer's own insecurities. By damning these other "characters," the writer feels she is somehow defeating her own neuroses. Take, for instance, the line where Mary says Brad's hair is uneven. You're presupposing that's a reflection on his character when there could be other explanations. Maybe his regular barber was sick and he had to get his hair cut for the date by a nervous, chain-smoking fill-in. You also made fun of Brad's zipper, but that seemed contrived, because it's almost certain that on a first date Brad would've checked it before he stood up. In another instance, you seem to think the device of having Brad "flirt" with the waitress characterizes him; however, it actually says more about Mary than it does Brad. Brad just seems like he's being friendly, while Mary's jealousy makes her seem shrill and histrionic. Likewise for the way Mary makes fun of the way Brad eats. What does it matter if he puts gravy on everything? Her distaste seems stuffy and frigid.

Usually it's better when a story's protagonist is not an innocent who goes from one scenario to another being victimized and manipulated precisely because she is innocent; usually it's best to make her complicit in what's happening. You need to humanize her. It could be something insignificant. Perhaps there was a very visible makeup line separating Mary's jaw from her neck like a crude line drawn on a child's map. Or maybe Mary reeked of cigarette smoke and was dressed like a Grateful Dead groupie going on a job interview. See? These changes would be simple. You could also insert a scene in which Mary goes to the bathroom and stares at herself in the mirror and realizes how petty it is to be so disparaging of Brad when *she's* the one who initiated the date.

Of course, it's not just beginners who make these kinds of mistakes. Look at the best-seller lists. What's there? Nothing but a bunch of distorted mirrors. Books that give readers an idealized version of themselves, whether that version is heroic or self-pitying. Books that tell them what they want to hear, whether they're tawdry thrillers or literary drivel. So maybe I should say full steam ahead, your work will likely soon be sparkling with diamonds of praise. Welcome to the great delusion that is American culture.

Sincerely yours,
Wendell Newton

Dan Federman

Lesson 6

Dear Mr. Newton,
Your new lesson 6 struck me as sort of odd. I thought the story read like a parody of my own opening chapters. Your characters were similar to mine, and were also in a similar situation.

Were you aware of this? I know that sometimes the style of whatever book I'm reading will start seeping into my own writing, but what you did seemed pretty direct. And maybe I'm being too suspicious, but given our previous correspondence, the advice to get an editor also seemed to be directed toward me.

I guess I'm still going to pass on your offer to read my novel. I think our relationship has gotten some kind of odd kink in it that just won't straighten out entirely. Please know, though, that I have no hard feelings. I've learned some things from you, and for that I'm grateful.

46

Chess Malone was fifty or fifty-five and looked like Kenny Rogers with a bad hangover. He wore a green sport coat too tight in the shoulders and black ankle boots with zippers up the side. We were a few minutes late getting to Brockton's because Bobo had gone by his house to get a pistol, which was now in the back pocket of his pants; when we walked in the showroom, Carrie's desk was empty, and there was no sign she'd been there at all that morning.

Brockton was behind his desk, leaned back in his chair, tight-lipped and angry. Chess was sitting in front of the desk, and Fee and Fluke were in chairs off to the side against the wall. Fluke had a gauze bandage taped across his nose and was leaning forward in his chair as if he were ready to spring, while Fee was sitting back staring placidly at no one.

There were two empty chairs in front of the desk. I sat down in the one next to Chess, but Bobo scooted his out of the way and sat down on the corner of Brockton's desk. He smiled at Chess.

—Have you told them yet? he said.

—Not yet, Chess said. He nodded at Bobo and me. So are you boys going steady or what? he said.

Bobo laughed.

—Nah, we're just gonna go to the fair together, he said.

—Faggots, Fluke muttered.

Bobo swung around and faced Fluke, then kept looking at him.

—I hear you tried to kiss a dog, he said.

Fluke's expression darkened and he started to reply, but stopped when Brockton shot him a look.

Bobo swung around and smiled at Brockton, who looked back at him, expressionless.

—These gentlemen are already aware of the death of Bill Peterson last night, Chess said.

—As the Lord willed it, Fee said.

—So did He happen to will Eton Brockton's death, too? Bobo said.

There was a long, heavy silence. At first Brockton looked stunned, but then his eyes turned hard.

—He wills it all, Fee finally said. We're just instruments.

—Yes, well, be that as it may, Chess said, clearing his throat, Bill Peterson's death leaves some situations that need to be resolved. When we informed Mrs. Peterson, she of course became distraught and went home. It's tragic to see a woman widowed so young.

Then he started coughing like someone in a Dickens novel. Everyone watched, waiting for him to stop. I shifted my weight in my chair—a 1950s model with padding like a slice of ham—but it didn't make me any more comfortable.

When Chess finally quit coughing, Brockton leaned up in his chair, its springs squeaking like mice.

—Look, he said, I've got someone coming in at eleven-thirty, so let's just cut to the chase.

—Cut to the chase? Bobo said. He made a production of looking around the room. Is there a camera in here?

Chess reached into the inside pocket of his jacket and pulled out an airplane bottle of Jack Daniel's, screwed off the top and turned up the bottle and drank until it was empty, then set the bottle on the desk.

—For the cough, he said.

Bobo had one leg hanging off the desk, rocking it back and forth.

—Brockton, he said, you need to understand one thing, and that's that we're in a position to do whatever we want, whenever we want. He pointed to the telephone. I'll pick that up and order Chinese if I feel like it, and then we'll all sit here smiling until it arrives. Understand?

Brockton stared at him.

—You're in high water, son, he said. Higher than you realize.

Bobo grinned. Could be, he said.

Then Chess leaned forward and picked up a paperweight from Brockton's desk. It was clear glass and had tiny seashells and fake seaweed inside. He examined it, turning it this way and that, then brought it down hard on the empty airplane bottle, shattering it. He tossed the paperweight back onto the desk, where it landed with a thud.

I had no idea where they were going with this.

—Okay, I think that's enough chitchat, Chess said.

He said he had drawn up a document that morning outlining the events of the last twenty-four hours and also the information Bill Peterson had given about the drug operation. Copies of it would be placed in a lockbox, he said, and in the event any harm came to me, my family, Bobo, Tracy, Carrie, or Tommy, copies of the document would be sent to the *Cleveland Plain-Dealer*, the DEA, and an associate of Chess's who knew how to contact the right people in Colombia.

—You see, Chess said, those Colombian businessmen wouldn't be too happy if they knew they were setting up an operation with people who have no judgment. Small-timers who tried to save a couple of hundred dollars by kidnapping a driver instead of hiring one.

Brockton was staring over the top of Chess's head. He didn't look angry anymore, just blank.

—And there are a few other things that also need taking care of, Chess said. Mr. Farnsworth needs his car back.

Brockton looked over at Fee, who nodded.

—His wallet needs to be delivered with it, too, Chess said.

Fee nodded again.

—Also, your niece won't be working here any longer, Chess said. And if any of the problems with your bookkeeping ever come to light, you'll say you made the changes, not her.

Brockton nodded.

—And you'll give her severance pay in the amount of two-hundred and fifty thousand dollars, Chess said.

Brockton looked at him like he'd seen a frog hop out of his ear.

—What? he said.

—She's a widow without a job, Bobo said. It's the least an uncle could do.

—Just consider it the inheritance she never got, Chess said. The one you cheated her out of after you got him—he nodded at Fee—to trick your brother's own son into killing him.

Brockton didn't answer. He kept staring at Chess, who stared right back. The room was chillingly silent, except for the muted voices coming from the showroom.

—Look, Brockton said, I'll help her get on her feet. But I'm not—

—This isn't negotiable, Chess said. You don't pay, the information goes to the Colombians.

Brockton's face stiffened and he leaned up in his chair.

—Then go ahead, he said. We'll just see how it plays out.

—By God right, Fluke said, and we all looked at him.

47

His hand was at his ankle, fiddling with the cuff of his jeans. When he raised up he was holding a pistol, a little .22 with a taped handle. He waved it in the direction of the desk.

—Ain't nobody telling the Colombians nothing, he said.

—Dammit, put that down, Brockton said.

—No sir, Fluke said. I can see this ain't gonna end good for somebody, and I ain't gonna be the one on the bad end. I'm gonna take these fuckers to the woods and put them on their knees, then throw 'em in a cave and let the rats finish things off. He pointed the gun at Brockton. You got a problem with that, you can go too.

—How're you going to get all of us out of here at midday, holding a gun on us? Bobo said.

Suddenly Fee shut his eyes and started muttering to himself. Everyone glanced at him.

—We're goin' out the back, Fluke said. Through that door over there. He nodded toward the end of the room opposite the desk. There was a door there with three metal filing cabinets in front of it so that you didn't really notice it.

—You go through a little room there and then you're out back of the building, Fluke said.

—If you had to fire that gun, you wouldn't be able to get away, Bobo said.

—Maybe not, but if that happens, you won't know nothing about it, will you?

He motioned at Bobo with the pistol.

—Turn around and pull up the back of your coat, he said. I need that gun.

Bobo slid off the desk and turned his back and pulled up the jacket.

—Get that gun, Fee, Fluke said.

Fee stopped muttering and opened his eyes. He looked at Bobo standing in front of him, and then looked at all of us one by one except for Fluke. Then he twisted in his chair and threw a tremendous right hook that caught Fluke dead on the nose. Fluke let out a wail and the pistol flew out of his hand and he was knocked out of the chair. The pistol came to rest at my feet and I picked it up.

—I once killed me a Chinaman in Korea with one punch, Fee said. He shook his head.

Fluke was standing on his knees, holding his nose, a stunned look in his eyes. Fee nodded at him.

—I was just sick of hearing him talk, Fee said.

48

Fluke got back in his chair and sat with his head tilted back, holding the bottom of his T-shirt up to his bleeding nose. Chess and Brockton argued for a while about the money Carrie would receive, but Chess wouldn't budge and the figure stayed at a quarter million. Brockton said my car would be delivered in running order to Tracy's house that afternoon.

Then we left. Chess headed back to his office, and Bobo and I got into the Escalade to go to Tracy's. After we pulled out, he winked at me.

—I told you the clothes would work, he said.

49

Tracy and Carrie were asleep in the same bed, on top of the covers. We left them alone and Bobo fixed lunch. He fried half a package of bacon, then scrambled a whole carton of eggs in the grease, and we washed it all down with glasses of milk that had a splash of bourbon in them. When we finished, we each lit one of his thin cigars and had another bourbon and milk. Then Tracy walked into the kitchen wearing her robe, bleary-eyed.

—There she is, Bobo said.

She nodded groggily, then went to the coffeemaker and got a pot going.

—Is Carrie still asleep? I asked.

—No, she woke up too, she said. It smelled like you guys were roasting a pig in here. She wants you to come in there, and she nodded toward the bedroom.

—All right, I said. I pushed my chair back and stood up.

—The plot thickens, Bobo grinned.

—You, Tracy said. She moved behind his chair and put her hands on his shoulders. You've got some explaining to do.

—In the kitchen? he said.

50

Carrie was propped up on the pillows, wearing another long football jersey, a yellow one, smoking one of her thin cigarettes. I climbed in beside her.

—Hey, I like the new clothes, she said. Real retro.

—Bobo picked them out, I said. He insisted we wear the same thing.

—Well, they look good. You look like you should be driving a convertible.

—Yeah, a used one.

She blew out her smoke and laughed prettily.

—So what happened? she asked. Since you're here, I take it things didn't go too badly.

—No, they did. The world ended while you were asleep.

—Well huh. Is the cable still working?

—Yeah, all we lost were the talk shows.

—CNN?

—Still on. They're sitting in a scorched building arguing about whether it's really scorched.

Then I told her about the meeting and that all of us, including her brother, were going to be okay. I told her about the two hundred and fifty thousand dollars she was getting.

—Right, she said. She shook a finger at me. Not funny.

—I'm not kidding, I said, then explained the whole thing to her, how Chess had negotiated and that she'd soon be getting a lump sum cash payment. When I finished, she had tears in her eyes. I pulled her close and she put her head on my chest. I stroked her arm, her hair, until she finally stopped crying and looked up at me.

—My father, she said. This would've made him happy.

—I'm glad, I said.

She put her head on my chest again and nestled up as close as she could and threw a leg over mine.

—So when are you going home? she asked in a small voice.

—I don't know. I guess when they deliver my car.

—Can't you stay just one more night?

I thought about it. It was what I wanted to do.

—Yeah, I can. I'll call and say they can't get my car fixed until tomorrow.

—Good.

Then we were quiet awhile. I played with her hair.

—So your little girl, she said. How old is she?

—Six.

—I bet she's a doll.

—She is.

—You know, I think you should probably go home, she said. If you were my father, that's what I'd want you to do.

I didn't answer, and she didn't say anything else. I could feel her heart beating against my chest. Pretty soon she fell asleep. A few minutes later I did, too.

51

When I awoke I was alone. The room was hot and uncomfortable, with sunlight pouring through the windows on the west wall. I looked at the alarm clock. It was half past four. Carrie had left two of her cigarettes next to the clock, along with a box of matches and a clean ashtray. It took me a moment to figure out that meant she was gone. I sat up and smoked one of the cigarettes. The house was completely quiet.

I got out of bed and went to a window to look for my car. It was there on the street and it even looked like it had been washed. The tires were pitch black and the red paint was bright and shining.

My clothes were on the dresser next to the bathroom door, washed and folded, which surprised me, because Bobo had put them in a trash bag with his to take off and burn. I picked them up and found a note under them. It read:

Sorry, didn't think I could do a good-bye. Love, C.

I took off the clothes Bobo had bought me, then showered and dressed in my old ones. Someone had done a nice job of sewing up the gash in my pants leg; however, that just gave me one more thing to explain to my wife. I left the clothes Bobo had bought in the hamper—I figured Tracy could give them to Goodwill. I found the toothpaste and brushed my teeth with my finger, then took an unused pink disposable razor from under the sink, lathered my face with a bar of soap, and shaved.

The living room was empty and dark, the shades drawn. I checked all the bedrooms and didn't find anyone. Then in the kitchen I found a note on the counter:

Doug,

Hey, me and Trace just got engaged! Sorry you missed it. She liked the ring. Your car showed up about 1:30. We thought about waking you up but figured you needed the sleep. Carrie said it'd be better for you if you could wear your old clothes, and I think we're out of this deal pretty clean, so I said okay. If you haven't found them yet they're on the dresser in the bedroom. Sorry we had to leave, but business calls. I know Carrie's gone too, but if it makes you feel any better she felt bad about it.

Hey, whenever you put on your new jacket and pants, think about old Bobo, and next time you come through, stop and have a cold one.

Bobo

I went back to the bathroom and got the clothes he had bought me out of the hamper, found a paper grocery bag in the kitchen and put them in it. I didn't want to hurt his feelings.

I tried to find a way to lock the front door without a key, but there wasn't one. I figured they weren't worried about it.

The car was running just fine.

Out on the interstate, I stopped at the first rest stop and put the bag of clothes in a trash can. I had considered keeping them, but there was just no way to explain them to my wife.

52

It was dusk when I got home. The air was hot, muggy and still. I got out of the car and stood in the driveway a moment, listening for the hum of the air conditioner. I didn't hear it.

As soon as I stepped in the front door it felt like I'd stuck my head in an oven. I put my briefcase down in the foyer and went to the living room doorway. Joan was on the couch, wearing a pink maternity outfit. The top was sweaty around the neck and arms and her bangs were stuck to her forehead. She didn't notice me because she was staring at a sitcom blaring on the television and a tall oscillating fan was blowing loudly behind her. An empty quart of ice cream was on its side on the coffee table, a spoon sticking out of it. There was no sign of Katie, but her toys were strewn all over the floor, along with two or three days' worth of newspapers. The wind from the fan was flapping the pieces of newspaper up and down like little waves.

—Hi, I said.

She jumped and looked up.

—Oh, you scared me, she said.

—Sorry.

She used the remote to lower the volume on the television.

—You made it, she said.

I nodded. Where's Katie?

—Over at the Paulsons' spending the night. The heat was really getting to her.

—Schmeils hasn't been here yet? I asked.

—Oh, he's been here. She shook her head. He said what was wrong with it wasn't covered under the warranty. He wanted almost a thousand to fix it.

—Son of a bitch, I sighed.

—I didn't know what to do, so I thought I'd wait until you got home.

—All right.

—Why didn't you call and tell me you were on the way? she asked.

—My phone was dead, I said, which was the truth.

She nodded, then took a long look at my pants.

—What happened there? she said.

—I caught them on a piece of barbed wire when I was walking back to town after I broke down. I was trying to take a shortcut across a field. I got them sewn up at a laundry in Marsburg.

—What'd you wear while they were doing it?

—They let me wait in their bathroom.

Then her nose wrinkled and her eyes narrowed.

—Did you start smoking again? Doug, I told you I wouldn't—

—I was in a garage all day, Joan, waiting for my car, and they were all smoking. That's why it's on my clothes.

—Oh. All right. Sorry. I shouldn't have jumped to conclusions.

She used her forearm to wipe the sweat from her forehead.

—Do you want supper? she said. I've got some leftover macaroni salad and I could make a grilled cheese.

—No thanks. I just want to take a shower and go to bed.

—Okay.

I went through the living room and down the hall to the bathroom. I shut the door, then lowered the commode lid and sat down. I put my elbows on my knees and clasped my hands together and stared at the floor a moment, then stood up, opened the window, turned on the vent fan, and took out the pack of Camels I had bought the day before at the country store. I lit one, then stood at the porthole-sized window and smoked, staring out at the row of perfectly spaced, almost identical houses across the street.

Love. I knew it wasn't the excitement of having a pretty woman on your arm or the different sort of vanity of marrying just so you'd have some children on the planet, and maybe it was having someone you could talk to, but there had been plenty of women I could talk to and after about an hour most of them made my ass hurt. All I could come up with was that it was an unexplainable connection—the kind that might've gotten Carrie's father murdered because he couldn't stay away from his brother's wife, but I'd never know that for sure now. I did know that you were lucky if the one you loved happened to be reasonable, sane and available, but even if you woke up every Friday night for a year with her holding a butcher knife under your chin and you finally left her, love didn't end, it just waited until the next time you saw someone who looked like her and then that pleasant ache came back—I knew that was going to be happening to me a lot from now on.

I dropped my cigarette butt in the commode and it hissed out. Looking out the window, I lit another one.

[Mr. Newton: That's the end of book one. At the beginning of book two Carrie shows up in town, and the story continues.]

Famous Writers School
P.O. Box 1181
Fayette WV 32111
July 18, 200—

Dear Dan,
Good work here. This section is a nice close to the Marsburg part of the novel, and I have only one suggestion for revision. I'm not sure the final paragraph is entirely effective. Its elegiac tone makes it sound like something that would come at the end of a

book, not in the middle, and besides that, the sentiments it expresses are ones we've seen a number of times before. I suggest you cut the paragraph and try to come up with something new.

I've been thinking about some ideas for book 2, so I thought I'd offer them up in case you might find them useful:

1) At the beginning of book 2, Chess and Bobo have been murdered.
2) Have Carrie dye her hair brunette.
3) Have Fee's daughter, Melinda, reenter the story. I believe you can make some more hay there.

All right, now it's confession time. Until I got your last letter, I was not aware my new lesson 6 was similar to the opening of your novel. I think you're right about what happened—what I had been reading just seeped into my own writing. I hope you take that as a compliment, even if it happened unconsciously. I think it goes without saying I would never do something like that on purpose.

I want to thank you for letting me know you had learned some things from me. It's not often that a teacher gets to hear that, and coming from a writer of your ability, it certainly means a lot. Since we're on this note, I should tell you that I, in fact, have learned things from you. For one, you opened my mind to the rich possibilities of genre fiction.

I'm glad we're parting on friendly terms, despite our rocky start. I do have a final request, though. I would still like to see how this story ends (or should I say, I would like a preview, since I'm sure your book will be published), so would you consider sending me a summary of book 2 so I don't have to wait to satisfy my curiosity? I'm really interested in where you're going with this story.

I'll sign off now, but please know, Dan, that even with the rough patches, working with you has been a pleasure.

All the best,
Wendell

Famous Writers School
P.O. Box 1181
Fayette WV 32111
July 31, 200—

Dear Dan,

Hi, I just thought I'd drop you a quick note and see if you had given any thought to my request to see a summary of book 2 of your novel. I don't mean to push, but it's been about a month and I hadn't heard back from you, so I thought I'd let you know I was still interested. I got so hooked on your story that I guess I'm going through withdrawal—ha-ha. Anyway, I've enclosed an SASE, and if you get a minute or two sometime, I would really appreciate it if you could stick something in the mail.

As you can see, I've also put something else in this envelope, a vintage copy of the Chandler classic *Farewell, My Lovely.* I know our disagreements were smoothed over long ago, but I thought this might serve as a final peace offering to make up for my brief period of ill-considered behavior. I thought you would like owning the book since it is by a master of the genre you are quickly becoming a master of as well. I don't know if you're at all interested in book collecting, but this war-era Pocket Books first edition is fairly valuable, despite the cracks in the art deco cover, the yellowed pages, and the hilarious inscription inside the front cover. I paid a pretty penny for it in a bookshop in Bruges, Belgium, during my trip to Europe while I was in the air force. It was one of those dim, airless, crowded shops where everything seems stacked, and the proprietor sat behind a table in the middle of the room, smoking one cigarette after another and talking in broken English about movie posters. At the time, I bought the book as a lark, but now I'm delighted to be able to give it as a gift.

I hope your work is going well, and I look forward to hearing from you soon.

Best wishes,
Wendell

August 11, 200—

Dear Mr. Newton,

I'm not quite sure what to say at this point, except that in no uncertain terms I am not interested in having you as a reader for my novel, and I also won't be sending you a summary of part 2. Sending the Chandler book was nice, in a way, although as you can see I'm sending it back. I guess I don't appreciate being lied to. You told the story about how you got the book, but then I found a receipt stuck in the back of it that said it was bought at the Book Nook in Pittsburgh.

I don't know what else to say at this point without being re-dundant. This is just getting weird. Please stop writing me.

Dan Federman

Linda Trane Has Done All She Can

Because he is sleeping with the housekeeper, my husband never questions me about money. I get the five thousand for the visa by telling him I need gum surgery. He writes the check before he leaves for work, standing at the dresser in his shirt and socks.

That afternoon, I sit at the dining table with a cup of coffee. I'm wearing sunglasses. Nancy is doing the once-a-month dusting, tak-ing down pictures, opening the china cabinet. Her boy came with her today. He's playing dinosaurs with my children. They run around the house. When they want something, they go straight to Nancy, not me.

Nancy is cleaning the shelves in the china cabinet when my daughter runs up and asks her if they can have the glue.

What for, honey? Nancy asks.

To make fins, she says.

Fins? Nancy says.

My daughter nods.

How're you going to make fins? Nancy says.

We're gonna cut out some purple paper and put it on our shirts.

Oh, you don't want to ruin your pretty shirt, Nancy says.

I don't care, my daughter says.

It's a shirt I got her last Christmas, pink with a glittery horse on it.

Well, hmm, let's see, Nancy says. She has her hands on her hips, thinking. What if we got some old T-shirts out of the rag bag and made dinosaur shirts that way?

Yeah! my daughter says.

Nancy looks at me. I nod.

Okay, Nancy says. Let's go.

They leave. I stare at the open china cabinet, the empty shelves. In the laundry room, the children squeal. I admit to myself, for the first time, that my children would be better off without me. I'm no kind of mother. I want to be, but I'm not. I've tried. I take the drugs, but they don't work. Years of therapy, and I'm still screwed up. I want to be normal, but it's not in the cards. Tears come behind my sunglasses. That's what they don't know, I wear sunglasses inside the house only when I know I might start crying at any moment. I know how to keep the tears in my eyes, keep them from falling. You have to blink a lot.

Nancy comes back.

I've got them making *T. rex* shirts in the laundry room, she says. That's okay isn't it?

I nod.

Do you want some more coffee? she asks.

I shake my head.

Well, if you do, just holler, she says.

She starts reloading dishes onto one of the shelves in the cabinet.

This is such a pretty pattern, she says, her back to me.

They're yours, if you want them, I say.

She stops for instant, then continues stacking dishes.

Oh, I couldn't, she says.

I want you to have them, I say.

She turns around and looks at me.

But Mrs.—she starts.

No, I say. Take them.

I get up and go across the room to her. We stand face-to-face.

It's okay, I say. Really.

She looks at me a moment. She understands. She looks down at the floor.

You just be good to my children, I say. I love those children. You might not believe it, but I do. I want them to be happy. That's why I'm doing this. I don't want them to be like me.

She looks up. Her expression is both angry and embarrassed. She walks around me and goes to the kitchen. I go back to the dining table and sit down. I hear the dishwasher door open, the rattle of her unloading it.

A couple of minutes later, the front door opens and closes. My husband walks in. He sees my sunglasses. Disgust comes into his eyes. He says a terse hello.

Nancy's in the kitchen, I say.

So? he says.

She's got something to tell you, I say.

He looks tired. He sets his briefcase on the table.

What're you talking about? he says.

It's all right, Bob. I'm not going to give you any trouble.

I'm blinking like crazy behind the sunglasses.

I said what're you talking about? he says.

You and Nancy, I say. I know.

What? You're crazy.

Really, there's no need to pretend anymore. I'm not going to try to get a dime, I promise.

Oh good Christ, this is just perfect. He rolls his eyes and shakes his head and says he needs a beer.

He goes to the kitchen. Nancy comes straight out. She goes to the china cabinet without looking at me and starts putting dishes back in it.

Okay, Wendell, no more kidding—this *is* me, Lana. I don't know if there's a way to prove that to you now, short of us meeting face-to-face, but I've decided that's not going to happen. However, I want you to know that I appreciate the fact you were the only one who ever took me for what I am. When I wore sunglasses inside, it didn't bother you. When I panicked in a theater, you left without complaint. When I wore the same outfit every day, you told me I looked nice. Of course, when you poured gravy over coleslaw, I didn't say a word. When you played the same song over and over, I kept dancing. When you ranted, I listened.

But I'm sorry, I just don't think this is going to work out. You never should've broken up with me the first time, whether I was married or not. I'll never be able to trust you again. And I've decided I can't go to Prague or anywhere else, for that matter, because I can't be that far away from my children. They need to see me at least some, such as I am. Don't worry, though. I'll put the visa in the mail. I owe you that much, and when you get it, I guess you'll know for sure this has been me.

Good-bye,
Lana

Famous Writers School
P.O. Box 1181
Fayette WV 32111
December 11, 200—

Hello Folks,

Sorry I've been out of touch for so long, but I've recently been on a sojourn of sorts, and it's taken me awhile to get situated back at home. Believe it or not, this fall I was living for a time in Humpolec, Czechoslovakia.

Humpolec is a small town on the edge of the Bohemian-Moravian highlands, about 130 kilometers southeast of Prague. It's well known in Europe for its brewery, and although it wasn't my first choice, things still worked out better than if I had ended up in Prague, which was my original plan. Certainly Prague was nice, and I enjoyed my one visit there, but for a writer Humpolec was a much better place to land. It didn't have the museums, plays, readings, concerts, and other endless distractions of Prague, and besides that, the sickly sweet smell of fermentation from the brewery hung over the whole town and kept me indoors and working—ha-ha. At first I wasn't too happy, though. I spent several nights roaming the dark and dank streets, wondering what I had gotten myself into. There was only one place in my neighborhood that stayed open late, a bright bustling restaurant with plate glass windows, but my mental state was such that I never felt like going inside, and it seemed a bad omen to me that almost every time I passed the place, a dog in the alley next door would give a funereal bark.

However, I see now that the small-minded official I dealt with when entering the country actually did me a favor by sending me to Humpolec instead of Prague. I wrote at a Balzacian pace, anywhere from five to ten longhand pages a day. I had come to Eastern Europe in the first place to research and write a Cold War spy novel, since I figured there was no better spot to do that than at ground zero of that battle. The book took off like a rocket. Its protagonist is a salesman for a state-owned Russian tractor company who, on a business trip to Czechoslovakia, gets mixed up with a corrupt party official who's selling heroin. Think *French Connection* meets *Gorky Park*, but add the twist that the salesman's love interest is the ward of the party official.

However, as I shall explain, my own life in Humpolec took a sinister turn, forcing me to reconsider my dream of living and writing in Eastern Europe. I'm now back home in Fayette. There are still a few problems here that need to be ironed out— the hippie family who leased my house has refused to leave, and of course I'm way behind on my responses to your lessons—so please bear with me. But there is one bonus for you in this situation—the postage for mailing your assignments is now free! Enclosed in this letter are enough stamps to cover the cost of mailing at least thirty pages of text for each of the lessons you have left in the course, and please consider this small gift my apology and my amends for my absence.

Once you current students finish your lessons, the *Famous Writers School* will be no more. All good things must come to an end, alas. But I do want to let you know about an exciting new venture I've just started. *Upward Spiral* will now be published as an e-zine! (I've finally entered the electronic age. Who knows, could a cell phone be next?) The magazine will no longer be published in paper, and we are now sponsoring a fiction contest. For an entry fee of $15, you will have a chance at a $1,000 first prize! Runners-up will also receive publication on the website. Submissions are by email only, and entry fees are paid by credit card on the website (don't worry, we use the best security software available). Just go to upwardspiralmagazine.com for all the details.

I'm sure you're all wondering what it was that sent me packing back to the USA. Well for one, my voltage adapter didn't keep my typewriter's motor from burning up the first time I plugged it in. There was just one shop in Humpolec that repaired office equipment, the proprietor was a dour man who spoke no English, and he kept the typewriter for six weeks, almost my whole stay. When I would go to the shop, he would just shake his head and shoo me away, babbling in Czech. There were also difficulties with the post. Sometimes the carrier would pick up my outgoing mail, but sometimes he wouldn't, and if I took the mail directly to the post office it was often returned to my flat with a phrase stamped on it that I could never translate accurately. I'd take these envelopes to the window at the post office for an explanation and they would all but ignore me. I think it was because I was an American.

But it wasn't all bad over there. For instance, I made the acquaintance of a young woman who worked in a stationer's shop near my flat. She was tall and lanky, with long brown hair and a shy smile. She always wore sunglasses—sometimes they were up in her hair, sometimes down over her eyes. Just depended on her mood, I guess. Her dress was usually simple, a pair of loose-fitting jeans that looked creased and crisp as if she'd ironed them, and she wore no jewelry except for a silver watch that had a face the size of a nickel. Her smell was sweet and delicate, like a scent of flowers that reaches you on a breeze—I couldn't tell whether it was perfume or the soap she used. She was a graduate student in anthropology with everything finished but her dissertation, which, according to her, had been hanging fire for two years. She spoke passable English. I stopped in most every evening for a candy bar or some other notion, and our exchanges were always pleasant. She was interested in America and hoped to visit someday, and I let her know I'd be happy to help any way I could.

Finally one evening I asked her if she'd like to accompany me to the restaurant I mentioned earlier.

"Okay, sure," she said. "We can make talk about America."

We talked a moment longer, then the phone behind the counter rang. She answered and had a short conversation in Czech, then hung up. She said, "I'm sorry, but I cannot attend with you tomorrow night."

"Really?"

"Yes, there is a meeting already. I forgot."

"I see. What about the next night?"

"No, I'm afraid it is not possible."

I decided to go to that nice restaurant anyway. I'd been having supper each night at a cheap café near my flat, but I figured this other place would at least have an entrée other than pork roast and dumplings. Outside the restaurant, a waiter was standing in the doorway shooing a dog away, clapping his hands and shouting coarsely. I realized it must be the dog I often heard when passing. I looked through the restaurant's windows to see how crowded it was, and, lo and behold, I saw the girl from the stationer's sitting by herself at a table near the back. At first I thought I was in luck, but then she was joined by a man. He was at least fifteen years her senior and built like a linebacker. He had jet black hair, a bodyguard's suspicious cast to his eye, and a scar as thick as your finger running from one ear to the tip of his chin—a Le Carre character if I've ever seen one.

I started to turn away, but then decided I just had to go in. I wanted to observe the girl and her muscular oaf.

Inside, the waitress led me on a zig-zag through the room until we reached a table of eight with an empty chair sitting at one end. The family at the table went silent to stare at me. I stared back. The waitress gestured impatiently toward the empty chair, and the father in the party smiled and nodded at it. I sat down, grateful to be partially hidden from the couple across the room. The waitress put an empty glass and a menu in front of me and the father, sitting on the opposite end of the table, started the water pitcher my way. He was a handsome man just starting to bald, and his wife was a thin woman who looked a few years older. A girl of three or four was next to her, and to my right was an old woman in a high-necked blue dress who didn't acknowledge me, but just stared vacantly across the room. To my left a girl of eight or nine with long ponytails sat next to two identical twin boys a bit older.

I picked up the menu and looked at it, and they fell back into their chatter. Then the father spoke to me.

"You are American?" he said.

I looked up. "Yes."

"I made studies there," he smiled. "I remember some English not much."

"Then maybe you could help me with this menu," I said. "I want a beefsteak."

He called for the menu and I handed it up the table. He pointed to the pitcher of dark beer on the table.

"Please take," he said. "Is from Humpolec."

I had yet to try the local beer. I poured myself a glass, then drank—it felt like I had swallowed a pound of sausage.

"Good?" the father asked.

"Yes," I said with watery eyes. Then I took my first look across the room at the man and the girl. He was staring at me, and when my eyes met his he didn't look anyway; if anything, his expression grew more menacing.

The waitress returned and the father placed my order. Then he began asking questions about American football, most of which I could scarcely answer. Each time I spoke he translated for his wife, who would smile and nod.

And whenever I looked up, the man across the room was still staring at me. It was unsettling. Then the waitress brought the family's food. When they were halfway through their meal, she brought my steak. It was overcooked but the fries were excellent.

The father started talking about a Dean Martin movie, a western he'd seen while in America. After a minute, I did remember seeing a Dean Martin western some years ago. He wore a fringed buckskin shirt in every scene. But I couldn't remember the title or any plot details and I didn't know if it was the same movie he was talking about. By then the continuing stare of the huge man had me completely unnerved. I only ate about half my steak, and ended up wrapping what was left over in paper napkins. After we paid our bills, we stood up to leave. The old woman scooted her chair back with difficulty, then stumbled as she tried to stand up. Already standing, I caught her by the arm before she fell back into the chair.

"*Dekuji*," she said, which means thank you in Czech.

Then she took hold of my hand. I could tell she wanted me to walk her out of the restaurant. The father nodded and smiled, and the rest of them went ahead, while the old woman and I carefully made our way around the crowded tables. I was holding her with one hand and carrying the napkin-wrapped steak in the other. Then the huge man stood up and came toward us. The girl's sunglasses were down, so I couldn't tell what she thought. The man stopped in front of us, right in our path. His expression was cold and empty. The old woman kept her eyes averted, as if through years of practice at avoiding the ire of government thugs.

The man hovered over us, but didn't speak for a moment. He was at least a head taller than I, and had such a strong odor of garlic it nearly sickened me. Up close his scar was pink and angry. Then a waitress with an armload of trays stepped around us, and that's when he leaned down and spoke in my ear.

"Be safe," he said in a perfect British accent.

Then he turned around and went back to his table.

Outside, a cold rain was falling. The street lamps looked foggy. The father and his children went down the street to get their minibus. Shaken, I stood under the restaurant's awning with the old woman, who was still holding my hand. I saw the taillights flare on a white Volkswagen minibus. It did a tight U-turn out of its parking spot and speeded back toward us, its motor rattling, then jerked to a stop right in front of me.

I guided the old woman across the sidewalk, helped her down off the curb, then up into the passenger seat of the minibus. The father put her seatbelt on her, then reached across her lap and handed me a slip of paper. It had his name, address, and phone number scribbled on it.

"You will come for dinner," he said.

"Yes, thank you," I said.

Then one of the twin boys said something and all of them laughed, even the old woman. The sliding door on the other side of the van banged shut.

It was at precisely this moment that I had what I can only describe as a Proustian epiphany: the gods had spoken, and Eastern Europe wasn't where I was supposed to be. For better or worse, I knew that my fate lay in America, even if it was just to be a voice crying in the wilderness.

The van nudged into gear and then pulled away, making that peculiar thumping sound tires do on a cobblestone street. After the van disappeared around a corner, I stood on the sidewalk a long time, staring at the ornate metal light pole on that corner and the rest of the near-empty street. Then I turned and looked back through the restaurant windows. The man and the girl were still at the table.

Though it seemed foolish to tarry at all, I started toward the alley. I stopped at its mouth and called the dog—nothing happened. I took a couple of steps into the alley—the sour smell of restaurant trash was strong—and called again. I waited until my eyes adjusted to the near pitch dark before going farther, then walked to the end of the alley. I saw metal trash cans, litter, broken glass, a couple of lightless doorways, but no dog. I had expected it to start barking, but it must've been gone, so I turned around and left. The steak would make good sandwiches.

Yours,
Wendell